CRITICAL PRAISE

MW01045549

{ *A S*

"An emotionally charged saga of love and war—
a tapestry of Canadian history with the legendary Princess
Pats at its centre—by a consummate novelist."
DOUGLAS GLOVER, Governor General's Award-Winning author of *Elle*

"Franco-Ontarian writer Daniel Poliquin leaves
nothing to chance. Words... come together to form music.
He writes as much for the ears as for the eyes."
JOURNAL DE MONTRÉAL

"... rich in colour, at once funny and smart, historical fact
and destiny are blended with narrative virtuosity."
LE DEVOIR

{ *In the Name of the Father* }

"His honest prose turns Quebec's official history on its
head in a tragico-comedic way... Why has it taken so long for
Canada to secrete a social critic of Poliquin's stature?"
BOOKS IN CANADA

"... it could only have been written by
someone who cares enough about Quebec and the rest
of the country to criticize it with such passion."
MONTREAL REVIEW OF BOOKS

"... a fierce, memorable little book."
THE GAZETTE

{ *The Black Squirrel* }

"This is a hopeful and ultimately happy book, told with
a master craftsman's skill… With extraordinary economy and
style, Poliquin shows himself to be a master of the compressed
human spirit, and this is a wonderful, warm-hearted and
incisive novel filled with mordant humour and compassion."

GLOBE AND MAIL

{ *Visions of Jude* }

"… a testimonial to Poliquin's consummate fictional skills.
Writers like Poliquin do more than hold up a mirror
to our lives; they turn an x-ray on our most carefully hidden
dreams, the closely held myths that tell us who we are."

VANCOUVER SUN

"Poliquin has once again captured Canadian society,
with its divisions of language, culture, race, and geography.
He provides a unique view of our history and of the present
state of our political, social, and cultural affairs."

QUILL & QUIRE

{ *The Straw Man* }

"Characters are quirky, earthy and endearing.
The narrative is also laced with humour, much of which is
delivered with a sly wink to the modern reader."

VANCOUVER COURIER

"Wildly inventive, *The Straw Man*
is rich with the power of true storytelling."

QUILL & QUIRE

A SECRET BETWEEN US

a novel by

DANIEL POLIQUIN

TRANSLATED BY DONALD WINKLER

·A·
SECRET
Between Us

DOUGLAS & MCINYTRE
Vancouver/Toronto

French edition © 2006 Editions du Boreal, Montreal, Canada
Originally published in 2006 as *La Kermesse*

07 08 09 10 11   5 4 3 2

Douglas & McIntyre Ltd.
2323 Quebec Street, Suite 201
Vancouver, British Columbia
Canada v5t 4s7
www.douglas-mcintyre.com

Library and Archives Canada Cataloguing in Publication
Poliquin, Daniel
[Kermesse. English]
A secret between us / Daniel Poliquin ; translated by Donald Winkler.
Translation of: La kermesse.

ISBN 978-1-55365-272-4

I. Winkler, Donald II. Title. III. Title: Kermesse. English.
PS8581.O285K4713 2007   C813'.54   C2007-901941-2

The passage on Father Brébeuf quoted on page 24 is taken from
Word from New France, the letters of Marie l'Incarnation, translated by
Joyce Marshall (Toronto: Oxford University Press, 1967).

Editing by Mary Schendlinger
Cover and text design by Jessica Sullivan
Cover illustration by Ryan Heshka
Printed and bound in Canada by Friesens
Printed on acid-free paper that is forest friendly (100% post-consumer
recycled paper) and has been processed chlorine free.

We gratefully acknowledge the financial support of the Canada
Council for the Arts, the British Columbia Arts Council, the Province
of British Columbia through the Book Publishing Tax Credit,
and the Government of Canada through the Book Publishing Industry
Development Program (BPIDP) for our publishing activities.

．

．

．

．

．

I AM THE FLESH MADE WORD.

A particularity that was my stock in trade when I was a journalist: secure in my role as arbiter of opinion, I overthrew governments between two morning coffees, denounced liars and rained down honours on the virtuous. In my novels it was simpler still. With circumstance obedient to my whims, women fell in love at first sight with the man I dreamed of being, and I rewrote history according to my tastes. All I needed was a credulous public for everything to be true.

When I write now, it is to beg my father for subsistence, and my only readings are the classified ads that offer work to those who lack it. I would love to make an honest man of myself, gainfully employed, but my brain mocks my dim ambitions: it continues to weave fantasies without my consent, spawning and altering universes for which I no longer have any use. My mind plays this game against my will, leaving me drained of strength. And wanting one thing only: to become one of those trivial creatures who materialize and dematerialize in my head, only to melt away during one of my periodic spells of amnesia. I must stop dreaming during the day and confine to the night those visions that vanish with the coming of dawn. For now I know that the imagination can hold freedom in thrall.

My memories are of no more use to me, I must be done with them. A difficult task, as despite myself I retain all the stories that others have told me, as if I didn't have enough of my own. My mother would have said that this curse was my punishment for a life of sin.

She died just before the battle of Vimy. The telegram was signed by the village postmistress, who must have pitied my illiterate father, otherwise she would never have written to the happy reprobate I was: "Your mother is dead. Pray." I sought out my warrant officer, hoping that my loss might garner me a two-day leave that would free me to go and ask Nurse Flavie from the Vendée if she might one day love me. The officer had a good laugh: "My ass, Sergeant, that's the fourth time she's died, your old lady! You should try doing in your father for a change!" I protested a little. I even swore that this time it was true. He told me to screw off. I consoled myself with the thought that the imminent death of my mother had already earned me two leaves in Droucy, where Nurse Flavie's unit was encamped. She was the first woman in my life whom I'd desired more than once.

Had I known my story would break the heart of Private Léon Tard, my friend and subaltern, I wouldn't have told him anything at all. We were digging graves for our comrades killed in action, and when he insisted on knowing why I wasn't singing as much as usual, I told him about the warrant officer's coarse laugh. He fell into my arms, sobbing. Impossible to calm him down. "I'm sorry, but I'm so sad for you. Your mama…" A colossus like Tard who weeps hot tears is hard to resist. I managed to console him, promising to make him a corporal one day.

Our job was to bury, the two of us, half a dozen lads who'd not made it through the night. As it happened, they were amputees whose coffins weighed almost nothing. A light workday. And so to ease his pain a little, Tard told me how, at the age of seven, he had lost his own mother. She died in childbirth while he was playing in the farmyard with a stick and hoop, and he had given a kick to an old hen that was in his way. "When they told me that Mama had gone to heaven, I thought right away it was my fault because I'd been mean to the hen. Then I asked myself how we'd manage for supper that night, since Mama wouldn't be there to cook for us, and that made me hungry. I still get famished every time I think of her." He began again to moan so loudly that he almost dropped the little corporal from Ontario who'd been gutted by a shell, and whom we'd liked a lot because he whistled so nicely when he was shaving. Seeing Tard with his orphan face too large for his age, I thought I might shed a few tears along with him, but he had already drenched my handkerchief. I can still, from time to time, respond to the suffering of others, even though my own leaves me cold. It is all the fault of my fickle imagination, which finds me unworthy of interest.

Tard had had the misfortune of being adopted by his uncle and aunt, who already had nine children and could well have done without the four new mouths to feed that the death of their widowed sister-in-law landed on their doorstep. For the rest of his short childhood he was accused of taking up too much space and eating like a pig. His uncle sent him to the woods as a kitchen helper at the age of ten, and there, frightened by all the lumberjacks, who cursed as though the good Lord were dead, he missed his mother even more, and even the adoptive family that was so happy to get rid of him. After five or six years he got tired of handing over all his wages to his uncle as compensation for the man's goodness. He fled the forest for the factories in Massachusetts, but after six months he crawled back to his Quebec hole like a beaten dog returning to its master. "Yes, I understand why you're laughing at me, Sergeant. It's true that our house smelled of piss, sweat, cabbage soup. What else? Oh yes, it also smelled of sour milk, overcooked meat, dirty laundry, but it was still my nest, my place. It's hard, when you're homesick..." So as not to add to his troubles, I drew on my pipe like a man who is wise to life's mysteries, and said no more. He would not have wept so hard had he known my mother.

•
•
•
•
•

HER NAME WAS MARIE, SHE HAD BEEN A SCHOOLMISTRESS for four or five months after leaving normal school, and she was still single at the age of thirty-six. Her father was the biggest market gardener in the region, but his money attracted no suitors. The reason was clear: there was a streak of madness in the family. Marie was touched by it, as were three of her aunts and her grandmother. They said in the village that it was the fault of a few savage ancestors who had interbred with her forebears. In that township where no one's lineage was a secret, attractive young men were told to beware of this woman whose father had money, yes, who was not hard to look at, no, but who sang her head off at mass and told everyone what she had confessed to the priest, always contending that her penance had been too lenient.

The market gardener's wife, who did not appreciate her youngest being mocked, undertook one day to change this holy Josephine into a woman. There was soon to be a wedding in her family, and she let the whole village know that Marie would be there with an escort. No one believed it, of course. What they didn't know was that she had arranged with the horse dealer Lusignan that his son, who looked as though he too would end up a bachelor, would come to the wedding and invite her daughter to dance at least once. The horse dealer coveted the market gardener's wife's money, and the deal was made.

He was Lucien: the most skilful cabinetmaker in the village, with the kindest of hearts, and not a mean thought to his name. He was then a boy of barely thirty-eight years, reserved, like so many individuals with a speech impediment, and as far as anyone in the village could remember he had never addressed a word to a young woman without stuttering three times more than usual. The youngest of the family, with no rights to the paternal land, and dead last in class, he had been removed from school and apprenticed to a carpenter in Trois-Rivières, after which his father had set him up in the village. It was said that he worked well but priced his work too low, which made him the laughingstock of the entire township, including the horse dealer, who managed his son's affairs. "He can call himself Lucien if he likes but he's no bright light," he quipped, having studied Latin in his youth for a couple of months (*lux, lucis*).

The obedient son, Lulu to his friends, went to the wedding, where, in the opinion of the market gardener's wife and the priest, he acquitted himself very well. At church he took communion, which meant that he must have confessed the day before. After the banquet, instead of taking a swig behind the barn and trading blows with the local youths to show off his strength, he stayed with Marie and made sure she had enough orangeade all evening long. He even asked her for the first dance, as had been agreed, then went to smoke his pipe outside. He also escorted her home without being asked.

The next week Lucien discovered that he was engaged. The horse dealer was elated: "Consider yourself lucky, my Lulu. For the dowry your future father-in-law is going to lend you for life, free of charge, his little house in the village, so you'll have more space for your workshop; there'll just be the taxes to pay, which are almost nothing. But I've added on to the contract, just for you, the land with the duck blind on the river. You can also be sure that Marie will have a big inheritance later on. You'll never lack for anything, my boy. Don't thank me, it didn't cost me a penny." For the wedding Lucien put on the suit his father had worn at his own, and which he'd sold him at a good price.

How do I know all that? I learned some things from the cruel folklore of my village, and I invented the rest as best I could.

Nine months later a son was born to these two innocents who had come together at the pleasure of others. The priest had to explain to them how to make me. In the confessional, of course. I was put out to a wet nurse on the day of my birth, and I was already walking when my parents took me back. I believe I even had to make my way to them on foot. My memory embroiders, I know, but that's the only way to respect the truth.

Years later, when my mother had been placed in the Quebec Asylum, where the province's madmen and women were shut away, my market gardener grandmother put the blame on me: "It wasn't enough ripping her up when you came into the world, it's 'cause of you she went wild in her head. Before, she was fine, she was sweet, everyone loved her for her learning. Her only pleasure was going to mass. I should have kept her with us instead of giving her to your father, that no-account!" Her accusations didn't bother me; she was usually much less agreeable than that.

There were no others after me: doctor's advice, priest's orders. It became clear to the village that my father was being deprived of that thing, and they stopped calling him Lulu to rebaptize him Good Saint Joseph. The nickname became such common currency that one day someone slipped and called him Good Saint Joseph to his face. My father said nothing, the nickname stuck. He never corrected anyone, he got used to it. After a few years people stopped laughing when Good Saint Joseph's name came up in conversation, which was a small triumph over the village's meanness.

The village called me Little Jesus. As a joke, of course. My mother had decided at my birth that to expiate her sins I would become a priest. So absolute purity was my lot. To make sure I wouldn't be exposed to the neighbour children's coarseness, she had a fence six feet high built around the garden. With her nimble fingers, she fashioned me a cassock, a surplice and a stole when I was four years old, so that I could play in the yard dressed as a little priest. The village children laughed at my costume, and as I was always trying to get away to tear it off my back, my mother tied a cord around my ankle and attached it to a stake in the ground, just like the neighbour's goat. During the summer the village children glued their faces to gaps in the fence and whispered: "Little Jesus, come and play! Take off your robe and come swim in the river..." They laughed and I cried. Sometimes my mother stormed out of the house screaming like a raving maniac, and the nasty children, shouting like Iroquois, took to their heels, only to return and torture me again the following day. When I cried for too long, my father came out of his workshop. He removed my priest's clothing, dressed me like a little boy, took me to the general store and offered me sticks of licorice or mint candies wrapped in papier-mâché, and sometimes both at once. At such times I knew he was the only one on earth who loved me as I wanted to be loved.

When I mentioned candies, Tard squirmed with pleasure in our corner of the bunker, near the privy: "You see, it wasn't so bad for you. Better than for us. At least you had candies..." It's true, but we prayed a lot. I learned to pray before I learned to talk, and I spent half my childhood on my knees. That's why the day a man knelt down before me to make love to me with his mouth, I thought of my mother.

When she came into my room in the morning she immediately got on her knees at the foot of my bed to thank the Lord for allowing her to find me alive. In church the family always had to stay prostrate longer than the other parishioners, to prove to them that we prayed better than they did. When I was six I knew all my prayers in Latin, an exploit that in the deranged mind of my mother confirmed my vocation.

No respite. Never. If we passed by the church while out for a walk, we had to go in to recite an act of contrition; if we encountered a statue, the tariff was three Hail Marys; if Father Lajoie crossed our path, we had to throw ourselves at his feet to ask his blessing, which he always accorded us, but rather grudgingly it seemed to me. I now think our ostentatious piety embarrassed him.

One day I asked my mother why Father Lajoie didn't kneel before other people. Yes, he kneels before his Bishop, she replied. And the Bishop? Before the Cardinal. And the Cardinal? Before the Pope. And the Pope? Before God. And God? No, it stops at God. Then, I said to her, when I am big I want to be God. She cried blasphemy and washed my mouth out with soap. I had to promise never again to say such a thing, but for a long time afterwards I continued to want to be God so the whole world would one day prostrate itself before me, especially her and Father Lajoie. A dream I was to renounce the day I myself desired to kneel forever before the only man who cared about me and whom I knew I loved, Essiambre d'Argenteuil.

Come the religious festivals, my mother's piety veered towards delirium. On the eve of Pentecost, when I was nine years old, she lit candles all over the house so that God could see us better. When we went to sleep, my father wanted to put them out; she objected violently. My father replied gently that the house could catch fire and we would all die. She insisted: "No, the crucifix is on the wall, we couldn't possibly burn to death, are you crazy?" After a long sigh, he managed to stutter: "Even... a crucifix... can burn." She went to bed furious, and for a month afterwards we had to recite three extra rosaries a day as punishment.

When one fantasy had run its course, that of my priestly dress, for example, of which she relieved me by the time I was six, another instantly took its place. It was the statues that proved fatal to her. She had ordered statues of saints from Montreal and had set them up all over the house, and at night before going to bed she said, "Excuse me, I have to feed my children." And then she filled her apron with bits of bread and deposited one before each statue. My father said nothing. He went out, smoked his pipe and waited until she was done. He was used to it, as was I, and we would never have dreamed of laughing at her newest obsession. But the day when the priest came to collect his tithe, she confessed to him, "Saint Jude isn't happy, I gave him a smaller portion than Saint Paul. He's sulking..." Then she began to laugh. It was doubtless her laugh, too shrill, that convinced the priest that she had to be interned at the Quebec Asylum. It was December 8, the day of the Immaculate Conception, and my birthday. The next day her bag was packed, and I did not see her again until two years later, just before entering the seminary at Nicolet.

Sometimes, to please Private Léon Tard, who venerated the mother he had barely known, I said nice things about mine. And I did have things to say, because when she was right in her head, her heart was in the right place. On those days she let me sleep in her bed in the morning, near the stove, and she made buckwheat pancakes while singing something other than hymns. As soon as she finished a pancake she tossed it onto the bed so it could absorb the heat of the body that had slept there. We ate them with molasses and tea. I loved her smile of goodness that enveloped the smoky kitchen. Tard was delighted by my story. "Your memory has made me hungry. Do you have another?" He was persistent.

To give myself some peace, I told him how much I enjoyed duck hunting with my father at our blind on the river, the market gardener's wedding gift. I couldn't stop babbling when I was with my father, even as I ate; there was no other way, he never opened his mouth, I had to talk for both of us. I never tired of watching him as he worked with his big hands, browned by their contact with wood and varnish; I loved his grey eyes that went green when he gazed at the river and blue when he looked towards the sky. He was beautiful in his silence. But I said nothing of that to Tard, afraid that he would take me for a fairy.

The next day, while I was delivering a message to head-quarters, a German mine blew up the bunker. All I saw when I got back, in the place of Tard's face smiling serenely at the thought of pancakes in a lukewarm bed, was a smoking hole. There was nothing to do. The lice had already deserted his corpse. He was so unrecognizable that while digging his grave I began to wonder if it was really him. I rummaged in his pockets and found the watch he'd stolen from me a month before. It was truly my very own Léon Tard, the giant pilferer made ravenous by the memory of his dead mother.

TOO BAD HE DISAPPEARED SO EARLY, POOR PLUMP
Tard, I was just going to tell him about the seigneur's bread.

Every New Year's Eve, while she was still half there, my
mother baked a homemade loaf of bread we were forbidden
to eat, on which my father had the honour of inscribing a
cross with his hunting knife. The next day we all got up very
early to deposit the bread, wrapped in a white cloth, at the
seigneurial manor's door. We left immediately without waiting to be thanked by the master of the house, and rushed to
church to be sure of arriving before the priest, or even the
beadle.

"The offering of bread to the lord is an important custom," my mother said each time. "That is how the populace pays homage and expresses its faith in their lord ever since New France." We also never missed the manor's maypole ceremony. We were the only ones in the village to go, but I didn't dare ask why.

It would have pleased Tard to hear how my father offered our seigneur the fruits of his hunting and fishing: smoked eels in the spring, wild ducks in the fall, ritual gifts that for the villagers represented a past long dead, but for my mother very much alive. The seigneur thanked us with the smile of a man accustomed to entitlements. Certain that my mother would refuse, he asked us in with exaggerated courtesy. "Stay for tea at least..." Blushing like a debutante, my mother replied that we had to rush off. People with class, she explained to us later, never accept invitations from those outside their world. You must say no, but politely.

Our seigneur could not have been very flattered to have as his sole zealous subject the most educated madwoman in the township, and he must also have realized that our family was the only one to feign a belief in his nobility. But to honour these obsolete conventions gave us great satisfaction. For my mother the seigneur stood for a temporal immutability derived from the miraculous, and therefore from God. By prostrating herself freely before this make-believe seigneur who was frozen in history-book time, she set herself apart from her contemporaries, on whom she looked down: those she termed the "riff-raff" of the village, who had forgotten everything of ancient servitudes. What is more, she kept to herself the wellsprings of her ancient knowledge, sharing them only with Father Lajoie, himself the author of a monograph on the local seigneury, and an authority on long-ago refinements. As an adult I could never blame our seigneur for his smiling acceptance of my mother's extravagant tributes, because she was the one using him: she ennobled herself through her voluntary servitude.

As I learned shortly after entering the seminary, the little man was no more a seigneur than was my behind. Two of his sons, in fact, were my fellow students, whom their mother, with the showy flair of the social upstart, had baptized Vincent de Paul and Antoine de Padoue, doubtless so they would accustom themselves to the noble "de." Our sham noble was a Poitras, a family name whose sonority faithfully reflected his plebeian thickness. He was a notary who had enriched himself in his Montreal practice through a variety of investments. His family had made no mark on the history of New France, but he had developed an aesthetic affinity with ancient times that he had the means to cultivate. Having purchased the former communal mill to make it into his summer residence, he warmed to the game and decided to revive for his own benefit the former seigneury, which had been left with no heir. Little by little, the way others become stamp collectors, he played at making himself a seigneur. As the local notary died around the same time, Poitras took over his clientele and set himself up permanently in the region. He had bought the ruined manor for a song, and with it a house full of old furnishings that my father restored. And so the cabinetmaker readily tolerated his wife's infatuation with his best client.

I benefited as well. My mother's veneration for the seigneur tempered our pious regime. By inviting me to join her in acting out her comedy of obeisance, my mother afforded me some of the rare bright spells in my devotional childhood. For example, I often accompanied my father during his restoration work in the manor. Maître Poitras loved watching my father work, and while the mute cabinetmaker planed and sanded, the apprentice lord reeled off a long discourse on Canadian history that interested no one but me. Madame Poitras, distressed that none of her children shared the seigneurial tastes of her husband (which did not come cheap), compensated by displaying for my edification a generous bric-a-brac of porcelains, snuff boxes and spittoons that evoked the worlds of Louis xv, the three Georges, Napoleon and Queen Victoria, and I pretended to admire her possessions while sneaking cinnamon biscuits behind her back. Thinking back, I suspect these European artifacts were of quite recent manufacture; their distant provenance was what gave them value, and in any case, in our country twenty years is ample time to make an antique.

What I loved was the old carriage with worn velvet seats that the notary had stored in the barn and that he dreamed of converting into a coach bearing his own coat of arms. While my father worked inside, I was sometimes allowed to play alone in the carriage, and I could easily conjure the horses with which I travelled back in time, becoming myself a French Canadian seigneur. My mother had not really succeeded in giving me a taste for God, but she had, all unknowing, infected me with a passion for the illustrious long ago.

As Maître Poitras entertained a lot, my mother sometimes had the honour of serving at his table, and I of admiring the august company from the back of the kitchen. They were all, like the notary, old gentlemen mad for history, some of whom had served in foreign armies. I especially liked the former corporal in the Southern army who had fought at Shiloh; he at least seemed more authentic than another gentleman with a white beard and a disagreeable voice, an old Zouave who claimed to have defended the Pope against Garibaldi. The least convincing of all was a bald Frenchman who said he had been decorated by Emperor Maximilian himself in Mexico, during the Juarez insurrection. Entranced by their tales, I hung on every word of their reactionary conversation while my mother served tea with the smile of a contented slave. They often discussed, I remember only too well, the reestablishment of the monarchy in France. Should they recall the Bourbons or the Orléans? A grave question in which I feigned a lively interest, but that leaves me utterly indifferent today.

The last time I saw my would-be seigneur, I was wearing the uniform of a Nicolet seminarian, cap and green belt, and at my neck the wooden crucifix designating children promised to God's service. He asked me what I wanted to do when I grew up. I replied that after the seminary I would join the Foreign Legion in order to find fame and become a French citizen, doubtless something I had heard around the table from one of his guests. Enchanted, the seigneur gave me an écu, and I had to hold myself back from kissing his behind in memory of my mother, who had admired him so.

I WAS TEN YEARS OLD WHEN MY CHILDHOOD BEGAN. My mother had just entered the Quebec Asylum.

All at once, no more interminable prayers, no more reciting of the rosary on my knees morning and night. No need to burn incense to exorcise the spectre of our defecations, the stench of the devil as my mother called it. We also stopped hearing the adage that was always on her lips: "Better safe than sorry." My father threw our old curtains into the fire and opened the windows wide to let the sun shine in. He remained as silent as ever in his suffering, but at least now, in our house, it was bright.

Ended, above all, were my mother's dark rages, stirred up by trifles. Such as the time when I was six years old and went to play with the little neighbours, Hector, Donatien and Gertrude, who, along with the others, had tortured me when I was disguised as a child priest. Their uncle had died a few days earlier, and Hector, eldest of the family, had been present at the funeral. He came back impressed. The lowering into the earth, the grave blessed by Father Lajoie, everyone dressed in black, and above all the little cousin who had wailed like a banshee when the coffin descended into the hole. "Don't put him there, he's my papa, he'll never get out, he'll die! Don't do that! You're bad!" When Hector told us about it, we immediately began to play funeral.

Because I was the oldest of the four and I already had a solid liturgical background, I played the priest. Hector was the gravedigger and Donatien, because he was the smallest and lightest, was the corpse. Their sister Gertrude played the role of the cousin who threw herself into the grave. With the sure instinct for theatrical convention common to children all over the world, we performed with talent. I thought I was doing a convincing imitation of the priest's oratory by adroitly placing an *omnipotens Dei* here and there, without, of course, knowing what it meant. Hector, beside me, kept his head lowered, his two hands resting on his little shovel; Donatien lay on the ground like a real cadaver. The ceremony over, Hector and I took his little brother by the shoulders and the feet and threw him into the trunk we were using as a grave. That's when Gertrude hurled herself on

Donatien and tried to wake him up, pretending to cry. Considering the inexperienced actors, only one of whom had seen the real play, it was very well done.

Of course, the game often turned into an argument. Hector wanted to be the priest, but he couldn't because he didn't know how to read. He ended up saying he didn't want to play any more, and went off. Other times, Donatien complained that we were hurting him when we threw him into the grave, and he started to fight with Hector. Or it was Gertrude who wanted to be the priest. We replied that a girl wasn't allowed, and she went away crying.

When my mother learned from the postmistress that I was playing funeral with the little neighbours, I got the thrashing of my life. "You have no right to play a priest," she cried. "You don't even speak Latin, God's language. And those others, they're little criminals who only want to do evil!" I was forbidden after that even to wave to my playmates when I passed them on the village's only street.

With my mother gone to the asylum, the priest enrolled me in the village school. I was a mediocre student, being poorly prepared for learning. Afraid that school would corrupt my soul with knowledge that would compromise my ecclesiastical vocation, my mother had taught me at home, in a small room my father had equipped for this purpose with a blackboard, a platform for her and a desk for me. She taught me what she knew: a bit of arithmetic, a few rules of grammar, handwriting, drawing, a lot of biblical history and an enormous amount of catechism. But as she often had terrible migraines, she had to lie down and the class was cut short, which allowed me to spend the rest of the day in my father's workshop.

At school, naturally, I reunited with my former playmates. As I liked the history lessons given to us by our teaching nun, Sister Felicity, the most beautiful woman in the world to my child's eyes, I appointed myself leader of the pack for our historical reconstructions outside of class. We especially liked playing Father Brébeuf. "Some cut off their feet and their hands, others removed the flesh from their arms, legs, and thighs, part of which they boiled and part roasted so as to eat it in their presence. While they were still alive, they drank their blood. After this brutal cruelty, they drove burning firebrands into their wounds. They reddened the blades of their hatchets, and made collars of them, which they hung around their necks and under their armpits. Then, in derision of our holy Faith, the barbarians poured boiling water upon their heads, saying, 'We are greatly obliging you. We are giving you great pleasure. We are baptizing you so that you will be very happy in heaven, for that is what you teach.' After these blasphemies and a thousand like taunts, they removed their scalps." Hector and Donatien asked me, "Can things like that still happen?" They were disappointed when I tried to reassure them.

We played Brébeuf after Sunday mass. Naturally, I was often the Jesuit and Gertrude was Mother Marie de l'Incarnation, transfixed by my suffering. She also had the right to go to the kitchen for biscuits to feed the famished Iroquois. For authenticity's sake Hector and Donatien stripped to the waist, and I allowed myself to be tied to the stake, saying, "Forgive them, Lord, they know not what they do." We never failed to tell the story as we went along, as children will: "Me, I'm wounded in the chest, you're attacking me with the tomahawk."

There too things went badly from time to time. One day when it was Hector's turn to be Brébeuf, he who had been a decidedly cruel Iroquois, Donatien and I tied him solidly to the torturers' stake and left him out in the rain for an hour. Hector Brébeuf yowled, "Come untie me, damned asshole Iroquois! I'm going to tell the good Lord!" On that occasion the good Lord took the form of their father, who saw red when he got angry. I escaped in time.

Another time it was their mother who punished them, because Donatien had invented a new torture that consisted of tying up Father Brébeuf so he couldn't move, and farting in his face. That day I was the Jesuit.

We stopped playing together when Father Lajoie told my father to make me a boarder in school. He took this decision because the postmistress, who had the nastiest tongue in the village, told him that Gertrude and I were playing dirty at night behind the presbytery. It wasn't true. We did talk about it a lot, she and I, but we never did anything. I was much too dense to take any such initiative.

WITH FATHER LAJOIE'S AGREEMENT, MY MARKET GARDENER grandfather enrolled me in the Nicolet seminary, which he supplied with vegetables and dry goods. I didn't have the same advantages as the wealthier students, but I was easily provided with all the delicacies my father sent me, courtesy of the family delivery boy: jam, chocolates, ginger biscuits and spice bread. That would have made Tard happy, now that I think of it. I still talk to him frequently—I ward off solitude by conversing with those absent from my life.

Overall, I was quite happy at the seminary. Unlike many of my school friends, I shed no tears during my first months there, so relieved was I that I had at last left behind me the pious gloom of my home. Conversation with my companions was a welcome change from my father's resigned silence. As for rising at five in the morning, and the interminable prayers and edifying readings in the refectory, I had known so much worse that it never occurred to me to complain. What I was taught went down easily, and I took a natural liking first to Latin, then to Greek.

Having already encountered the seigneurial whims of old Poitras, I was well primed for my meeting with Brother Mathurin, who was supposed to teach us biblical history but preferred to stray from his subject and talk to us of the glorious annals of French Canada, hoping, doubtless, to make us into fearless and virtuous knights in the service of Church and Country.

I was bound to be of interest to Brother Mathurin. Like Maître Poitras, who sought to invent a noble lineage, and like Napoleon on Saint Helen's Island lamenting the shallow roots of his dynasty, I too already dreamed of being my grandchild.

At his first class, Brother Mathurin called the roll, and as soon as he came across my name he said, as though in a trance: "Is your name really Lusignan? Why then, you are the descendant of the fairy Melusine, fated to turn into a serpent every Saturday because of a sin she committed, and who gave birth to a large family, including Guy de Lusignan, who was King of Jerusalem and Cyprus and battled the Sultan Saladdin at the time of the Crusades. Another Lusignan later came to Canada, and his son made war on the English invader, was commander of Fort Saint Frederic and died a Knight of Saint Louis. You are blessed, young man!" A fairy, a king, a knight—I was overjoyed. During the days that followed I walked around in a kind of happy fog. I was no longer the son of Marie, the Lord's madwoman, and Good Saint Joseph, who made the whole township laugh. I was the offspring of history, and it was written that as soon as the opportunity presented itself, I would renew my ties with my glorious ancestors.

Brother Mathurin's words didn't make me arrogant. I was wise enough to keep these heady dreams to myself, and if at times I got carried away, I only had to think of the men in my family to know that an illustrious name is no hedge against accidents that can so easily cut a noble family down to size. It was strictly impossible for me to reconcile Father Mathurin's accounts of my celebrated namesakes with the image of my grandfather, the horse dealer with the coarse laugh, whose underhandedness was legendary in my village. I saw again the desolation of my father, labouring with his brown hands while silently enduring the villagers' taunts. Or my uncle Socrate, penniless fisher of eels who farted at the dinner table, or Uncle Jérémie, indolent game warden and discreet comforter of widows, all those whose prophets' and philosophers' names were belied by their indifference to any expression of knowledge or beauty. I belonged to a desperately democratic family in which everyone was a bit of a landowner and a bit of a smuggler, paid no taxes and hardly any tithes, where no one except my grandfather knew how to read, but everyone cast a ballot all the same. Those Lusignans were a far cry from the fairy Melusine and the King of Jerusalem. But I, the first of the family to be educated since the Knight of Saint Louis, began to think that my mother had had a brilliant idea in initiating me so early on in seigneurial ways. And in my heart I asked her forgiveness for having prayed so often, at night in bed, that she might die.

At Christmas vacation that year I went home on skates as usual. We set off in groups assembled according to the origins of each, and it took no more than a day to make the trip. I think that's what I liked best about my years at the seminary, the permission to skate back and forth on the river. Perhaps because I delighted in that sacrilegious privilege, to be able to walk on water like Christ.

This time I quickly outdistanced my group and sped off alone, head lowered against the wind, indifferent to the cold, because I had only one wish, to share with my father the secret of our noble lineage. I also wanted to tell him that our decline into anonymity would come to an end with me. But when I saw his brown hands once more, I chose, along with him, to hold my peace.

．
※
．
．
．

I NEVER CONFIDED THESE SORTS OF DETAILS TO MY
friend Tard.

I did, however, tell them to Essiambre d'Argenteuil, the
only man who loved me in my flesh. To this day I talk to
him passionately every time his likeness comes to mind. He
listens to me with his wide, understanding eyes, and nothing gives me more pleasure than to dredge up stories that I
never got around to telling him. Sometimes I say to myself,
"Ah yes, that one, he doesn't know it. He'll like it." He liked
all my memories, even those I thought were of no interest to
anyone.

It's almost two years since his body was ripped apart at Passchendaele, almost a year since the war ended, but I still talk to him as though he were more alive than I am. I can't help it, it does me good, and I'd rather talk to him than to fat Tard, who only liked my stories about food.

•
•
•
•
•

ESSIAMBRE PARTICULARLY ENJOYED MY TALES OF
school, which were not at all like his, as he had been a good
student.

When I arrived back from my first Christmas vacation,
I made the first friend of my life: Rodrigue, a new arrival,
who had only one thought in his head, to get away from the
college as soon as he could. Like me he was the first of his
family to receive an education, but he had decided to be
the last. Nicolet was his third school. He had managed to
get expelled from the seminary in Quebec after a fight with

a lay Brother. With the Fathers at Chambly he had tried to asphyxiate himself by crawling into a steamer trunk and smoking cigarettes of dead leaves and tobacco rolled in missal paper.

We met when my French teacher told us to read Corneille's *The Cid* together. An exercise whose futility became obvious when he refused to believe that his first name could be the same as that of the play's hero. He asked me just one question: "Does your Rodrigue ever get into Chimène's knickers?" My answer made him laugh.

Despite the protests of my still pure conscience, I adored the litany of his transgressions, which set him apart from all the rest of us. He who never spoke to anyone sometimes confided in me when he got fed up with being alone. He wanted to become a sailor someday and to live on a desert island in the South Seas. He would have crucified me had I dared to say it aloud, but beneath his facade of a hardened ruffian I sensed something chivalrous. One day, for instance, he went to the aid of a classmate whom the others were mocking because his nightshirt in the morning showed traces of adolescent dew. His disinterested pugnacity even made me somewhat jealous, especially when I saw the grateful look he received from this school friend after the altercation.

I considered myself his friend, but I'm sure he didn't think in the same terms. He was wary of all his companions, especially docile students like me. Today I think he was afraid of becoming like us, and thus prolonging his captivity in the college. To best keep his distance, he scornfully rebuffed the least expression of affection. When the class-mate with the stained nightshirt tried to offer him a piece of chocolate to thank him for his intervention, Rodrigue told him to shove it up his ass. And so I was very careful how I approached him, because I could not have endured it if this friend, whom I had never dreamed of having, rejected me in so brutal a fashion.

And so to please him I made up my first lies. I who had never before complained about the college food now asserted, like him, that it was inedible. And I felt guilty when I ate with gusto behind his back, especially the dish we dubbed "the lung," a sort of omelette swollen with water that we were served on Fridays. As soon as I saw him com-ing I hid the history books I was reading over and over to learn by heart, or I feigned boredom. Call it a callow lack of backbone at the onset of first love. You deny yourself so as to knowingly ape another.

Tough as Rodrigue was, there was one man at the college whom he feared: Brother Isidore, desiccated and tall, his face made unsightly by asceticism, and who dreamed of being a saint. He was in charge of the library but said he would rather have cleaned the latrines, would this task not deprive him of the pleasures to be had from burning books as evil as Boccaccio's *Decameron* or Suetonius's *Lives of the Caesars*. As librarian, it was he who snipped the ads for female under-garments out of the pages of newspaper provided in the priv-ies. In order to spare us any unclean thoughts, no doubt.

Brother Isidore urged us to emulate his methods of mortification. He forced himself to keep his eyes lowered at all times; he forbade himself from speaking except to pray and only opened his mouth if spoken to by a superior; if a witty remark occurred to him, which could not have happened very often, he held it back.

According to him, one had to rapidly swallow the foods one liked, and slowly chew those one found disgusting. It was also forbidden to touch one's own face, or even to let one's gaze stray outdoors or linger on a pleasing image. If he inadvertently assumed a comfortable position, he at once replaced it with one that was constrictive. He swore he would die were he to commit the slightest venial sin or neglect to cross himself when passing before the Blessed Sacrament. The memory of my mother made Brother Isidore's obsession seem perfectly normal to me; he could almost have been a member of my family. But it was not the same for Rodrigue.

One day he said to me: "Listen, I've got to do something, I've got to get out of here. I'm afraid of him, he'll be the death of me if I stay." The day before, Brother Isidore had summoned him to his cell, and once the door was closed he had stripped to the waist and handed him a whip. "Perhaps I am risking the sin of pride, but I want to share in the suffering of the Son of Man. You are the younger, I am the elder, and that is why I am asking you humbly to apply the scourge. Will you render me this great service, my young friend Rodrigue?" The young friend Rodrigue began to stammer at this point in his story.

"You understand, I'd never done that. And I pitied him because he was thin as a rail, with these tufts of hair around his nipples. I didn't want to..." Brother Isidore insisted: "The love of Jesus demands that we suffer for Him, like Him. Go ahead, do not curb your zeal! You will deal the first blow as soon as I have joined my hands." Rodrigue obeyed, he who had never even beaten an animal.

Brother Isidore did not know that Rodrigue came from a family of powerful men. At fourteen he was already strong: he had begun milking cows at the age of six, he was splitting wood at ten and haying at twelve; by thirteen he was a man. And so he did what the Brother asked. At the first blow, the Brother collapsed face down onto the ground, at the second he cried out as though he were being murdered, and at the fourth he said, "Thank you, young friend Rodrigue, I believe that Christ is happy..." Rodrigue was panicked by the blood spurting onto the walls and the bed, and he took to his heels. He couldn't stop saying, "I'm afraid I'm going to go crazy here, like Brother Isidore."

I loved Rodrigue so much that I had him expelled the next week, denouncing him for a theft he had not committed. And as soon as he left, I resolved to compensate for his absence.

That was my first stab at metamorphosis. I began to wear my hair the way he did, to mimic the wolfish grimace that was his smile, and to talk through my nose as he did. My game did not go unnoticed by my teachers, who for the first time became concerned about my behaviour. But I couldn't help myself, I had to become the twin of this boy whom I so missed. And in taking his place I felt that I was absorbing his strength and his courage, that from now on I'd be more attractive and more complete.

With the approach of Easter that year, and its customary sacrifices and mortifications, Rodrigue's aversion to false callings came back to me during evening prayers in the chapel. I decided then, as a token of our lifelong friendship, that I would never be a priest, and suddenly weary of our rote responses, I had an idea. I would do something outrageous to commemorate Rodrigue's passage through my life.

I raised my hand to talk to the supervising Brother: "I humbly ask permission to go to the cell upstairs and to submit myself to the discipline on my own. I am impatient to feel the suffering of Christ." This mortification, although not much encouraged by the college administration, was practised by certain students during Lent. I must have seemed so sincere that the good Brother said yes.

Once inside I took the whip off its hook, stripped to the waist in case someone came in without knocking, and started whipping the wall while howling as if in pain. Below in the chapel my fellow students could hear everything. I was later told that they began by exchanging terrified glances, but soon understood that my torment was only playacting. When I came back down, it was to hysterical laughter. During the very real correction inflicted on me subsequently by Brother Isidore, I was comforted by the thought that our young friend Rodrigue would have been proud of me.

· · · · ·

AS AN ADULT I HAVE OFTEN ASKED MYSELF HOW, being such a pure-hearted child, I could suddenly, and so light-heartedly, have entered into disrepute.

I knew nothing of the facts of life. As I was not a farmer's son like my schoolmates, I had never seen a bull approach a cow, or a cock rousing the chickens at dawn. Had one explained to me the circumstances of my coming into the world I would have rolled on the ground, consumed by laughter. I could not even imagine how one might derive pleasure from touching oneself, and after breakfast in the mornings, when Brother Mathurin, who was often on duty in the toilets, circulated between the ranges of stalls and repeated at regular intervals, in a funereal tone, "Remember, boys, to behave yourselves," I thought he was referring to those so disrespectful that they might wipe themselves with the obituary page.

Yes, I know what innocence is. The proof? It was only after I met Essiambre d'Argenteuil years later that I realized what had almost happened to me during a certain summer. To counteract the unwholesome influence of Rodrigue, the study prefect had sent me to the seminary's vacation camp. It was at Wolf Lake in the Laurentians. The camp consisted of a large chalet, a few outbuildings and a small farm that provided us with eggs, dairy products and meat. We ate fresh food every day, a real luxury compared to college fare. I loved the smell of the fields and the farm animals, something I had not known in our village. I was at last as happy as the real little boy I'd never been able to be. As a result of my Easter shenanigans I was assigned every day to wash dishes, but I could still take advantage of all the leisure activities offered us; it was there I learned to swim and to paddle a canoe.

One afternoon when we had free time, I went strolling along the lake's edge with lay Brother Marcellin, a little man with pleasant manners who didn't seem that old even though he must have been over thirty. At a certain point, just off the path, an abandoned barn gave promise of coolness. Brother Marcellin suggested we go in out of the sun.

Once inside he said, "Let's roll in the hay, it will be fun!"
I couldn't ask for anything more, I who had dreamed of this
kind of game since I was small. We laughed our heads off
and tumbled in the hay. After a little while, both exhausted,
we sat down on some logs near the door. Our clothes were
all covered with straw, and I said we would have to stay
there for the rest of the afternoon if we wanted to get them
free of it. But Brother Marcellin had another idea: "What if
we took off our clothes and rolled in the straw naked?" He
said it with a wink so I was sure he was joking, especially
as he had a prankish side, and I didn't reply, I just waited
for the rest of the joke. After a pause that seemed a bit long,
he added, in a serious tone of voice: "We could also snuggle
up and play with our birdies. I'd hold yours and you'd hold
mine. In a barn you can do it, if you have your superior's
permission." With that I couldn't hold myself back, I almost
split in two I laughed so hard, I'd never heard anything so
funny in my entire life.

I began walking back towards the Fathers' chalet, shak-
ing the straw off my pants and exploding with laughter every
two steps. Brother Marcellin seemed to have chosen to
laugh at my laughter. But when he offered to brush the wisps
of straw off my back, I drew away: "Oh no, Brother Marcellin, you're such a joker, you're going to start tickling me and
I've already laughed so hard that I'll go in my pants if you
don't stop!" I started to run. Brother Marcellin followed me
at a slow pace, his expression glum; he seemed sad when we
arrived, I even thought for a moment that I'd hurt his feelings by laughing so hard at his proposition.

Every night around the campfire, we told each other stories. That night when my turn came, I said: "You'll never guess what a funny idea Brother Marcellin had today..." I was the only one who found my story amusing. No one said a word. Ashamed, and distressed to have missed the mark so badly, I thought for a moment that my cheeks were being burned by the flames. In the silence that followed, the crackling of the campfire was deafening. To this day there are times when I can still hear it.

.

.

.

.

.

ONE NIGHT IN THE TRENCH, DURING A LULL, ESSIAMBRE

asked me where I had got the idea of using what I learned at

the seminary to make my way in the world. The bombing

started in again just at that moment, and I was never able to

finish my explanation.

What I came to understand was that if Monsieur Poitras

could be a notary and pass himself off as a seigneur, I could

do even better. I therefore mended my ways to the point

where I was selected to wait on the Teaching Fathers' table,

a domestic duty that was highly prized. Their breakfast

consisted of bowls of milk and thick slices of bread grilled in butter, which they ate slathered in slices of onion and garlic cloves marinated in vinegar. It was a dish that would have made me queasy had I not reaped such benefits from listening to their conversations.

One day Father Moisan was fulminating against the profession of journalism: "None of them know how to write, and if they have any talent at all they write poems to seduce women, or novels that corrupt youth while making themselves rich. The worst are those who use their art to serve politicians, who become ministerial secretaries, and end up governing us!" Delighted, I decided to become, successively, a journalist, writer and statesman. My path was clear, thanks to Father Moisan.

But to achieve my goal I would have to make contacts on leaving the seminary and I'd need to study literature in France, and so I would require money, a lot of money. I would find it.

I had heard talk of Father Foisy's *Sainte Oeuvre des vocations* in Quebec City. I wrote him:

Dear Father,

As a student at Nicolet College for the past five years, I feel stirring in me a priestly vocation that may have no future, given my financial situation. My father, a pious and sober man, lives by his hands, and his meagre gains are wholly monopolized by the care he bestows on my sick mother. Might you be so obliging as to make a gesture which would secure for the Mother Church

the ardent zeal, for life, of a young man? If you can offer me some
help, please write me directly at the college, for I am determined
to protect my father's dignity. My kind regards, etc.

I stole a stamp and mailed the letter.

I did not stop there. Having asked Father Foisy for two hundred dollars to cover my annual board, I thought it natural to address myself to other benefactors, notably the Bishop, three friendly priests at my college, a wealthy Nicolet lady and the notary Poitras himself. And while I was at it, why not solicit all the well-disposed, well-endowed souls across the province, Canada and the United States? A hundred sheets of paper, a bottle of ink, a book of stamps, and within a year I would have a hundred thousand dollars. As a person of independent means at the age of eighteen, I would have ample time to settle in Paris, to write a great work and to become a member of the Académie Française by the time I was thirty. I would marry a duchess, or a countess at least, I would be put in command of an army in Africa, and I would retake Palestine from the Turks, thereby restoring my good name.

Three days before Christmas I was summoned before the Father Director, who had spread out three of my letters on his desk. "And I understand that you have been stealing stamps as well?" As I was not only a liar and a thief but also a coward, I denied everything, I shed real tears, I tried to convert my rage at being unmasked into indignation, I insisted that someone had copied my handwriting, but to no avail, I was banished like a lowly poacher.

I had to leave immediately because I knew that my trunk would be returned by mail and that the school would write to Father Lajoie so he could inform my father. It was imperative that I reach the village before the letter expelling me. The ice on the river seemed frozen for all eternity, the sun was shining; the skating would go well, I would be home by the end of the day.

I sped across the frozen water to drown my humiliation in fatigue. When I stopped to warm up my face, I thought vaguely that my greatest crime had been my poor choice of addressees. But when I realized that I had only a few miles to go before arriving home, I stopped dead in my tracks. I knew that what I deserved was to drop into the first hole in the ice along the way and drown in order to expiate my sin. Around me the snow had taken on the roseate tint that a winter twilight bestows. In a few more minutes, with nightfall, the whiteness would fade to blue in the lunar light. I was astonished, then, to find that a little beauty around me was enough to exorcise the hopelessness I felt. My remorse had vanished. With one aesthetic impulse the artist had absolved the criminal, and more than ever I wanted to live. I continued on.

At nightfall, having arrived at the headland where my father's duck blind sat, I saw a house that had not been there the last time I was in the village. The light inside drew me in. My father was there with all his tools, he was making a chest. He didn't seem at all surprised; it was as though he were waiting for me. "You look to me like a fellow who's cold and could do with a good hot meal. Make yourself at home.

Sit down." The soothing aroma of pine logs burning in the stove left me at a loss for words. I sat and ate with the appetite of a prodigal son.

I never had to explain myself. Not a reproachful word on his part, even after the priest had talked to him. We spent a wonderful Christmas. Now he was making my mother's pâtés and pork stew, with much better results, as if he had entirely taken her place. And I learned to bake in her stead. At first my pies and my bread were not as successful, but my father said they were good all the same. I helped him in his new workshop, and we even had conversations. He had sold the house in the village to pay for my mother's stay in the asylum, and over the autumn had built himself the house at the duck blind.

I had to leave again. The debacle at the college had made me want to go away and never come back. Obsessed with myself as I was, I was persuaded that the entire province of Quebec was aware of my epistolary fraud, and that I had no future but in exile. I dared not set foot in the village, which I was sure knew everything. But the silence of the paternal workshop weighed on me, and my fantasies were all criminal and vengeful. I had only one thought left: to wipe out the memory of my false start in the literary profession.

With the coming of spring I put a few possessions into a duffle bag and asked my father to lend me a little money, enough to visit my mother at the asylum. He pretended to believe me. "You'll come back when you like." His violet eyes conveyed so much goodness that for the rest of my life I wished I could believe in God.

．

．

．

．

．

THE NEXT DAY THE TRAIN LET ME OFF IN MONTREAL.
The journey had taken only six hours, but I had aged twenty
years by the time I arrived, because I had come to the real-
ization that like everyone else, I didn't amount to much.

All the cars were crammed with lumberjacks down
from the woods for the seeding. From Trois-Rivières to
Montreal not a seat was free, and I found myself on my feet
beside a big pine box that took up a lot of space. Next to it
was a folding seat occupied by a sad-looking lady, modestly
dressed; her two small children slept on her lap when they

were not crying. It didn't take me long to figure out that it was their father in the box. When tired men asked to sit on it for a few minutes, the lady told them her story to keep them away. I must have heard it a dozen times.

Her husband had died in the forest where he went to cut trees every winter, somewhere far up in northern Quebec. He had wandered into the woods on Christmas Eve and it had taken days for his workmates to find his frozen body. She had only heard of his death a month later, in a letter from the company that she could not read, and that had in any case been written in English, and she had had to wait until the snow melted, in other words for two more months, before she could go and collect his body. She had made the long trip by train with her small son and her daughter, who was barely weaned. They had presented her with the coffin that held the love of her life, and she had left immediately, still exhausted from the journey up.

Twenty times she had to tell her son not to climb on the coffin to play. Weeping, she said, "Get off of there, you! Leave your father alone!" The little one didn't listen, and the girl cried because her mother was crying. Around them, the men stared into the air or at the ground.

At first the lumberjacks were polite to the lady because it was one of their comrades in the pine box, but at each stop the new arrivals were less accommodating. Certainly the sight of the coffin inspired some respect, but as time passed they thought less and less that the man she had loved was inside it. Some began to grumble that the woman took up a lot of space in the passageway with her corpse and her brood.

Almost all had begun to drink their pay from the lumber camp; they played cards and told the crude jokes common to men who have been deprived of female companionship for too long. The crassest among them were not above making obscene remarks everyone could hear. "If she misses her husband so bad, the widow, she can come see me, I'll show her a live one if that's what she wants!" When the conductor tried to restore order, a drunk felled him with one punch. Men started fights around the lady, her children wailed along with her in fear, a lumberjack even fell right across the coffin, fortunately without doing any damage. I would have liked to escape, but there was nowhere to go.

Soon the train was so full that the nastiest in the crowd proposed to put the corpse off at the next stop. The men were all exhausted or drunk, and they didn't want to stay standing in the aisle all the way to the next station. And so when the woman dozed off, some took advantage of her being asleep to sit on the coffin as though it were a bench. The first time she awoke with a start and immediately chased away the man who had dared set his behind on the final dwelling place of her husband. But it wasn't long before she grew weary, then took pity on them for their fatigue. And so when a man who was not too drunk asked politely if he could rest a bit, seated upon her husband, she no longer had the strength to refuse. She replied that her husband, kind as he was, would not have said no either.

Dead tired, she fell into a deep sleep at last. When she awoke, two men were straddling the coffin, playing cards, laughing, and drinking gin out of small glasses. I saw in her eyes that she wanted to protest, but that she was afraid of waking her little ones, asleep at her feet. She just wept in silence. The two men saw her tears but for all that didn't get up; they just continued their game, laughing a little less loudly.

What broke my heart was the man with an overlong beard who cracked hard-boiled eggs on the coffin and tossed the shells on the ground. He took huge bites without even offering the woman a taste. I'd have liked to be strong like Rodrigue and chase away this profaner of the dead, but I didn't dare open my mouth. It got worse when the man started asking her indiscreet questions about her husband, with no sense of decorum whatsoever. The hairy nuisance had just started inquiring whether her husband had any insurance when a young lumberjack appeared and said, "Stop that! Leave the lady alone! She has enough troubles!" The busybody left, wiping his nose on his sleeve like a real villain in a true story.

When I got off the train in Montreal, the young lumberjack and the woman were engaged in a lively conversation; he offered sweets to the children and entertained them with magic tricks; the woman laughed. In my innocent heart I had the widow marrying the good Samaritan a short time later and founding a large family, and I noted the episode of the eggs and the coffin, to be included in a story I never wrote.

ONCE IN MONTREAL IT TOOK ALL THE COURAGE I
didn't have to leave the station. Half dead from fear at the
sight of these streets crowded with horse-drawn vehicles,
not daring to ask directions because I didn't speak a word of
English, I barely managed to make my way to the newspaper,
La Presse: "Good day, I'm a journalist. I'm looking for work."
Having got used to imagining myself other than I was, I had
delivered my sentence with a carefully contrived accent. The
stifled smiles with which I was received did not escape my
notice, but I took no offence. I didn't believe myself either.

There were of course no openings for an overgrown child like myself, but the gentlemen were good enough to redirect me to their competitors, who paid badly but had the virtue of hiring all comers. They were for the most part nationalistic publications that didn't last six months. I changed employers four times in one year, but at least I got some experience in all the crafts: typography, layout, subscription sales, gossip columns, I did everything. It was fine, except that I was starting to get hungry.

One could find salvation from such a precarious existence in the French-Canadian colonies of New England. They were so much in need of French-speaking staff that they hired almost anybody. I made the trip. Their lack of personnel worked to my advantage: I was immediately made assistant editor of the *Patriote* in Woonsocket, Rhode Island, under the direction of an Oblate missionary who mistook my errors in French for the modern style. I edited all the texts, from obituaries to sports, including the handing out of prizes at the end of the school year at Saint-Michel Archange Academy. It was excellent training for someone who wanted to learn how to write. The price to be paid was the scrutiny to which one was exposed in these weavers' hamlets, where the slightest breach of good conduct could lead to banishment. Hunger-induced emigration tends to clothe itself in morality to ease the shock of exile. Small adventurers of my ilk would be well advised to get themselves drunk in private and to keep their distance from proper young girls.

That is why I didn't stay long in Woonsocket, Rhode Island, nor Lowell, Massachusetts, nor Falls, New Hampshire. But I was never seen drunk or with a girl on my arm, and no one knew I was defying the Index by gobbling up all the novels of Hugo, Zola and Flaubert, sold freely in New York and Boston. I also learned English from American girls, who made it impossible for me ever again to tolerate the narrow little world of French Canadian New England. Among them was a widow of about thirty, who cherished me as though I were the last man on earth. I should have said goodbye to her. I thought of writing to her at one point, and still remembered her address, but I had forgotten her name.

Back in Montreal I again approached *La Presse*, and they took me on as a proofreader.

MY PUBLIC LIFE HAD BEGUN. I WAS WRITING, AT LAST! It's that part of my life that Essiambre d'Argenteuil liked best. From time to time he would say to me, "Tell me again about when you…" From time to time, yes, but not as often as I would have liked.

I had neither style nor a sense of story, but I was a master at toadying. The current fashion was for patriotism, and so I wrote historic fables: *The Knight of Malartic,* featuring a moustachioed male musketeer who every twenty pages killed an Iroquois with his rapier; *The Fiancés of the Scaffold,* a moral tale where young and valiant French souls perished at the hands of the cruel English invader. And I never failed in my prefaces to rail against British imperialism and the spinelessness of our governments. Critical acclaim was assured. There was nothing simpler than to become one of the province's intellectual elite: one had only to think like the other opinion shapers and that did the trick. No question, conformity paves the way to the future, and what is more, it's not the least bit demanding.

It wasn't enough, however, to set down feelings on a page, one also had to be adroit. I was. As I did freelance work to finance my self-published books, I was accepted in most circles. A Quebec paper one day published this anonymous notice: "Rumour has it that a young and talented novelist named Lusignan will soon be publishing a novel whose hero is a valiant French knight. We expect that strong emotions await us." One month later, Oscar Petit of *The National* wrote: "A magnificent book, a confident style, etc." Samuel Legris, in *L'Étincelle*, after praising me to the skies, concluded: "It does not surprise us to learn that an important Paris publisher has made a tempting offer to this promising writer." My pseudonyms worked like a charm, the rest of the press followed suit, and I became almost well known in a short time. My publisher, the bookseller Crépeau, received new orders every day: he was ecstatic, I was doubled up with laughter.

For *The Fiancés of the Scaffold*, after the predictable chorus of praise, I upped the ante by having Oscar Petit write that he had expected more of me. Samuel Legris offered a vehement rebuttal the following Saturday. Oscar Petit defended himself, while still acknowledging that my talent was beyond question. I kept the controversy going for a good month.

Having heard mention of a certain Nobel Prize, which honoured the great writers of the time, I decided to inform myself. I learned that universities were invited to nominate candidates, and so Oscar Petit contacted the rector of Laval University.

Monseigneur,

We have among us a worthy candidate who is surely more deserving than all the foreign writers whom we ourselves have never read, knowing them for the most part to be Protestants or atheists. The soul of this young man is Christian, his pen Canadian. Given that the prize is accompanied by a sum of fifty thousand dollars, I can pledge that should he receive it, he will donate half to your university, which I never would have approached had it not been Catholic and French. I humbly thank your Grace, etc.

The rector never deigned to reply. I would exact my revenge with my next book.

My success with the pen had revived my altruistic inclinations. I therefore took a few days' leave to visit my mother. She talked of this and that with a cheerfulness I had never before observed. Her gaze was no longer bright with the madness of God, her serenity became her. As I was leaving she introduced me to a friend: "My son, Father Lusignan, I told you about him. He's a missionary in Japan." The two women asked me to bless them, which I did. This was not, after all, my first imposture.

I wanted to see my father again too. It had been six years since I left. He was doing well, he had even stopped stammering—almost. My greatest surprise was that I experienced a certain pleasure in revisiting my village. Nothing had changed, other than that the notary had now gone over the edge and was travelling about in a carriage with false arms that my father had prepared for him. I saw my uncles Jérémie and Socrate again, still as drunken and blasphemous as ever. When they asked me what I was doing in life, I replied without blushing that I was a novelist. A good profession that pays well, I boasted, to impress them. Ah, good, they replied.

This vacation filled a void in my imagination. My inspiration was renewed by the contact with my roots. As I had been keeping company, for some time now, with a group of Montreal freemasons I considered influential, I wanted to please my new friends by writing a novel that would not simply pander to current tastes. It's the book of which I am least ashamed.

Its title was *Franchonne*. It was as badly written as the first two, but instead of celebrating the French race and its sacred soil, it was set in my childhood village, with all its flaws. I went further than I need have in mocking Father Lajoie, his servant (the Franchonne of the title), the churchwardens and the notary Poitras. Chamber-pot humour pervaded the story, and for that I drew on off-colour passages from seventeenth-century novels. Naturally the publisher Crépeau wanted nothing of this sulphurous novel, he who made his living from edifying works, and I had to bring it out through an English-language bookseller who was totally indifferent to the content.

As a novelist I had created and destroyed worlds with the ease of an absent-minded god, but this time I was up against real life. Of course I was secretly delighted to see my novel placed on the Index by the Archbishopric of Montreal, but I quickly saw the downside of being a scandalous author. The first to turn away from me were my Freemason friends, who, to my great surprise, had remained believers. All the critics who had praised me earlier recommended that the book be banned. My lucrative freelance work vanished, and I lost my job as proofreader for *La Presse*. "Our readers are Catholics," said my boss, "you understand that we can't keep you on. Good luck all the same." The publisher Crépeau no longer knew me. He sold all the copies of my previous books to a discount merchant, for a song. Later I had to do the same with *Franchonne*.

The worst was reading the condemnations levelled at me by my pseudonyms. Oscar Petit said that he had never read such a piece of trash. Samuel Legris challenged me to a duel for defaming the Mother Church. A third, whose articles I had lovingly crafted in my glory days, Jacques Levasseur, declared that I was a traitor to my country. I will doubtless never know who commandeered my bylines to turn them against me. I never inquired, being rather badly placed to carp about betrayals.

At a time when the four or five Montreal aesthetes were offering me their hospitality, I had made the acquaintance of a senator whom I liked to mock in secret because I was jealous of his fortune. I went to grovel at his feet, that he might save me from starvation. I hadn't a cent left, and my landlady had asked, respectfully, that I move out. The senator relished the company of artists, and he gave me a warm welcome. I thought that he was going to provide me with an ambassadorship or have me elected to the House of Commons to relieve me from my setbacks. Instead, I walked out of his office as a parliamentary translator in Ottawa, which was better than nothing.

I, who had already been utterly insupportable in my happiness, surpassed myself in my misery. Newly arrived in Ottawa, set apart, in my imagination, by the prestige of banishment, I spoke to no one. I presented myself as an unbeliever and let it be understood that I was an adherent to Maurras's Action Française. I was the victim enamoured of his own wound and wallowing in his misery, the arrogant outsider indifferent to common pleasures. What was most true and most amusing was that I was happy without meaning to be so, but I was careful not to breathe a word of it to a living soul. With my salary of three thousand dollars a year I had never been so rich, and I was content in my little Sandy Hill apartment on Besserer Street.

It was during this new exodus that I lost forever the desire to make a name for myself. A good thing, because here names just come and go. That is why for a long time I kept this page, ripped out of the Jesuit Relations, in my wallet:

We give a child his name sometime after his birth; passing from childhood to adolescence, he changes his name as the Romans changed their robes; he takes another name when he becomes a man, and yet another when he is old; and so he has different names according to his age. Escaped from some danger or released from some great sickness, he takes a name that he believes must augur better than the name he owns. Sorcerers or soothsayers will sometimes change the name of a sick person, imagining that death or the manitou who wants to attack this man will no longer know him under his new name. In a word, they believe that there are unhappy names and happy names, and a dream is enough to make a man change his name. It is often said that we bring the deceased back to life by giving their names to the living, and that is done for several reasons: to revive the memory of a valiant man, and to motivate him who carries the name to emulate his generosity, or to wreak vengeance on his enemies. He who takes the name of a man killed in war is obliged to avenge his death, and to come to the aid of the family of the dead man, especially as he who brings him back to life and who represents him carries all the responsibilities of the deceased, nurturing his children as if he were their own father, and they his children.

Lusignan no longer has any meaning, I said to myself, with a sense of relief that had been too long in coming. The devil take the fairy, the king and the knight: give me the freedom of anonymity!

At the office I was relentlessly loathsome. Convinced that my career as a translator would be short-lived, as the senator surely had more important duties in mind for me, I persecuted my colleagues with my sulking. All were still inflamed by the Dreyfus affair and I would have loved to take part in their discussions, but to be sure to displease everyone I let it be understood that I thought Dreyfus was innocent, despite my monarchist convictions. Overall, however, office life was disappointing. I wanted my colleagues to be scornful of me, but on the contrary they were totally understanding, they rewrote my translations without complaint, and all had experienced a more difficult exile than I, including Garneau, our boss, notoriously anticlerical; Sulte, a historian hostile to the Jesuits; and Roby, a poet whom I pretended never to have read.

I thought of altering my behaviour the day a colleague placed a press clipping on my desk and shook my hand without saying a word. The article reported on the fire that had incinerated the discount merchant's shed where my books had found their resting place. My work had disappeared, my identity as a novelist had gone up in smoke. I leaped to my feet and kissed my colleague on both cheeks. I invited the whole office out to a tavern and bought the first round of beer. I had to celebrate this accidental auto-da-fé; it's not every day that one lays to rest a mediocre novelist. We made merry the whole afternoon, my only pleasant memory of the time. But the next day, I couldn't help myself, I was once again that odious persona who draped himself in make-believe contempt in order to conjure the moral superiority he lacked.

．

．

．

．

．

THE PRESENT IS SO DISCOURAGING THAT I AM COMING to like my past. We will soon be celebrating the first anniversary of the armistice. Great festivities are in the works. At least, that's what it says in the newspaper.

The war. I cannot really say that I fought it, but what is certain is that I was there. When I am told that it's been over for a year now, I would like nothing better than to believe it, but I am not so sure that it's as over as all that.

That's because, since my return to Ottawa, a drunken ghost has been following me in the street. When he addresses me we immediately launch ourselves into passionate conversations. I have a hard time recognizing him when he appears, and as soon as I begin to see my own features on his face he vanishes, leaving me alone with my arguments, convincing as they may be. It really is me, however, whom I continue to meet, my twin, utterly drunk and slovenly. On these occasions the amused faces of the people around me alert me to the fact that I had best make myself scarce. I hear some saying, "You'd think he'd been gassed." Gassed, the word from the war that here and now means drunk. As soon as I manage to pull myself together and act as though nothing has happened, I move on, followed at a distance by this reassuring shadow that is so obliging as to accompany me on my latest migration.

Migrate, that's all I've done my life long. It's exactly that that Essiambre d'Argenteuil liked in me, I don't know how many times he said it. At thirty-five I'm already on my fourth or fifth life, to the point where I've stopped counting.

For the fun of it, my double and I sometimes switch roles. I'm the one who overindulges in polluted ginger wine, while he becomes this vagabond dressed as a lieutenant from the Princess Patricia regiment who roams the streets of Ottawa in search of some means of subsistence, or of a woman who might take him home as a kept lover. He is so desperate that he would accept just about anything, even work.

Go ahead, my beautiful drunken ghost, talk for me while I sober up a little.

The drunken ghost bows his thanks and picks up where I

left off. He talks better than I do, and listening to him gives me a respite from my own life.

Poor dear Lusignan...

To think that five years ago the city was at his feet. The soldiers setting off to chase the Kaiser out of Belgium were then objects of worship. Now no one gives him the time of day. His uniform impresses nobody, especially since, as they say, it's out of style. His regiment was disbanded last March when it returned to the capital. Only forty remained of the thousand who went off, and the absent ones had been replaced twenty times over. All were demobbed; each received the balance of his pay, enough to buy a three-piece suit and a one-way train ticket home. He wasn't there, our poor Lusignan, for the last parade. He had already quit in England to join the international expedition that was going to checkmate the Bolsheviks in Archangelsk. He was let go for unsuitability, meaning, in his case, for excessive drunkenness, and he arrived home in June, after the others. (It's true he drinks too much, I should know, I'm his guardian angel and I can't help but drink what he does, only I'm the one who gets drunk for both of us. It's a bit hard to explain, but I know what I mean.)

He received his discharge papers in Quebec, and after celebrating his return all by himself in the Lower Town dives where he had once been so happy with his friend Essiambre d'Argenteuil, he remembered that he still had a father who was alive, the Good Saint Joseph in the village. When my Lusignan saw him again, his father was restoring a harmonium, his pipe between his teeth. He who had never studied music had just brought back to life an instrument thought dead of old age. He was still as modest as ever, like a magician who is the only one blind to his heavenly gifts.

The father would have liked his son to settle down with him for good, he wanted to take him on as an apprentice in his workshop and to teach him what he still had to learn about the craft, but he wasn't interested. He sobered up and took his leave.

Before the war he was a translator in Ottawa for the Senate. He imagined, naïvely, that he could easily pick up where he had left off, but, poor man, he had forgotten his vile behaviour towards his colleagues and his superior when he was assigned, by the senator who was his protector, to the Princess Patricia Regiment as an officer-interpreter. He had a superb uniform made for himself and he paraded it in the office with his cap on, caressing his boots with his stick, even more arrogant than usual if that was possible. He demanded the rest of his pay, refused to shake hands with the colleagues who were so glad to see him leave, and for good measure butted out his cigarette on his boss's desk, uttering words I will not repeat.

But dear Lusignan forgot all his wrongs. And so his reception was less than warm the day he turned up to ask for his old job. Stifling a huge desire to laugh, the chief translator reminded him, pleasantly, that he had refused the leave without pay he had been offered and had preferred to resign, an act that deprived him of all his rights. His position had been filled. And the senator who had got him hired and who used to cover for him when he stepped out of line had now, so sorry, passed away.

After he left, furious as he was, he craved a drink, which might help him regain his composure. Impossible. With prohibition in Ontario there were no more watering places and no longer any way to buy alcohol in the light of day. For that one had to go to Hull, in Quebec, on the north shore of the Ottawa River. Fortunately it was not very far, just across the Alexandra Bridge, and we went on foot. A good thing I was with him, he drank so much beer that afterwards he could barely stand. That night he slept on a park bench, and I held his head so he wouldn't hurt himself. I also kept at bay the petty thieves who wanted to get their hands on his empty wallet.

I try to reason with him. With no result. He has to stop drinking, and above all to take off that uniform, it will only bring him trouble. The war is over, Lusignan, you have no right. It's true that it's his only respectable outfit and that he still cuts a fine figure wearing it, but it's against the law and it could land him in prison. Might as well try to argue with a cat, he won't listen.

He just pulled another one a little while ago. We were in the streetcar, he drunk as a skunk (I only appear to him when he takes to the bottle), and to please a lady who had just got on and who looked distinguished, he rose with difficulty and offered her his seat. The problem was that the streetcar was almost empty, and the lady must have thought that it was because of her age that he was being so gallant. She accepted the offer to put him off guard, but then skewered him with her gaze, so much so that I felt sorry for him. So I took him by the arm and had him get off at Le Breton Flats, that neighbourhood tucked away on the south shore of the Ottawa River that people here call simply the Flats.

He's staying at the Couillard Hotel these days, thanks to an admirer who is being paid in kind. I took him there, and fed him a small bowl of soup. And now it's time for me to go, he'll be sobering up. Let him pick up the story.

MY DRUNKEN GHOST HAS DISAPPEARED. ALL HE'S LEFT behind is a horrible gingery migraine.

I see that he's brought me back to the hotel. Very thoughtful, this guilt-inducing ghost. But I don't want to be here.

As soon as I feel a bit better I will put my uniform back on and take the streetcar to Union Station. I like that place, with its scents of coal and cigar, house smoke, man smoke. Good things happened to me there. When I was appointed translator to the Senate, my superior, Monsieur

Garneau, son of the great historian, himself an accomplished writer, was waiting for me on the station platform. It was the first time in my life that someone came to meet me at a train, and it took a lot of effort for me to hide my pleasure.

It's from there that in the autumn of 1914, the Princess Patricia Light Infantry Regiment, the unit to which I first belonged, departed, and it is there that I spotted Essiambre d'Argenteuil for the first time, in front of the newspaper and tobacco stand that has not budged.

Finally, it's there that I met this young woman whose name escapes me and who is giving me shelter in this hotel room, she whom my drunken ghost calls my admirer. She's the one who approached me, I don't know on what pretext; I don't quite know what I told her, I could barely stand I was so hungry. Thirsty as well.

She invited me to the station restaurant I had dreamed of visiting for three days. I must have wolfed down the meal of my life: two helpings of soup, pork chops, potatoes, raisin pudding, with strong tea. Suddenly I felt better, much better, and I began to feel well disposed towards my benefactor, whose plumpness had not attracted me at first sight. She watched me gorge myself, with such tenderness that to show my gratitude, I did what Essiambre d'Argenteuil used to do for romantic women in whom he had no real interest, but whom he wanted to leave with fond memories.

"To thank you, if you like, I will read your palm." She accepted like a child being offered a big gift. Having listened to her while I ate, I had no problem reeling off some plausible generalities as I turned her hand this way and that. "I see a sick old man, an aged mother who is crying... they are slowly slipping from your memory... ah, a good-looking man, elegantly dressed... I also see a child asking to be born... he is awaited..." And I ended by promising her happiness, marriage, wealth, etc. Her misted eyes told me I had hit the mark.

Then she led me to the hotel, as naturally as can be. "We can go to the Couillard, if you like. It's in the Flats, the room won't cost me much. I'd invite you to my place, but I can't, because I'm still a girl. I'd look like a floozy." I couldn't say no, flat broke as I was.

She told me yesterday that the room is paid up for a week; she does my laundry and every day leaves me enough to eat. When her back is turned I take enough from her purse to buy drink. As I am no ingrate, I let her straddle me when I'm sober. If only I could remember her name, I'd be nicer to her.

Ah, here she is, all smiling. A welcome change from my drunken ghost, who always has something to reproach me for. The room smells good all of a sudden. She's not pretty, as I said she's too plump for my tastes, but she is so good. She'd like me to tell her about the war, but I have nothing to say. She insists. "My war was grotesque," I reply. "Grotesque." She doesn't know the word.

She has such a big heart that she makes me want to be honest. When she knows me better she'll leave, and that will be best for her. So I tell her everything.

"Look, for example, I never killed anyone. The only men I killed were already dead. When we were alone, my friend Private Léon Tard and I, we discharged our guns into the corpses. We did that to practise for when we would meet Germans who wanted our skins, and since we would already have got used to shooting holes in human flesh, it would perhaps be less of a problem. We fired on English, French and Australian soldiers that German guns had killed, but never on Canadian bodies; we had principles, after all. Once, on our way back from our chores at the cemetery, we almost soiled ourselves when we came upon the cadavers of German soldiers raised from the mud by the last downpour of shells. They were erect there, eyes vitreous, skin green, and we rekilled them to the last man. An hour later the grave-digger shells had buried them again. That's what grotesque means. You understand?

"My only medals are those that everyone got just for being there, even the cooks, who all survived. I was never wounded. Just gassed twice, that was nothing. When the Princess Pats arrived in France in 1915, I'd already been demoted to private, and I took no part in the first battles that killed off half of our men. After two weeks I had to undergo a medical inspection because I was feverish. The doctor discovered a virulent syphilis I'd caught from an Englishwoman whom I'd been too eager to sleep with, just because she was English. I felt powerful in her arms because I couldn't imagine the same thing happening to me at home, a bit like the black American soldiers I knew who were so delighted to go with white women who spoke French. In their arms they felt more masculine and less Negro, also cleaner. The same thing with me and this little English redhead who walked the streets behind the sumptuous Salisbury Cathedral. But a syphilitic in uniform is not well regarded, never mind where the illness stems from, the Queen of Norway or a sailor's tart. I was sent back to England on the first boat, along with some others.

"I spent more than three months in the hospital for shameful diseases at Etchinghill. It seems there were complications; I also caught pneumonia. Once cured, I was court martialled and dismissed for immorality, a formality. As I didn't know where to go, I drank the money I had on me, and in Liverpool re-enlisted in a company of Canadian Infantry Pioneers. The company had arrived in England only two weeks earlier, and it was already short twenty-two men as a result of desertions, sickness and so on. And so it was engaging as fast as it could. No one asked what I had done before. I was alive, I was Canadian, that was enough. This is how I returned to the front and met Tard. The Pioneers were responsible for heavy manual work such as digging trenches and burying those who really fought."

I know my tale is riveting, but the little one's eyes are heavy with sleep. I have just explained to her how Tard deloused me before our monthly bath, and how I deloused him in return. She said, "That's enough for tonight. Come to me, I want you." I don't want her, but I can't say no.

·
·
·
·
·

THE LITTLE ONE SLEEPS SOUNDLY. HER YOUNG BODY,
fresh and chubby, winds itself about mine, which is too warm.
I would love to talk to her about Essiambre d'Argenteuil, I'm
wide awake. Never mind, I'll talk to her about him anyway,
it will do me good. But I will talk in my head so as not to
wake her.

It was at Union Station in front of the Château Laurier,
where I wanted to go a while ago. The Princess Patricia
Regiment was on its way out of Ottawa. He was talking to
a tall woman with a beautiful pale face when I first noticed

him. I was told later that this privileged beauty was in some sense his fiancée, an intimate of the viceregal court, someone very well placed. As for me, I was being told off by the colonel in no uncertain terms because I had turned up at the station without my uniform. I had given it to my landlady, Madame Latendresse, to be pressed, and I had left with my suitcase, forgetting to pick it up. After leaving his lady, Essiambre approached the colonel, who bellowed, "And is this our lieutenant-interpreter, who's going to war dressed like an accountant?" Essiambre calmed him down, and offered to lend me one of his spare uniforms. The colonel put me under two days' arrest, which I never served, and forbade me to parade with the regiment before our departure.

After changing in the toilets, I installed myself in the compartment reserved for officers. Essiambre came and sat beside me as though nothing had happened. Gratitude is an aphrodisiac, and goodness as well. I didn't know it then, but I know it now.

Before meeting him, I thought I knew English. He quickly disabused me of the notion. He spoke English with an ease I had never seen, even with a certain flair. And he often interpreted for me, as my military vocabulary was non-existent. He knew everything. How to salute, how to address inferiors or superiors in rank, how to drink to the King's health in the mess, everything. I'd had to go to great lengths to be engaged as an officer-interpreter, and in the end it was to take me off my chief translator's hands that the senator had found me this posting. Essiambre, on the other hand, had been singled out instantly as officer material, even without his uniform.

I had known him for barely an hour and already I was wishing I could have lived his life. He was a seigneur, a real one, not like Poitras. The first Canadian Essiambre had been a sergeant in the war with the Iroquois. Having made his fortune in the fur trade, the second of his name had acquired the Seigneurie of Argenteuil at the beginning of the eighteenth century. His great-grandfather had been killed at the siege of Quebec, before the Conquest. His grandfather had been a member of parliament, president of the Legislative Assembly, in the following century. That same Argenteuil had been one of the leaders of the Patriot Party during the 1837 Rebellion. His great age spared him the gallows, and he died in exile in Australia. His uncle had been a member of parliament and a minister in Ottawa, an influential Liberal. My Essiambre's father had been first and foremost a grand alcoholic who had squandered the family fortune at the gaming table and in foolish speculations. All that remained to my new friend was his noble title.

He had grown up on the ancestral seigneurial lands before his father had sold them off, then he had studied with the Jesuits in Montreal. His mother, a Wingham of Boston, had persuaded a rich cousin to finance his law studies at Oxford. He returned an accomplished oarsman and a lawyer. Proud of his British accent also, but in no way an imperialist like other Canadians who had followed the same path.

Before enlisting, he practised law in a large Montreal firm, and made his own fortune. Once when I found myself alone with him on the train, I asked him why he had wanted to go to war. His reply: "To have fought it." I understood then that this man was incapable of lying, he was as authentic as a character in a novel. A born leader as well, who could have said, like Bonaparte: "I win my battles with the dreams of my sleeping soldiers." Without knowing him, I attributed to him the power of dissolving all my inadequacies.

"And you," he asked me, "why the war?" Taken by surprise, I babbled the first truth that came to my lips. "Well, for the pleasure of being seen as a lieutenant. To serve the King as well. I would have preferred the King of France, but I took what came my way. I'm a monarchist, but only to get the goat of those who are not. I wanted to be beautiful and different, that's all. The aesthetic is my only guide in life. There you are..."

I remember that while speaking these words I glimpsed, over his head, my mother's face, and for once she was vaguely smiling. I so much wanted to please him by seeming profound, that I truthfully said everything that entered my head. Before Essiambre, that had never happened to me. It was often like that between us: I shared confidences that I myself was hearing aloud for the first time.

Our training camp was in Lévis, facing Quebec City, where we went to chase girls. Once, back from one of our excursions, Essiambre took me aside. "A friend gave me this book. Look..." It was *Franchonne*. He was the first of my readers whom I had seen in the flesh, and I was touched. That same evening, around a campfire, I tore the book to shreds, and invited my new friend to join me in burning its pages. I told him, "We'll make another novel, you and I." The little holocaust caused me no pain. It was essential that this book be reunited with the others in the flames.

In the camp, the officers had to learn everything. The shooting manual, the manoeuvres, the artillery guide, military etiquette, in approximately that order. What we learned one day, we had to teach the soldiers the next. We served our apprenticeship self-taught and in a group. Essiambre was always the first, I the last. There was one other who did very well: Lieutenant Garry of Winnipeg, the rich heir of an aristocratic family from the West, one of the rare Canadian officers in the Princess Pats, the others being almost all Englishmen nostalgic for the mother country.

He could be tough as well, Essiambre. One morning when he was replacing the captain charged with our training, he had Lieutenant Garry step out of the line. "You are the worst officer in the regiment. When I look at you, I'm ashamed for us. We're going to correct that right away." He made him sweat blood and water all day with a fifty-pound sack on his back, and he humiliated him with his brilliant sarcasm in front of the whole regiment. I felt sorry for poor Garry.

The next day, after the inspection in front of the colonel in full-dress uniform, Garry asked to speak. "My colonel, I am convinced that I am an unsuitable officer. I ask permission to surrender my commission and to serve in the ranks as an ordinary soldier." The regiment was stunned. After reflecting for a few moments, the colonel gave his consent, and Garry went to take his place among his former subalterns, who applauded him like a hero.

We laughed a lot in Quebec, Essiambre and I. When we went off in search of girls at the dance music kiosks on Dufferin Terrace, I willingly played the role of his straight man. The girls did as we did, strolling in twos, one pretty and one plain. Essiambre spotted a pair of girls seeking adventure and approached them with style. A consummate tactician, he began by courting the less attractive one, forcing the other to feign interest in me. After dancing with his, he handed her off to me and turned to the other, who lost no time pressing herself against him. The less pretty one didn't reject me, perhaps thinking that it was too early to regain her lost advantage. We offered them drinks, and it all ended in a room where a diaphanous curtain separated the two beds. Our pantings mingled without our being the least embarrassed by it; we played at who could finish last. We arranged to meet the following Sunday, when he contrived to ignore his new conquest in favour of the other; to punish him, the prettier one consoled herself with me.

I was able to tell him my life's story without feeling the slightest shame: my twisted ambitions, the dreams that had stayed with me. He listened with an expression of sincere interest. I had such confidence in him that I dared to take him to the asylum and introduce him to my mother. She was charmed, and when I told her my friend's name, she recited her family tree without missing a single ancestor, as though her madness had left intact her genealogical erudition. She even talked to him in an accent she thought was French. When we left, he kissed her hand and clicked his heels, and she curtsied. I had never seen her so radiant. As we were walking out she caught my eye for an instant, and whispered in my ear: "He's very nice, that boy. I have a son who looks just like him. But he's a priest." I was glad to have granted her that moment of happiness. By treating my mother with sincere respect, devoid of pity, Essiambre had revived in me an affection that wiped away my ancient grievances.

The colonel sometimes asked us to keep in touch with the rest of the contingent, stationed at Valcartier on the north shore of the St. Lawrence. One day when we found ourselves there, nothing was on the schedule but a morning briefing, and Essiambre decided we should picnic on the shores of the Jacques Cartier River.

It was to be the last beautiful September day, and it was warm. We were in light fatigues, he walked in front and I followed, out of breath. It was the first time in my life that I had gone walking in the forest. I had never strayed from the villages that embraced me, and in these woods I was like a foreigner landed here in the country's first days. He strode ahead as though he were in his own garden.

Towards the end of the morning we bathed in the river, naked of course, to harden ourselves to the cold. I was frozen when I came out, he too. "Come on, we'll climb the hill, that will warm us up!" The race was worth it. The river at our feet was greener than ever, and far off, under the sun, the steeples and chimneys of Quebec City shimmered in the noon light. As I was still trembling from the cold, he began to rub me from head to toe. Then he asked me to do the same for him. I had a stiff erection by the time I was done, and so did he. He had, then, the same indulgent smile he had shown to my poor sick mother. A moment later he was at my knees, holding my fists tight in his hands, as he deftly assuaged this desire of which I had never thought myself capable. I was still moaning when he rose, visibly moved, to fix me with his gaze. He had not opened his mouth, and I thought, naïvely, that he wanted to return to me what he had just taken. I told him that, and he gave me a tender smile. Then he turned to press himself against me and he pleasured himself with the help of my hand. Not a word afterwards, except: "Come, let's go down. I'm hungry, what about you?" We did not speak of what had been for me a blinding epiphany. And yet I would have had so many things to describe: the tired green of the autumn foliage, the river that had stopped flowing under the sun, the city resplendent on its headland. But his impassiveness ruled out any exchange.

Nor did we speak of it in the days that followed, or ever afterwards. Neither the bottle of red wine with its inviting paunch, the hard-boiled eggshells that stuck to our fingers, the bread that had dried out too quickly in the open air but that had the yeasty smell of pleasure made good, the meats and fruits that no longer had the same taste. Not a word. Nothing had happened, all that remained was a secret between us.

When we got back to the camp at Lévis that night, there was a party going on at the officers' mess. The colonel had restored to the soldier Garry his rank as lieutenant. The officer who had replaced him had had a bad fall from his horse on leaving Toronto, and as the non-commissioned officers were always lauding Garry's zeal, the colonel decided that his humiliation had lasted long enough. Delighted to be back with us, Garry treated us to one round after another.

Three days later, with the two captains absent, Essiambre was once again in charge of the regiment's training. He had me step out of line: "Lusignan, you really are pathetic, you'd think you were crippled!" He gave me a few orders, I couldn't execute them. "Good, fine. You're ripe for a little lesson, and the regiment will learn by watching you perform." So I, as well, was accorded a forty-mile forced march in the rain, with the fifty-pound sack on my back. I thought that Essiambre would show himself more humane towards me than with Garry; his words were even harsher. "Faster than that, sissy! The worst soldier in the regiment is an intrepid warrior next to you!" I wanted to die of exhaustion before his eyes, just to punish him.

The next day, at mess, I ate at the same table as Garry. I couldn't bring myself to look at him even once during the course of the meal. At night, while we were playing poker, our eyes met, and I think we understood each other very well. His eyes said, "But what do you want to talk about?" Mine replied with the same aplomb, "Me? Why, nothing at all. I'm just waiting for the next bid." Two marble saints could not have done better. Essiambre d'Argenteuil had united us in a brotherhood we could only escape at peril to our lives.

To put him off the scent, I forced myself to be more than friendly with Garry. He remained courteous, but no more.

We held our positions. As for Essiambre, he ignored us, his eyes constantly buried in military manuals.

After having been one with him, I was now more alone than ever in my life. It was as though he had forced me to emigrate to a country where every man is on his own and facing death, the no man's land of our instruction book. I, who had never desired a man, now was in love with a man. The worst was that he had not changed. Always the same: considerate of everyone, intelligent and funny in conversation, penetrating in his observations and curious about everything, with not a trace of sham in his behaviour. No, that day in the Jacques Cartier Valley, you would think that I'd been the only one there.

Did Garry suffer? I don't know. And Essiambre, what did he think about all that? Impossible to say. I know that I was jealous of the subaltern who shined his boots and polished the butt of his pistol, not because he was his lover, not at all, but because he followed him everywhere. I would have waited on him at table if he'd allowed me to do so. I read his books without understanding anything, and I loved the headaches they gave me. When no one was looking, I gathered up his cigar butts and smoked them in secret. I also drank from his glass when his back was turned, I prayed for him before going to sleep, and I refused to caress myself because I was saving myself for the next time. Always, I carried around in my mouth that taste of cold ashes that succeeds amorous incandescence.

We left Quebec in October along with the rest of the expeditionary force. I who had always dreamed of the day

I would cross the sea for France, that land I had not seen for at least two hundred years, I remember that the morning of our departure, leaning on the ship's rail, I thought of nothing. Except him. Ever since that day I have detested the ocean. Now I travel only on solid ground.

BEFORE MEETING ESSIAMBRE D'ARGENTEUIL, I HAD
never in my life suffered from solitude. To remember his
embrace was to realize that I had always been alone, and
suddenly I experienced actual physical pain, all the harsher
in that it was unfamiliar, and I had no remedy.

The promiscuity on-board ship aggravated my distress.
We were always together, he and I, but never alone. What is
more, it was our responsibility to teach our fellow officers
some rudiments of French, which put us in frequent contact.
I also found it hard to have Lieutenant Garry as one of my

students, because I constantly imagined that the others could hear what we were able to say to each other in our minds.

To introduce his students to the art of French conversation, Essiambre staged little dramatic scenes, such as the one where a unilingual Canadian officer had to marshal his meagre vocabulary to find the way to his hotel. I was always cast as the French gendarme who offered to guide the officer through the beautiful Paris neighbourhoods in which I had never set foot. When I played this scene with Garry, we were both blushing from start to finish. We were also poor actors, and his voice quavered when he said, to thank me, "You are kind, monsieur." I despised the amused expression on our director's face at that moment.

My career as officer-interpreter came to an abrupt end about a month after our arrival in England. We had been visited by the officers of the British General Staff, all of them highly educated, and those among them who spoke Sorbonne French didn't understand a word of what I said. I, unfamiliar with British speech, caught one word in four of what they said. It was as though I had one accent in the mouth and another in the ear.

One evening, I asked the colonel to receive me. "I can see that my place is not here, and the regiment would do better to take on a competent translator. Corporal Davies is a McGill graduate, his mother is French, permit me to recommend him. As for me, I want to serve as an ordinary soldier." To my great chagrin, he acceded to my request with joy.

He could have made a bit of an effort. He could have said,

I don't know, something like, "We need all our men, you are already trained, don't worry about others' opinions…" No, nothing, he instantly signed my demotion order before I could change my mind. He was even smiling.

I got none of Lieutenant Garry's applause when I rejoined the ranks. I had to fight for a corner of the tent, no one was interested in my company. Naturally, no one helped me put my equipment in order. At my first blunder, my corporal kicked me in the behind with such enthusiasm that I knew he'd wanted to do it for a long time. I also found myself, during my first months with the troop, doing chores and keeping watch by night more often than was my due.

At first, of course, no one spoke a word to the former officer I was, but the quarantine eventually came to an end. The first words I heard were, "But are you out of your mind to have come in with us? You were fine where you were, no? We were at your beck and call, we did whatever you wanted, you think we're going to admire you because you're marching with us in line? My ass!" He who addressed me thus was Rooney, my former batman. In time I was accepted, and when I was excluded from the ranks due to syphilis, I became an acknowledged member of the band.

If only I could have met Essiambre's gaze from time to time to let him know of my suffering. Not a chance. The day of my voluntary demotion, he was sent to school with the imperial general staff because he was the best performing officer in the regiment. When we saw each other again, not a nod of the head, not a smile, nothing. I had disappeared from his horizon.

Not much chance either that the colonel would change his mind and recall me as he had done Garry, he whom the comrades in the ranks had been sorry to see leave. It must be said that he was a good soldier who was seriously wounded at Armentières, and was repatriated against his will. He was a man, Garry, a real one.

Still, I did well in joining the men, and I derived a certain pleasure from my reduced status. First, because I was happy not to be commanding my fellows any more. Had I remained a lieutenant with the Princess Pats, I would have sacrificed more of my men than the enemy would have killed. And then, because I found it agreeable to be invisible once again. Before, when I approached the men, they stopped talking immediately and stood to attention. Now I could circulate among them freely, and I learned much more about them and about myself than if I had stayed on the top of the pyramid.

And so I no longer wanted to be lord and master of my fellow man. My contact with ordinary soldiers was my apprenticeship in democracy. I renounced all my dreams of nobility, something that surely would have pleased Essiambre, and if I reacquired my officer's stripes in 1917 it was strictly the consequence of those deadly coincidences that made us all so equal so fast. After re-engaging in the company of Pioneers I became a corporal within two weeks because I was the only one able to read the orders of the day. I was named sergeant because all the other non-commissioned officers had been killed, and I became a lieutenant again for the same reason.

·
·
·
·
·

IN ORDER TO PUNISH ESSIAMBRE FOR HIS INDIFFERENCE
towards me, every day I imagined some new subterfuge
that might wound him. Once I managed to steal some letters from his trunk, hoping to find compromising information that would lower him in the eyes of the general staff. I
only took those that had not yet been opened. They all came
from the beautiful tall woman he had been talking with at
the station the day we left Ottawa.

I thought I would be jealous of her, but on the contrary,
she charmed me. She was not at all his fiancée, as I had

been informed. He had never spoken of her to me. But she was in his life, and so I decided I had a claim on her, as I did on everything that concerned him. Amalia Driscoll is her name. It's thanks to her that today I know everything about Essiambre. I am still proud of stealing the memories of this woman about whom he couldn't have cared less.

October 1914

My dear d'Argenteuil, my friend for life,

Before leaving Ottawa you said you would wish of my person a portrait from head to toe, unvarnished, free of vanity. Here it is. I hope you will be happy to read what I dared not say, you who gave me lessons in frankness whose memory is still seared into my mind and into my body.

You asked me once how I would earn my keep if one day I were obliged to do so. As of late I have found the answer. I paint my memories.

It is the only recourse remaining to an old maid who may boast of having had a past, but who no longer has any future. Happily, I still possess hope, which is a theological virtue. Just as are charity and faith, other virtues with which I am well endowed. Beyond that, I must confess that the balance sheet is far from impressive.

Never, never in the world would I have thought myself capable of talking about myself (I preferred to have myself talked about); less still of mining my past for commercial ends. But I no longer have a choice. I must unveil myself like those mercenary dancers in cabarets of ill repute, or I shall die of hunger. Famine spurs me on to practise art. Which distresses me enormously, for I have read too much not to know that true artists generally take the opposite path: it is art that leads them to hunger.

And so I exploit my worldly memories in the service of newspapers and magazines, which pay quite well, thank you very much. To augment my revenues, not only do I recount what I once witnessed in the time of my splendour and what I now see at the soirées to which someone is kind enough to invite me, but I also produce sketches in which I flatter some and dim the beauty of others. Under a pseudonym, of course, chosen by the editor-in-chief of the newspaper which is my principal client, the Ottawa Citizen. He has baptized me Deirdre Hawthorne, but that must not be known, because if it were, Amalia Driscoll would be invited nowhere, and I would lose the small livelihood of which I am a little ashamed, I who as a young girl swore never to do anything with my ten fingers.

Naturally you will promise me, Essiambre, to keep secret the clandestine activities of this Deirdre Hawthorne, rose ink and peacock's quill. She continues to pursue her career as chronicler of the best salons, and it is perhaps that which will one day save me from penury.

But when I play music I always refuse to be paid, that would be more than I could endure. I sing in churches, I play the organ there, and believe it or not, I am much in demand. Music ought always to be free for everyone: it is my sole concession to this democracy that I abhor.

I am eager to see the end of the war, Essiambre, I dream of recovering those days that I realize now were happy ones. Life was easy, Ottawa was brimming with eligible bachelors who were there for the taking, and had I a little more good fortune, I would today be the wife of a minister or of some diplomat. I would be living in a beautiful residence on Sandy Hill, I would have servants whom I would ask what to wear on such and such an evening, people would come to my home for tea, and I would welcome with indulgence those hangers-on of my kind who prefer the buffet table to the delights of conversation. I would perhaps have an automobile like my sister, except that I would drive it myself. Finally, I would not be obliged to earn my daily bread with my pen or my charcoal.

A good marriage would perhaps also have enabled me to leave this hole that is Ottawa. I was not born here and, I feel it in my bones, I will always be a foreigner in this outpost that takes itself for a capital. And of that I am proud. I was born in Dublin, I never told you that. I grew up in Montreal and I came to Ottawa as a young girl. I have been trying to escape this small town ever since my family settled here out of necessity.

It is easily forgotten, but the fact is that I come, like you, from what once was one of the best families. We were, in Ireland, what was called, with a bit of scorn and a bit of envy, "Castle Catholics," that is, Papists in favour with the viceregal court because of their fortune. My family was not titled as such, but my mother's lineage included some idle gentlemen, and that was more than satisfactory to me. My paternal great-grandfather, through patience and industry, raised himself from potato serfdom to become the steward of a stallholder in the county of Cork. His most gifted son was apprenticed to a ship chandler, and the *family's prosperity began with him. He was my grandfather. He acquired wool or cotton mills. Wool or cotton? I don't remember, and it is of no importance. It's best to remain ignorant of such matters if one wants to cultivate a certain mystery around one's name. It enhances one's charm.*

Now I am going to tell you what you do not already know, I have owed you this confession ever since you revealed yourself entirely to me. My father was a scholar. As a young man, disdainful of the family fortune that he had not amassed himself, because one is rarely loyal to money one has not earned on one's own, and in love with natural science, he undertook lengthy studies which led him from Dublin to London, and from there to Paris and to Munich. He met Pasteur in France, and he corresponded with the greatest scientific minds of his time. At a very young age he was received into the Royal Academy of Sciences in Holland, without having made the slightest discovery, it must be said, but strictly because he was appreciated as a dilettante enamoured of those scientific explorations that are rarely lucrative, but are essential to humanity's well-being. In those circles dedicated to investigation, he was seen for a long time as a future benefactor whom it was wise to cultivate for the sake of the rich inheritance that would surely one day be his, and in the meantime one settled for his passionate conversation and his freely dispensed opinions.

He always talked brilliantly; in that sense he was a master of blarney in the great Irish tradition; he could even have held his own among the Hibernian monks who once preached to the Germanic tribes. When I was young I didn't see the Irish braggart in him, I only admired his British veneer. He loved to say things like, "One day chemistry will triumph over nature!" Words I thought profound, and whose banality disconcerts me today. I owe my present poverty to his failings, which I have forgiven him ever since I became conscious of the same weaknesses in myself.

He married in his early thirties, a bit absent-mindedly no doubt, and it is perhaps the only commendable thing he did in his life, a bit like a clumsy magician who once knew a moment of grace and who has invoked this exploit for the rest of his days to divert attention from his failures. As a young woman I sometimes wondered, anxiously, if my parents ever truly loved each other. I am not so naïve as to ask such questions now, and all I can say with certainty is that both had the means to become enamoured of one another without concern for the consequences.

My father was not the only one in his family with no stomach for textiles. The eldest, who had no choice but to take responsibility for the family business, was a gentle incompetent who always abhorred accounting and machines. In the rough world of my grandfather he was but an elegantly dressed convict in a luxurious prison. He found it vulgar, for instance, to see the family name inscribed in large white letters on the walls of our factories. He used to say it looked common. As soon as Grandfather died he disassociated our name from the company and handed over its management to a businessman known for his prudence. So prudent was he that he didn't foresee the technical advances that were to render our family penniless.

The enterprise, as my father repeated a thousand times, never formally went bankrupt. The truth is that the business's honour was saved by financiers who bought up the factories and the machines for a song. The family still owns some tenanted farms in Ireland as well as a rental property in Dublin, none of which I have seen, and it is the meagre revenue from these assets that now constitutes the largest part of its members' income. Which does not amount to a great deal, as there are still five children sharing this rent, which diminishes every year.

My father settled in Canada at a time when the family was still riding high. He had finally set his sights on entomology, and at the invitation of a professor from McGill University he had come to do research in an experimental laboratory in Montreal. He was only to have stayed a year, but he ended up as one of those involuntary immigrants you can find by the thousands in this land. Of which I am one.

Not surprisingly, this country pleased my father from the start, as his conversation, here, passed for being brilliant. After two years it occurred to him that he had family responsibilities, and he had my mother cross the Atlantic with the children. This adventure, which was to be brief, continues.

For a long time he lived happily between his insects and his little family; he didn't notice the time pass or his money melt away. At the beginning of our life in Montreal we lived in a superb house on Sherbrooke Street, and it was my mother who one day had to convince her husband that if the situation continued to deteriorate, we would soon be unable to stay on. I did not witness the scene, but I can imagine my father extricating his pipe from his mouth and saying, in a solemn tone of voice, "How unfortunate..." Decent man that he was, however, he bore no grudge against that destiny which had smiled on him for so long, and for the first time in his life he looked for a job.

He had the good fortune that is typical of those with a carefree nature. My mother was from a family more Catholic than the Pope, but that had always been fiercely loyal to the English Crown; in return for this zeal, it had been rewarded with enviable positions in the Empire's colonies. And so we had cousins who were administrators in Egypt or India, naval officers or professors of classical literature in Australia, and, among the faithful servitors of His Majesty, there was this uncle who had been secretary to the minister of justice in Sir John A. Macdonald's government. The uncle had just been appointed clerk to the Supreme Court, and was able to use his influence on my father's behalf.

As a result, my father found himself in the House of Commons in Ottawa, with the august title of assistant clerk of the Crown in Chancery. It was a sinecure which required a keen sense of etiquette, a style tilting towards the pompous, and elegant handwriting, qualities that my father possessed, but that would have been of no use to him without the protection of our powerful relative. The public service is thus constituted: merit counts for nothing, and advancement is always a matter of influence. My family profited from this golden rule. Someone other than my father, doubtless more deserving, was perhaps deprived of a necessary livelihood, and this injustice has fed my own.

My conscience tells me today that I must pay for this wrong, and I resign myself to it with a stoicism that derives somewhat, as you know better than anyone, from a certain coquetry. You,

Essiambre d'Argenteuil, once my sham fiancé, saw it immediately. "Don't be afraid of displaying your dire straits, my dear, but bring to it all the elegance that is yours. We love suffering here, especially when enhanced by a dignified silence on the subject." It is words like that which bring me at times to despise your memory; I know very well that you were not seeking to wound me with your acuity, but your words had the effect of leaving me naked before an unflattering mirror.

And so the family set out for Ottawa, and my mother applied herself to settling us there with all the enthusiasm appropriate to the spouse of a senior functionary. She never liked this city, but she let nothing betray her feelings outside the family. She knew only too well that my father's position was our bulwark against need, and she would not have said a single word that might have compromised our situation. We had embarked upon a phase of our life in which maintaining appearances became an inexorable law.

My sister and my young brother quickly accommodated themselves to Ottawa life; I, never. As my mother was accustomed to saying that London was worth more than Dublin, Dublin more than Montreal and Montreal more than Ottawa, I always cultivated the nostalgia of exile to impress my superiority on my fellows. For a long time, in fact, I insisted on keeping company with other rootless souls, and together we indulged ourselves by evoking those charms beyond the ken of the uninitiated. This sort of company is beyond me now, I no longer have the means.

I don't know if it was already common knowledge in our circle that we were indigent. Doubtless it was, but no one ever brought it to my attention, and you, Essiambre, less than anyone, because you know as well as I do what it is to be déclassé. Perhaps you had a mother like mine, who knew how to mask her family's poverty. When our difficulties became obvious and beyond help, she adopted an aesthetic that never failed her; we had henceforth to garb the ugly and the naked with beauty, good taste would be our bulwark against penury, a pretty blouse would hide a threadbare dress. I can say these things today; my mother herself would never have wanted to be so candid. We did not talk about money at home; we never said that this or that was lacking; we preferred to loudly voice our enthusiasm for the colours in clothes when we could afford them.

The nearer I come to destitution, the more I admire this mother who dealt so well with adversity. She who had not known how to sew or cook or clean, applied herself to all the household tasks, and never did we sense the outrage to her pride.

There are times when I would like to possess her gift. For example, on the rare occasions when we entertained, one would have thought oneself in the best bourgeois household in the neighbourhood, with at least four maids at our beck and call. But it was my mother who put things in order and prepared all the dishes, and she only hired a domestic to serve at table. Once the guests were gone, the queen of the household donned Cinderella's apron once more to scour the pots.

I never helped her. The subject never even came up. It was as though it were understood between us that I would maintain a healthy distance from the household chores in order to protect the remnants of aristocracy the family still had the right to claim.

My mother upheld this code of idleness by design to preserve my chances of one day marrying well. If I were surprised in the act of washing dishes or baking a pie, I, the marriageable daughter of the house, could be taken for a servant, and so I had to avoid dirtying my hands.

I no longer see things in the same way. I am now somewhat ashamed of this indolence that made my mother's task heavier, and I see clearly that all our pretensions were in vain. I have remained a marriageable daughter for life, all the more so in that I would be incapable of running a house. No sensible man would desire me unless he were rich. I do not know how to cook an egg, I do not know how to light a coal stove, and I am hopeless at sewing. In fact I have only one gift: the skill of being served. You know it, Essiambre, you've seen me at work. When I am in a house with servants, no one knows how to address them more sweetly than I, to obtain the tiniest services. I want to be remembered as a kind mistress; I want one to take pleasure in shining my shoes or in hemming my skirt. In this sphere I have no equal: in all the houses where I have been received, the servants were delighted to be under my command.

I now suspect my mother of maintaining me in this state of sheltered uselessness in order to keep me near her for as long as possible, as a purely ornamental staff for her old age. It is not a very charitable thought on my part, but I prefer it to the explanation you gave, d'Argenteuil, casting a more disturbing light on my situation.

The day you received your commission as an officer, if you remember, I was in your apartment on King Edward Street along with some others. When someone complained of having eaten too lightly at the Minister of Militia's, you slipped on an apron and cooked up a proper meal for all who were present. One would have sworn that it cost you no effort whatsoever. After the meal, an officer friend having lost a button from his tunic, you took needle and thread and skilfully sewed it back on, only stopping to take a sip of port or a puff of your cigar.

At the end of the evening, you and your friend walked us home, Leona McIntyre and me. We passed Strathcona Park near my home on Blackburn Street, and as I was congratulating you on your culinary exploits, you offered this explanation, which is branded in my memory.

"You boast too much of your ineptitude, my dear Amalia, for there not to be some troubling motivation behind it. Does this active disinterest not mask a denial of your femininity? What do you think? It would seem that you fear being taken for a woman. Or that you insist absolutely on being treated like a princess. In feigning weakness or incapacity you are always sure to be served. You should not, however, confuse these services so kindly rendered with marks of admiration and affection. That said, you play the role of an incurable incompetent admirably."

I blushed from head to toe. Fortunately the two others had gone ahead of us and had heard nothing, otherwise I might have strangled you. As you were only talking to me, I contented myself with that little silvery laugh on which I fell back when I had no argument, and asserted that I found your theory extremely nebulous. I answered that I had fled domestic servitude all my life. Leaving to others the task of tending to my person, I had acquired an independence of which women are too often deprived. I admit today, Essiambre, that you clearly saw through my bogus suffragette's sermon, but you were gallant enough not to force the issue.

Yes, you were right. In fact, Essiambre, you were for me a sort of dark angel who knows all our faults and reads our most intimate thoughts. With the one difference that you never took advantage of those embarrassingly exact intuitions to mock me. Nor did you try to seduce me with vulgar stratagems. You let me come to you myself, and I have never regretted those moments of intimacy when you taught me pleasures I could only have imagined without you. I still find it remarkable that all that has remained of our adventure is a feeling of fraternity, or, if you prefer, of complicity. Your successors will instruct me, I hope, in tenderness and love.

You appreciated my learning, you said, but I was careful not to reveal that I had never received an education due to the lack of funds in our household. Now you know. Only my brother went to college; he is a doctor today, in Niagara Falls. My sister and I studied at home. My mother passed on to us the knowledge she had received while being taught by the nuns in Dublin. She was an excellent educator, in fact, and with great gentleness she instructed us in arithmetic, English, singing and piano. A non-resident seminarian taught us Latin and a little Greek; a retired professor took care of the exact sciences, aided by my father, whose courses in physics and chemistry, I have to forgive him this, often meandered onto the subject of beetles. A friend of my mother taught us French, which I still speak with the accent the Queen of England must have when she receives the French ambassador. It was, overall, a solid education for a modern young woman, and I have only happy memories of those times when for four hours each day our living room became a classroom.

The rest I learned through reading. And I was voracious. I read the entire Bible very young, and immediately afterwards Homer and Virgil in translation, all of Shakespeare, all of Milton, Victor Hugo, Alexandre Dumas, Coleridge, Browning. I learned at least fifteen thousand lines by heart, and I can still recite a quarter of them without hesitating. I also loved music, and above all, the theatre. I excelled at singing. I saw all the plays and operas staged in Ottawa over a period of twenty years—that is, the few productions available to us; I even acted a little, sang opera in a few, too infrequent, amateur productions, and I would certainly have pursued a career onstage had I been less straitlaced.

Another thing: my education turned me into a replica of my mother. We already resembled each other physically, and despite myself I learned from her all the stories from viceregal court in Dublin, the gossip there bandied about, the customs of the place, what one ate and drank, and so on. Her past as a smiling aristocrat was reproduced in me and frozen there forever. To this day, in my mind, Queen Victoria remains thin and pretty, the Prince Consort Albert goes riding every day and electricity does not exist. Should I find myself in the presence of one of the friends from my mother's youth—and this has happened several times—I can recount in the greatest of detail scenes from Dublin high society that took place forty years ago, long before my birth.

I never fail to mesmerize my listeners, who wonder, scratching their heads, how their memories have become mine. I have become her, and it is for that reason that I will forever belong to another place and another time. The woman I see in my mirror is not thirty-four years old, rather she is seventy, like my mother. And so I will be a centenarian before my time, and my century will always be foreign to me.

What is most strange is that my sister, the pretty Rose, who grew up in the same environment as I, has no such memories. She is utterly indifferent to this knowledge, which is of interest only to the old and to historians. I am not the least bit jealous of her, by the way. What I possessed in sensitivity, she boasted in energy. In her youth she excelled at tennis; that is how she met the son of an important industrialist in the region, Mr. Devon, who owns foundries. You know him, he lives in the grand style, with a beautiful house at Rockliffe, servants, and all of life's amenities, even a car with a chauffeur.

As for myself, I still live with my parents, who are very old. My father is retired. He spends all his days with his nose in books on entomology, between his pipe and his magnifying glass, and for twenty years he has been writing an article for the Royal Society of Canada. He seems so happy that I sometimes envy him a little. My mother is still living in her 1880 Dublin, and she continues to criticize severely certain outfits that displeased her at court in those days. She repeats the same stories without tiring, to the point where I could tell them myself were she to allow me a word from time to time. We live poorly on the paternal pension, and we owe our rare indulgences to the meagre income that *still comes to us from Ireland. In brief, we get by as we always have, and this small revenue will come to an end with the death of my parents; afterwards I will have to make my own way.*

My brother and sister tell me not to worry. Rose has ample means to take care of my needs, and my rich brother-in-law, with whom I get along very well, says that he would like nothing better than to welcome me into his home. As for my brother Doctor Driscoll and his wife, they have always said that they would be prepared to welcome me. But I have no wish to end my days as a poor relative who fades away in the familial greenhouse alongside the other exotic plants one displays to visitors on holidays. I do not want that fate, no. I believe I deserve better.

You said you wanted of your friend Amalia a portrait that was true, now you have it. I have made an effort to match your frankness, to pay you homage in my way, you who so deftly led me to open myself totally to a man. Keep this portrait even if you want no more of me, as one day I will want no more of you. We will long remain friends, nevertheless. And of course I count on you to return my letters on the day you return to Ottawa with your marshal's baton.

Write me in French, if you please. With all the aid we are presently organizing in Ottawa for those poor Belgian refugees, it is truly the language of the hour. Your friend, etc.

In a return to my early vocation, that of a specialist in fraud, I easily simulated Essiambre's handwriting and addressed a short lyrical letter to Miss Driscoll wherein I extolled the beauty of the Jacques Cartier Valley.

Unfortunately, nothing came of this small vile deed. Essiambre hated writing and never read his mail, other than the letters from his mother to which he barely replied. I had shown myself unworthy to no end. My only consolation: Amalia Driscoll has never since been out of my life. She has remained a constant, forever associated with the sometimes happy, sometimes painful memory of Essiambre. I will see her someday, it has been decreed.

I MUST HAVE SLEPT A LITTLE. I HAVEN'T BUDGED FROM Hotel Couillard, Room 27, and the little one is asleep beside me. In sleep her face is almost pretty; at any rate, you don't see her toothless smile.

She has just turned over in bed, sighing sweetly like a woman well loved. That has given me an idea: to go in pursuit of this Amalia Driscoll. I will present myself to her wherever she lives, will show her all the gallantry of which I am capable, will ask to see her again, will seduce her, marry her and live off her for the rest of my days. It's not very complicated. And as I will be living in this lady's shadow, Essiambre will never leave me again. That is what I desire above all.

To pay court to Miss Driscoll, all I have left is this uniform that I no longer even have the right to wear. I ought to be careful. Once, already, I've almost been caught out.

I was certain I would be treated like a hero in Ottawa, even if I'd waged a paltry war. I thought I would have my choice of jobs in the upper echelons of the civil service. Not a door opened, nothing. One day, while disguised as a lieutenant, I stood in line in front of a business that was hiring, and I was insulted by the other unemployed. "Just 'cause you've come from the front, you think you're entitled to everything! You're just like us, you've got no rights we don't have, so just wait your turn!" I regretted having been converted to democracy during the war, I suddenly missed my aristocratic longings.

This episode was nothing compared to the rest. I wanted to meet influential people to get back on my feet. It would be fine, I thought, to find a spinster to marry whose magistrate or minister father could get me an office job. But I don't have the means to play tennis or golf, and I don't know a club in town that would have me as a member. And so I started going to church, hoping to be noticed. On my second Sunday at the Sandy Hill Church of the Sacred Heart, a kindly gentleman, clearly intrigued by my uniform, asked me if I had been in France. I told him yes, that I was new in the parish, and so forth. We chatted for a while, and he invited me to dine with him the same evening. The meal was mediocre but nourishing. He had a daughter, Eugénie or Hortense, I no longer remember, who played a little something on the piano while her father went to buy tobacco and her mother did the dishes; the other children, I believe, were playing outside. It was a classic set-up to trap a future son-in-law. I couldn't have asked for more.

I was not invited back. The mother must have suspected something when she saw me take three helpings of stew and two of pie. Or perhaps it's because I had a little nap during Eugénie's or Hortense's recital. I snore when I nap, that doesn't make a good impression.

Fortunately, I switch religions with ease. The following Sunday I turned up at the Anglican Church, Saint Alban the Martyr on Daly Street, thinking I would find more rich people who might notice me. I went in with a drink-induced migraine that was making me myopic.

I left before everyone else to stifle my urge to vomit, and I was pretending to admire the church's architecture when a well-dressed colossus grabbed me by the arm: "I'm going have you thrown in jail, but I'm going to smash your face first, you dirty fraud!" Three men with menacing attitudes gathered round us, things did not look good at all. What may have saved me from a severe beating, was that I had no idea why the gentleman was so angry. It's hard to raise your hand against someone whose expression is clearly sincere.

The fact is I was behind in the news. I knew that the extremely wealthy Gault of Montreal had equipped my regiment in honour of Princess Patricia, the daughter of Canada's Governor General. What I did not know was that the daisy adorning our standard was the founder's own tribute to his wife, Marguerite. On my uniform, the 1914 version, the daisy was sewn on the right sleeve, at elbow height. I had not worn this jacket long enough to notice it. I had left it with Madame Latendresse, my Ottawa landlady, and as I had been obliged to give up my Pioneers' officer's dress when demobbed in Quebec, I was only too happy to rediscover that first uniform, a lieutenant's, on my return. Madame Latendresse had handed it back to me with joy, and she was even happier to see me leaving along with it.

What I truly did not know was that Gault had cast off his wife after falsely accusing her of adultery; to punish her he had had the flower removed from both the standard and the uniform in 1916 or 1917, following their divorce. The daisy had betrayed me.

A crowd had assembled. Among them were veterans who did not find it at all funny that the regiment and the dignity of its cuckold founder had been dishonoured. I was sure they were going to give me a bad time and alert the military police, when a voice rang out: "Let him go!" It was former Lieutenant Garry. I would have thanked him, but I really had to rush.

I have a confession to make that will not surprise you, my good friend d'Argenteuil: to pass the time, on occasion, I gaze at myself in my diary. I light one of the eucalyptus cigarettes with which I treat my asthma, and I rediscover myself with pleasure.

Take this entry for August 2, 1914: "Archduke Franz Ferdinand of Austria was assassinated today at Sarajevo. Judge Cummings said war with Germany was imminent. But these grave happenings do not tell me what I should wear this evening!" The frivolousness of my words unsettles me and charms me at the same time. I could not know that the war would send so many young people to the grave, and could have made me a widow many times over. (Which would have afforded me a small pension at least, and saved me from indigence for the rest of my life; I know it's bad to say that, but the ache of poverty provokes in me the vilest thoughts. I will make my confession to Father McBride next Friday, I promise.) But I cannot keep myself from recalling with pleasure those days when we were dancing on the edge of the abyss, and in these present grim times the value of those memories only increases.

I also have a photo album that I look at when I am alone. My favourite picture was taken by Trevor Carlisle during our stay at Bark Lake in July and August of 1914, a few days before our meeting. I had my hair knotted around an ivory barrette, and I wore that marine blue bathing suit with an anchor that I will doubtless never again put on because the woman who wore it is no longer the same. (I wanted to give it to my niece the other day, but she burst out laughing, exclaiming that it was far too unfashionable. If I were a rich old aunt on the edge of the grave she would not inherit a penny, that one, because in mocking my bathing costume it's as though she were laughing at me when I was inside it. That youthful merriment wounds me, because I will never be able to keep myself from wearing in my mind the finery I have loved, especially that which made me beautiful. But I forgive her. There, it's said.)

The photograph. I am wearing black stockings to protect me from the mosquitoes and the cool wind that was always blowing on the lake. You do not see very much of me, but I know what *is there under this ensemble. My celebrated alabaster skin (you remember—you, the first man to see me as I was born?), the shoulders of an experienced swimmer, the breasts of a woman who could give suck to all the orphans of Ireland, thighs that would make me loved by one man for an entire life. Pardon me for these details that you know, but I love playing the shameless one with you, I whom Ottawa society has always taken for the last of the prudes. The night before the day when the photo was taken, I swam naked in the lake at nightfall, as I often did. In those moments I felt so much a woman, so whole, so true; I was the water spirit who comes to the aid of the prince held captive by the evil fairies. (I hear you laughing from here; do not laugh.)*

Trevor Carlisle and his wife had rented the house of the former Finance Minister, Atkins. I was only to have spent the one weekend, but I enjoyed myself so much that the Carlisles invited me to stay on for the rest of the summer.

A word about Trevor, whom you do not know as well as he deserves. His father was a minister under Macdonald, but, having given his all to politics, he had left almost nothing to his children, other than an illustrious name. A bit like you. Once he had become a lawyer, Trevor practised politics, he was even Mayor of Ottawa. When the Conservatives regained power he was named Commissioner of Railways, a very lucrative post. He had been my younger brother's tutor at college, that is how we knew each other. We had flirted, he and I, in times past, but it was completely innocent. We were happy just trading meaningful glances when we saw each other on Sundays at Saint Joseph Church, on

Wilbrod Street. We adored skating, and often went to the Minto Skating Club to impress those less skilful than ourselves.

I would have allowed myself to love him, but I sensed that a man like him could only marry into a secure fortune. I am the one who introduced him to my friend Mabel Addison, who sang with me in the parish choir. Her family was in the lumber business, they were comfortably off. She had all it took to please Trevor, including beauty and intelligence. (I remember, in this regard, noting in my diary: "Money marries money.") It did not take long for Trevor to ask for her hand, and I strongly encouraged him in this initiative. I was bridesmaid at their wedding, and we are still friends, all three.

It's too bad that I have no photo of the house. It is superb, like all the other holiday houses at Bark Lake. The great wealthy families of Ottawa congregate there in the summer. Besides the Carlisles, who owe their prestige to politics, there are all the industrial clans: the Rogerses of the railways, the Woodses of steel, the Madisons of the flour mills, the Johnsons of electricity. The senior public service is represented by the Saint-John Smithers family, sergeants-at-arms in the House of Commons from father to son, and by the ineffable Judge Cummings.

It was a constant party, do you remember? Each had his day to invite the others, all rivals in refinement. It was tea at the Rogerses', dinner at the Woodses', sherry at the Carlisles', or port and coffee at the Cummingses'. Some houses, including ours, were so large that there were numbers on the doors to the rooms. In each there was the silverware and porcelain dishware indispensable in any good home in the city; even the maids and valets were so well dressed that one might have thought them wealthy. One could only tell their domestic status by the fact that they were never seen in casual dress. Informality was the prerogative of the affluent.

I had to myself a kind and very funny little maid who had been assigned to me because I was the only one who understood what she said. She couldn't put together three words of English, and so I became her interpreter, and she was constantly grateful. She was not pretty, no, but she was, how shall I say, fetchingly plain. At night, in my room, when everyone was in bed, I amused myself by teaching her English words and the rules of etiquette, and she forgot nothing of what I taught her. I also began to instruct her in reading and writing. She assisted me when I rose in the morning and when I retired, and I exposed myself to her gaze without the slightest shame; it was like walking naked before a cat, an exquisite sensation. She adored outdoing herself in her kindnesses, and in her presence I felt myself alternately a queen and a child. We became equals, however, when we talked as women. I had to teach her some of the rudiments of intimate care because the poor girl had not learned much in that way in the countryside where she was born.

I sometimes talked to her as to a little sister, a practice that greatly displeased Judge Cummings. "Really, one does not fraternize with the servants! They could develop bad habits, you'll give them delusions of grandeur and soon they'll be demanding higher wages!" These reprimands made us all smile, for we knew that the good judge was most particular where etiquette was concerned.

It is he who made me the reproach that became legendary around the lake. To go sailing with my friend Trevor I had worn my green sweater and my white skirt, because it was chilly on the lake this beautiful July day. I returned with my face tanned and my hair in disorder, and Trevor and I had laughed heartily at his docking manoeuvres, worthy of a Sunday sailor. Judge Cummings had observed us from his doorstep, and when we arrived for sherry in the afternoon, he declared for all to hear, in the gruff tone he adopted when delivering a lesson, "I find it inconvenient that a woman dressed in a green sweater should go sailing with a married man." We were all struck dumb, not knowing what exactly he found inconvenient, the green sweater or the married man. Everyone seemed to meditate on the question, and then we all burst out laughing, with no consideration for his august presence. The judge, as it happens, did not in any way take exception to our hilarity, but only requested another sherry.

Judge Cummings was not as sanctimonious as he seemed. He would have had a great deal of difficulty, I imagine, maintaining this posture of moral superiority before his sister Ophelia, who had been a well-known actress and had pushed immodesty to the point of pursuing a career under her true name. Widowed and penniless, she accepted her brother's hospitality during the summer. She had played all the great roles on the stages of New York and London, she had been Roxanne, Medea, Cleopatra, Antigone... I had boundless admiration for her, not only because I adore the theatre, but above all because she was the incarnation of all my desires to escape. This young woman from a good family had succeeded, thanks to talent and hard work, in leaving behind her the dark little town of Ottawa and charming the most sophisticated audiences in the world. True justice did exist here on earth, and her life confirmed it.

When her brother entertained, she performed monologues for us from her repertoire with a passion that only comes from a mastery of one's craft. When she was acting she was twenty years old once more, and her youthful stage presence clung to her long after the presentation. It was she, Ophelia Cummings, who convinced me, forever after, that salvation is to be found in art.

It was an athletic summer. I swam several hours a day, and I perfected my paddling technique. I adored the canoe races we organized on Sundays. In the evening we made music, and I sang more willingly than in the city, for the lake air seemed to lend more freshness to my voice. I will leave aside bridge and other social games that attracted me less. I preferred the pleasures of reading. I reread Milton's Paradise Lost, and, under Ophelia Cummings's influence, I conquered Sophocles, Euripides and Racine's Britannicus. This last, which I preferred to read out loud before my mirror, greatly astonished the little maid. "By us there are Racines on the poorest road in the parish. The boys are lazy, the girls are mucky. I don't think they're related to the gentleman you're reading there. They don't talk fine like that, oh no!" She asked me to teach her a few lines from the play. "If ever I see again one of the Racines from near us, I'll say these words right to his face. Will he be surprised..." I wonder whatever became of her resolution.

One evening when we were dining at the Saint-John Smitherses', a guest arrived whom no one was expecting, a certain

Essiambre d'Argenteuil. Do you remember? You did not impress me overmuch, excuse me for saying so; I even found you rather modest, not at all the sort to flaunt his merits in order to attract attention. A handsome man, yes, but as I was at the time considering several tempting prospects, I did not pay much heed to your appearance. I only noticed your literary erudition, superior to my own, and your manners, impeccable in every way.

I was, in fact, the only one not to succumb to your charms. And yet you needed only a few hours at Bark Lake to entrance all the other ladies. Especially the mothers who had marriageable daughters. Even the men adored you: the young boys whom you astonished with your skill at swimming and tennis, the fathers who admired your talents as a lawyer, and the snobs like Judge Cummings who only had eyes for your title as the Seigneur of Argenteuil. I enjoyed listening to this chorus of praise but did not join in, a lack of interest that irritated my good friend Mabel Carlisle: "But why are you looking down your nose like that? He's handsome, he's well-bred, he is destined for the most wonderful political future! Trevor says that all he has to do is to fight a good war and he will be Prime Minister one day. What more do you want? You're being so choosy..." Even my little maid noticed you: "Madame, this Monsieur d'Argenteuil, he's the most beautiful man on earth. If I were you I'd marry him right away."

I did not seek out your company despite the efforts of my friends Carlisle and Woods. Frances Woods, who prided herself on being a good matchmaker, had decided that we would see each other again in Ottawa, you and I. At the tea she hosted in your honour the day of your departure, she said quite loudly, so everyone would hear, and to compromise me a little, "You are looking for a commission, Monsieur d'Argenteuil. You should seek the help of our friend, who is with us here today. Amalia Driscoll knows everyone in Ottawa. She is a frequent visitor to Rideau Hall, the Governor General thinks most highly of her. She has only to open her mouth, and the deed is done. But she is modest, she does not like to flaunt her connections. I am sure that if you woo her a little, your efforts will bear fruit more swiftly than you might believe." The entire company concurred, while I blushed. We then agreed to see each other again, a public pledge from which neither you nor I could withdraw. Do you regret it? I do, sometimes, a little, I must admit. It depends on the day.

The summer grew cooler, and the vacationers began to thin out. I must have been the last to leave Bark Lake, much later than the Carlisles, who had left me their house to enjoy. There was no one remaining but the cook, the gardener and the little maid. My stay was no less agreeable for all that. I read voraciously in front of the fireplace, and walked in the woods instead of swimming. In my moments of reverie, I thought of those men I had known at Rideau Hall and elsewhere, and I wondered who among them would dare to ask for my hand. Would it be tall Gillespie, the Chamberlain of the Governor General's residence, who was promised a fine career as colonial administrator? Of course not, I could never wed an Anglican! Then it would be Richmond, His Excellency's aide-de-camp, also an Anglican, but he liked to say that to marry me, he would go to Rome to be baptized by the Pope. Playful words, of course, but widely enough heard that one could take them seriously. You, d'Argenteuil, who are Catholic like me, know that it was the sole advantage I allowed you at that time.

My friends exaggerated my influence, which was non-existent, but they were right to say that I had access to Rideau Hall. It had been so since I was a child. My father, given his high office, was regularly invited to all the functions at the viceregal court and Parliament. At century's end the family often attended the parties hosted by the Governor General, Lord Aberdeen, and my small girl's imagination was nourished early on by this sort of pomp. But as the family fortunes declined with no hope of recovery, my mother began to refuse more invitations than we accepted, given that we had nothing elegant to wear. As soon as we had exhausted our wardrobe we had to stay at home. My mother could muster marvels of inventiveness to lend us a bit of style, but there were limits to the mixing of blouses and the dyeing of dresses.

Winter saved me. The Countess of Minto, whom I had met often when I was a child, adored skating. She had lent her name to the Sandy Hill skating rink, and, intrepid skater that I was, accustomed to long excursions on the Ottawa River, it did not take long for me to make my mark at the Minto Skating Club. I let no invitation from the Governor General pass me by when his court paid a visit. My mother consented to these outings because no one would guess that my attire beneath my thick coat was so modest, and I was able to give myself a fetching air with a little white bonnet and scarf. My cheeks reddened by the stinging cold, I had no need of makeup.

I could do anything on a skating rink, and I had no equal at tracing threes and eights on the ice. I was also sought after as a partner for skating waltzes when the viceregal Foot Guard's little orchestra was present, which was quite often during the time of Lord Grey.

When Prince Arthur, Duke of Connaught, the cherished youngest child of Queen Victoria, replaced Lord Grey, he fell in love with the sport, to my great joy. I was chosen to introduce him to waltzing on skates, and he complimented me at some length for the grace with which I performed this task. As of that day I began to receive invitations to Rideau Hall in my own name. I thought my fortune was made.

This was the time when my sister had just married money, and as she had a well-stocked wardrobe I was able to borrow all the outfits I wanted and appear in the world without having to exhaust my brain.

Prince Arthur's favours cast a kindly light on many years of my life. He often invited me to take tea with him, and on occasion we even found ourselves chatting alone together. He loved my conversation, which was soon known in Ottawa and it earned me many more invitations. If I had been able to dress according to my tastes, I would have gone out every evening.

The prince said that what he liked in me was my moral sense. One Sunday in March when we were taking tea together he had had served a magnificent cake of nuts and apricots coated with vanilla cream. I refused the piece offered me, and he was astonished. "His Royal Highness will surely pardon his loyal subject for being Catholic. I am observing Lent, which is a period of mortification. In the forty days preceding Easter, I abstain from all treats of this sort." The prince said nothing, and I was afraid I had displeased him by showing myself more faithful to the Pope than to the King. But at Easter, exactly three weeks later, a valet from Rideau Hall delivered to me a cake identical in all respects to the one I had refused, with a note from the prince: "To his loyal Catholic subject, this token of respect. Connaught." It hardly needs saying that this gesture on the part of the prince had many tongues wagging in the capital's salons.

I had become a celebrity. To please me was to please his Highness. Men lined up to invite me to dance at the viceregal balls. That is how I came to know all the aides-de-camp at Rideau Hall during the Prince's tenure. At every dinner, I found one sitting beside me. When one of these gentlemen courted me, other men's gazes, increasingly, turned in my direction. Agreeable to men, I began to please women as well. That is how I became intimate with Dorothée de Villers, lady-in-waiting to the Duke's daughter, Princess Patricia. I became her confidante, and thanks to her I learned the secrets of the viceregal house.

There was not just Rideau Hall, its teas and dinners. There was also this passion I had never acknowledged, the moving pictures. I loved Mary Pickford's movies so much that I sometimes went to showings by myself, even if it was hardly appropriate. I left these spectacles under a spell, and told myself that could I choose one vocation in this world, it would be to play the piano in a movie theatre. I play well enough for that, and as it is a well-paid job I would lack for nothing, and I would have the great pleasure of participating in the making of a work of art with an immediacy that is constantly being renewed. But I would have revealed my poverty in accepting such employment, and my worldly status would have suffered an irremediable blow.

My nostalgia for those days is tempered by my memory of the pain I endured every time I became interested in a man of quality. What will he say the day he learns the true state of my fortune? Will he still want me? I expected, of course, that he would conduct himself like a perfect gentleman and say nothing! I also thought that in this world there must exist gentlemen who would be more than pleased to marry a woman in dire straits in preference to one who would be financially independent and perhaps more resistant to the authority of her husband. Surely, for some men, a good education and a keen artistic sensibility were attributes as welcome as shares in the railway or in big business. There had still to be wealthy men, like my own father in times past, for whom the qualities of one's mind counted for more than one's bank balance. No?

Well, no. The mind attracts only the mind, and when big money is at stake, morganatic marriages are novelettish rarities. When they live the life of the mind, men are poor, or they become poor like my father because they do not have the necessary toughness to protect or increase their holdings. The only exception I knew was you, Essiambre d'Argenteuil, but I did not appreciate this while we were seeing each other.

I was already an autumn leaf when Prince Connaught opened the doors of Rideau Hall to me, but I must have been the only one not to know it. Autumn leaves, that's what one calls faded debutantes of my sort who have never found a taker. I *am not distressed by this term, not at all. Especially since you, Essiambre, forced me to acknowledge my carnal desires; thanks to your schooling, all that reticence proper to an old-fashioned ingenue has dropped away. You initiated me with such grace and delicacy that I no longer fear my cravings, and I love this body that you claimed to find attractive. I know well that I was respected in the Ottawa salons for my aesthetic sensibility, my courage in voicing my moral convictions, but there are days when I realize that all that amounted to very little.*

My distress is now so complete that the idea of marrying beneath one's station does not displease me as it once did. After all, there are notable precedents. It is said that Princess Patricia herself, Connaught's daughter, intends to marry a man with no royal blood. He is Alexander Ramsay, who was naval attaché to the Viceroy in Ottawa, I knew him well. To marry him she will have to give up her title of Royal Highness, she will no longer be a princess, only Lady Ramsay.

By the way, I disapproved of this possible marriage when I heard talk of it, and I let everyone know how I felt. However, I would give anything to live the fairy tale that awaits this Ramsay, and today, to set me apart from the lowly commoner, all that remains to me is this celebrated moral sense that so impressed Prince Arthur. It's precious little.

I have no choice, I am trapped in this posture for life, I can no longer deviate from it. I have turned my back on too many promising Protestant suitors to change my ways. My past sacrifices have rendered me hard and severe, and I am sometimes the first to deplore it. I have always been known for respecting my religion's strictures, as though my Catholic faith enhanced my uniqueness in those salons where I was perforce almost the only one committed to my beliefs. To see certain movies or to read books on the Index, I asked permission of the Bishop through my confessor, and nothing gave me more pleasure than to talk of those constraints with my Protestant friends. I admit now that I was endowing myself with one more enticement, and I imagined that this religious armour would make me more desirable. I was the inaccessible Catholic, my religion heightened my appeal.

I attend mass every Sunday, I take Communion at least once a month, I go to confession the first Friday of every month, and I support all the good Catholic causes. And I do not hesitate to impose on my kind the same strict regimen. When my childhood friend Adelaide Johns married the Scottish Calvinist Hamish Robertson, I wrote to inform her that I was breaking with her forever. She did not reply, she did not dare. I saw her recently at the By Market buying cut flowers and I made certain she had clearly seen me before turning my back just as she was about to hold out her hand.

I lacked charity, my sister tells me, and she is right, but I cannot do otherwise, this ostracizing instinct is all that remains to me of the aristocrat I almost became.

And so there you are, my dear Essiambre, you who know better than anyone that I am only playing a moralistic role in order to intimidate those around me. You also know that the world in which I live hardly gives me the choice. A poor excuse, my friend, yes, I know.

I think of you often, you who have taught me so much about myself. I saw myself as a swan, I was but a goose. Thank you for setting me straight.

I have no rights over this woman or any other, but there are moments when I convince myself that Essiambre has willed her to me, or that he would have presented her to me in any case in order to compensate me for his absence. An instant afterwards I realize that I am lying to myself, as always, but I forgive myself with ease.

·
·
·
·
·

THE LITTLE ONE. SHE HAS JUST AWOKEN AND IS looking at me as though she were going to devour me with her eyes. In her place, I would have chosen better.

I say "the little one," but she is not little at all. She has large breasts of a becoming whiteness, a lot of stomach with rolls of flesh, and an ample behind with a little tuft of hair at the opening of her buttocks, but her goodness leads me to disregard her corpulence. Her straightforwardness charms me also. She just has one small flaw: to put herself to sleep, she babbles endlessly.

I only half listen, but I'm wrong. What she says would fascinate Essiambre, I'm sure, he who loved war so much because it brought him close to the commoner I am, as is she. Besides, his greatest pleasure in the army was to take part in those saturnalias where the officers served the common soldiers at table, and I remember that he drew on all his comic talent in the process. The men adored him. Say, my lovely Essiambre, I'm going to let you listen to the little one, you'll love it. I'll lend you my ears...

She's from Nazareth, a miserable parish on Allumette Island on the Ottawa River, two days' drive from here, one day by boat. "There was no future for a girl like me on the island," she says. "I wouldn't even have found anyone to marry, unless I went with some asshole, some no-good, or a bit of both. There was no work there either, no factory, no office, nothing but farms that can't even give people a decent living." She will never go back, she swore that on the heads of the children she can't have because the doctor told her she was sterile.

She fled the island a few years before the war. Her father always said that a daughter who leaves her family without permission is a good-for-nothing. She left anyway, seeing as she already felt she was good-for-nothing. Her mother said she didn't know how to do anything in the house; her father said she wasn't even good for coupling because he didn't find her pretty. Her mother disagreed, she said her daughter was in fact good for nothing else. "She's a little whore, that one. Made of arse skin!" The little one didn't agree with either of them, fortunately, otherwise she would never have left, and I, whom she calls "my beautiful captain," would perhaps have starved to death by now.

She doesn't know where her parents are from. They were born on the island, that's all she can say. Her world began with them; before, there was nothing. The father cut wood in the forest in winter and farmed his fields in the summer. There were sixteen children at home; she was the ninth. There's no one from the family left on the island. All the boys abandoned the paternal land. Some sought their fortune in the West, others are lumberjacks in northern Ontario. Where? She doesn't know and doesn't care. The girls have settled elsewhere, just like her. Her mother is dead, her father also. "If they were still alive," she says, "it would be another good reason never to go back to Nazareth."

That's what troubles and delights me about her, that way she has of recounting the worst horrors so casually. "When my three little sisters died of the Spanish flu, my mother killed herself by throwing herself into the well. That's the way it is where we come from: the men hang themselves in the barn or blow their brains out with a hunting rifle in the mouth; the women throw themselves into the well or the river. My father didn't kill himself. He died of cancer of the rectum. He'd been sitting on it for thirty years, you understand..." Her voice is musical, jolly.

One must never make the mistake of telling her that Allumette Island is a romantic name. The time I told her that Samuel de Champlain had wintered there with the Algonquins in 1610, she replied, "I don't know any Champlain out there, just one Samuel, a fat fellow with bad breath; it couldn't be the same one. Our neighbours were the Salvails, the Pellerins, the Métiviers. He maybe wintered with us, your Champlain, but he didn't stay, otherwise I'd know who he was." There's nothing historic for her about Allumette Island. It's just her story.

There was a school in Nazareth, but nobody went there. There was a church, but the people on her road only turned up at Easter, at Christmas and for baptisms and burials. "The only time we prayed in our house," she says, "was before the Holy Virgin's statue we'd set up in the garden so the potatoes would grow.

"As there was nothing to do where we were, everybody had only one idea: to whack yourself off, or somebody else. In almost every family the fathers tried to screw their prettiest daughters; the brothers were next in line. The same thing all the time. I started to be ashamed of that only when I met families where it didn't happen. Then I saw that our family was no better than the others, and that made me feel bad, because I saw that we had no more class than anyone else.

"The first one who tried me was my grandfather. He told me he'd give me candy if I made him feel good, but I didn't want to. I knew he had no candies in his pocket. My other sisters, Anna and Thérèse, who were not too bright, had already been had by him, so I knew what to expect. My father never touched me. He preferred Jeanne, the oldest, and Henriette, who made my mother jealous because she had beautiful thick hair. My other sisters said I was too ugly for him to touch me. It's because one time, my two brothers, Viatime and Ermille, made me climb into an apple tree. They left me hanging from a branch by my two arms, I was afraid to get down, so they took the opportunity to pull down my pants. I fell on my face and my nose has been crooked ever since. I was cross-eyed already, so it's true I wasn't a pretty sight. Anyway...

"Around us the girls began going with guys when they were twelve. Thirteen at the most. I started late, I was fourteen, and I didn't even do it on purpose.

"The first man in my life was my cousin Anselme, the handsomest and strongest man on the island. A circus artist from the States had taught him feats of strength, and he was respected also because he earned a lot of money as a boat pilot on the river. But you couldn't tease him for long before he got mean. When he was little, his father beat his mother when he got drunk and made her sleep in the barn, even in winter. When he got big, Anselme started beating his father so he would stop mistreating his mother. After she got sick and died, his father tried to hang himself. Anselme cut him down just in time, and his father was left weak in the head and paralyzed. In the family they said that Anselme had saved him on purpose so the old man would be left crazy. He spent all his time sitting in the kitchen, while his daughter fed him by hand and wiped his behind. His only pleasure was when the hired man brought the mare in front of the window, the mare he liked so much and that the family refused to put down even though she was old. The hired man had the mare turn around the yard three or four times, and the old man smiled because he remembered when he had been happy with his animals.

"To punish his father, Anselme sometimes took his revenge on the horse. When he came back from his tour on the boat he went to get the mare in the meadow, brought it in front of his father, and whipped it violently until it was on its knees. The old man cried, but said nothing because he could no longer speak. When Anselme told about what he had done, he said, 'And there, Papa blubbers and me, I laugh!' He laughed twice as hard when people told him it was wrong."

The little one tells me that it happened one August night on her parents' land, after a corn-husking party to which everyone in the parish had been invited. She didn't really want to be there because all the men who were drunk started to feel up all the unmarried girls, her included. Suddenly Anselme asked her to dance. She couldn't believe her luck! For the first time in her life, the women in the parish were jealous of her. Obviously, she didn't say no.

Afterwards, he took her behind the bar and gave her a swallow from his bottle of whisky blanc. She'd never liked the taste of alcohol, but she didn't say anything so as not to displease Anselme, who seemed happy to see her drink. Then he told her that four or five louts wanted to jump her so she would stop putting on airs, seeing as how she said no all the time to the guys who went after her. They wanted to screw her, they said, to bring her down to their level. "If you want, I know a hiding place where they won't bother you. And I'll be with you, they won't dare." She followed him, thinking he might have other thoughts on his mind, but because he was too handsome for her and she'd drunk a bit she wasn't afraid.

His hiding place was a little shed beside the river that smelled of chicken shit. It didn't take her long to realize that she had been silly to follow him. "Come on, take off your dress, Miss better-than-the-others. And down with your panties, I want some pussy tonight. We'll see if it's true that you don't want to do that with anyone…" They did it on two sacks of oats someone had left behind. He was gentle afterwards, he even lent her his handkerchief so she could wipe herself. He asked her if she'd liked it. She said yes because she was afraid he'd hit her if she said no. He told her to keep the handkerchief as a souvenir. After they left she asked for another mouthful of whisky, and she drank almost all the rest of the bottle. That helped her forget the soreness between her legs and, even more, in her heart.

Her troubles that night were not over. Once everyone was gone, she wanted to go to the toilet. But one of her brothers had locked the dog in the outhouse because he'd been too excited by the neighbour's bitch. When she opened the door the dog jumped at her face and bit her. She still has a scar over her mouth. "It hurt so much," she says, "and it bled so much, that I peed in my pants. As I was crying at the same time, everyone came out and started to laugh." As one laughs heartily when someone unsavoury gets his comeuppance.

They laughed at her for a long time after that incident. She heard about it hundreds of times: "She don't have much luck, the fatso! Weren't enough for her to be bitten in the face by a dog, she had to pee in her pants!" Every time someone new came to the house her mother told the story of her daughter who had got bitten, and everyone laughed as though it were being told for the first time. Had people known what had happened just before, they would have laughed twice as hard.

But you would think she doesn't know what it is to bear a grudge, as though the story of her life were a bit like everyone's. No, she doesn't blame anyone. Especially not the dog that bit her in the face, because he's the one that gave her the notion of leaving the island.

She asks me if she can go on. I say she's a good storyteller. She smiles in the darkness.

"Not long after I was bitten, the dog disappeared. Maybe he fell in love with some female gone wild with one of the packs of stray dogs that came through the parish of Nazareth from time to time.

"He was called Ti-Cot, the dog. He turned up again on our doorstep one morning, his flanks torn, limping, missing an ear. He seemed to have had a hard time away from the farm. We took care of him for a while in the barn, and then, back on his feet, he settled in with us like before.

"It wasn't long before we realized that we were missing some chickens. Then when we saw he was also killing kittens that he buried here and there to eat later, my father tied him to a fence post one night, took his hunting rifle and put a bullet behind his ear. I was looking out the window, I saw everything. Just as my father was loading his gun, Ti-Cot held out his paw. He looked up at my father tenderly, as though asking forgiveness for his betrayal.

"That night I dreamed that Ti-Cot came to wake me up so I could follow him with his pack of wild dogs. He talked to me in a language I was surprised to understand, seeing as I had never learned it. I woke in a sweat, and it's then I decided to leave home. I didn't want to end up like Ti-Cot.

"A few days later, when Anselme offered to take me to Ottawa for the day on his boat, I didn't think twice. *Adieu, Nazareth.*"

It was the best trip of her life. The only one also, because she has never gone anywhere else since. Anselme was a bit surprised when they arrived in Ottawa and she told him she wouldn't be going back home that night, or ever. She had to insist: "Anselme, you've got no choice, you have to help me. After all, you were my first." But his mind was a blank. "I was drunk that night, you think I can remember all the women I've had?" Finally it came to him that he had an old girlfriend in Ottawa who might help her: Virginie, a girl who had made a life for herself and who was a waitress in a restaurant.

"After they finished unloading the boat, Anselme took me to eat something at a restaurant. Apple pie and tea, I remember. I'd never eaten anything so good. It was my first time in the city, the first time I was waited on, everything seemed big and beautiful, I was laughing every two minutes. I must have stayed like that a good three or four years.

"Anselme explained that the place where we were was called the Flats, and that Virginie didn't live far. He went to find her. I had to wait outside all night but I didn't care, it was warm, it wasn't raining, and I was better off out in the street than on Allumette Island. When Anselme came back the next day, he introduced me to Virginie, who didn't seem too happy to meet me. But Anselme had been persuasive. Virginie had agreed to put me up for a while and to find me a job as a maid to some rich people from Quebec City, the Lamothe-Frémonts. Good people.

"I changed my name when I changed my life. Before Ottawa I was called Philomène, but as the Lamothe-Frémonts had a daughter with the same name, they asked me kindly if I wouldn't mind... They didn't want their guests to confuse their daughter with the maid. No problem, I didn't care. I would have changed my religion, even, to become a servant and never see Allumette Island again. The children in the family renamed me Concorde: it was the name of an old aunt on the Frémont side who they'd liked a lot even though she left them nothing in her will."

I jumped when I heard her say her name. Concorde... It's true that I had only known her for three days, but still, I was a bit ashamed to have already forgotten her first name. I promise never to forget it again.

"I like my life," she told me. She was a servant in great houses: not only with the Lamothe-Frémonts, who took

135

pleasure in improving her diction, but with the Atkinses as well, who showed her how to serve at table, and where she learned a bit of English. There are days when she dreams of working in the laundry for the Governor General of Canada, because she thinks she has enough class now to get into Rideau Hall as a servant.

She is also proud of the men she has known. "There were a lot," she assures me, "because here in Ottawa I've stopped being ugly and fat. But it's just because I'm not beautiful—anyway, I'm not as pretty as my friend Virginie—that I know how to make men like me. I have to make more of a fuss over them than the beautiful women, who only have to let themselves be desired. I have to work a bit harder, but it's not a problem. I have a way with men now, there's not one who can resist me, not even you, my beautiful captain."

The little one reminds me of someone, but whom? When I ask the question, she replies, "I can look like whoever you want. If it makes you happy, just choose." That's it, it's come back, she reminds me of Flavie. Flavie... I won't say anything to the little one, the comparison might upset her, you never know.

I've been sleeping for a few minutes, I think. Her last sentences went something like this: "I came to Ottawa to make some memories. Now I have so many I'm starting to forget them." She caresses my brow like a mother who loves her child, and curls herself around me.

FINE, ENOUGH HANGING ABOUT. THAT'S FIVE DAYS
I've been loitering here. Goodbye little girl, and thanks for
everything.

I dress quietly in the darkness, to avoid pointless
explanations.

But if I were a man, a real man who knows how to love,
I'd marry this young person tomorrow morning and put my
life in order. I'm sure she's an admirable individual who's
a hundred times more deserving than I am, but her amorous enthusiasm will not deflect me from my hallucinatory

wanderings. Without her charity, which moves me, I wouldn't have glanced at this poor girl, all of whose beauty is in her goodness. A bit of a coward too, I let my fatalism deter me: I've never been able to love the women who loved me, and those I desired never returned the interest. To complicate things, when two people love each other it's never for the same reasons or at the same time. Love is a sublime misunderstanding. Yes, that's what I will tell her if I see her again one of these days. She's intelligent, she'll understand.

Closing the door behind me, I hear the little one's cheerful voice: "Till next time, my beautiful captain!" I walk away as though I haven't heard.

It's a dark October night on the Flats, and it's cold. So much the better, the cold clears my head. In front of me, the stairs leading to the upper town. I climb them easily, my suitcase weighs almost nothing, and my drunken ghost has vanished.

I walk for the rest of the night: I'm in great shape.

Say, I'm going to have a coffee at the station restaurant. There I'll refine my plan to get back on my feet. I'll have to act quickly, winter is on its way. A shelter, a job, a bit of money, anything at all, I have to find a way out. Amalia Driscoll must fall in love with me, it's as simple as that.

Sitting in front of my coffee, amid the noisy bustle of arrivals and departures that always delights me, I have to stifle my laughter when I think about the last few months.

Back in Ottawa, I went to see Madame Latendresse to collect my things. She said she was happy to see me alive, but I sensed she was offering me a cup of tea just to be polite. I accepted, to be polite myself, and I lingered on purpose because it was raining and I had nowhere to go.

Her husband arrived at the end of the day. He proposed that I have a drink before leaving. I couldn't refuse. With prohibition, it's not so easy these days to fortify oneself. He had hidden in his basement a bottle of whisky of doubtful origins. I told him that I missed England, because there women had the right to drink in pubs. He couldn't believe it. I added that women also smoked in the street, and did the jobs of all the men who were off at war; I'd even seen some driving streetcars. The fellow found my conversation more and more fascinating. One glass, two glasses, three glasses, I stayed for dinner, and during the meal we drank, he and I, a gallon of poisonous wine under the furious gaze of his wife. It's not that we pretended not to notice her anger, the fact is that we no longer noticed anything. The husband and I fell asleep side by side on the couch. You would have thought us two drunks leaning against the first wall that presented itself.

To be certain that I would never again set foot in her home, Madame Latendresse led me the next day to a rooming house run by a lady she didn't like, and paid my first week's rent out of her own pocket. I couldn't pay the second, and the landlady had me thrown out by her fat son, swearing that it was the last time in her life she would take a tenant from Madame Latendresse, the old cow!

I found another room the same day in Sandy Hill, and I had to move again the following week because the lady didn't believe me when I told her I would be receiving my veteran's pension any day now. I'm still waiting for my pension, and I've still not paid any rent since my return. But I am past master at the art of skipping out.

There is a house where I lasted three weeks, a record. A boarder was staying there to whom I played the suitor, Miss Dumoulin, spinster and secretary to a Member of Parliament. She saw through me, it was clear, but I was still able to borrow five dollars, which I wanted to send, I said, to my brother who was a missionary in Africa. The fourth time the landlady asked for my rent, I threw my suitcase out the window during the night between Saturday and Sunday. In the morning I put on all the clothes I had and went out wrapped in my bulky military overcoat. I had trouble walking with my three shirts, my two pairs of pants and my six pairs of socks, but it was with an easy grace that I said to my neighbour on my way past, "See you in a while, Miss Dumoulin." Two hours later I retrieved my suitcase from the yard, while the household was at mass.

The hardest thing was to find food. The Indians used to fast to clarify their ideas. That must be why my mind is so clear and I'm a waking dreamer all the time. My last landlady, Madame Simoneau, on Cathcart Street in Lower Town, had cooked a roast pork for Saturday night's meal. She had let it cool on the kitchen windowsill. I was pretending to read in the living room, and the aroma of pork and garlic gave me visions of a wolf on a glorious hunt; I had turned into an Indian. Suddenly the lady said to me, "I have to go and see the neighbour. Can you look after the house?" Why of course, Madame...

She had hardly stepped out when I threw myself on the roast and consumed it in four minutes flat. Fifteen minutes later the lady came back and shrieked as though she were being murdered. "My roast! Someone took my roast!" Feigning astonishment, I swore that no one had been in the house, and since she could not imagine that a man might devour a three-pound blazing hot roast that fast, she didn't even suspect me. I told her I had seen a young man wearing a red cap pass in front of the window. "That Robitaille! It must be him!" "We should look into it," I added, to feed her suspicions.

As I commiserated with her in her loss, to thank me she invited me for supper; there was still some macaroni. I accepted, to keep her off the scent. I had dessert too, to be polite. That night I almost died of indigestion.

Recalling the expression on Madame Simoneau's face, I began to laugh so hard that a railway policeman tapped me on the shoulder: "Listen, the owner says you've been hanging around here since eight o'clock. You'd better move on now. You're going to miss your train..." I would have put him in his place, but the words didn't come. Another time...

．

．

．

．

．

FORTUNATELY THERE ARE CHURCHES WHERE YOU CAN
go to warm up. My favourite is Saint Francis of Assisi in the
Flats, which belongs to the Capuchins. But I don't just go
there because of the weather. I pray as well. I have not lost
my childhood faith, and I can easily summon up my prayers.
Today I'll pray that Flavie is still alive.

Essiambre didn't know her. That's something he missed.

When I remember the little hotel room we stayed in,
always too cold or too hot, then I know I exist. I can still
taste the bags of pale fries the Belgian canteen owner

handed us when we got hungry, and his beer, pale as well, which he served up in large blue and white faience bowls.

I was a sergeant in the Pioneers. Flavie's ambulance unit had come for the Senegalese infantrymen who had wandered into our sector and were in very bad shape. Flavie had been left behind with us because we were short of nurses, and when the time came to escort her back, my superior had volunteered me.

Nothing about her struck me at first; her femininity was concealed by her uniform, that of a little French Red Cross sister, as my humanity was hidden under mine. Her clipped accent intimidated me, obviously, and to put us on an equal footing I had brought along a copy of *Les Misérables* I'd picked up in Paris. As we drove along I looked for an opportunity to show her I was well read. Finally I said, "You know, I've just learned about the death of Jean Valjean." She replied, "I'm so sorry. Was he one of your comrades?" Her ignorance, so casually revealed, charmed me. All my life I had thought of the French as possessing the sophistication and erudition I so yearned for. I was a bit like my mother, for whom the lords and priests of our acquaintance might eat like everyone else, or even more so, but would never defecate afterwards.

I thought she was from Paris, of course, like her forty million compatriots. I told her that I had been there often and had loved Notre Dame and the chateau at Versailles. I feared she would respond with an advanced course in architecture which I was determined to counter with contrary opinions, but she answered, "Paris. Ah yes. I hear it's very pretty, Paris. I don't really know, I've never been there." This was more than I could deal with. Here was a woman placed on earth to teach me honesty.

It was when she told me where she came from that I became hers completely. The Vendée... the Vendée... "You know Flavie, I think God truly loves me..." And I began to dredge up my old readings like a senescent miser who has just remembered where he hid his gold. The Vendée, Cathelineau, the sublime paradox of Catholic resistance and Royalist revolt, the fraternal Republic that slit men's throats, raped peasant women and murdered children by shattering their skulls against walls. At last someone to whom I could talk about the ideas that obsessed me! Why did French Canadians, treated so unfairly in their own land, offer to serve the English Crown along with all the Natives, and Métis such as this Patrick Riel of whom I'd heard, who fought in a unit of sharpshooters side by side with the grandsons of his grandfather's executioners? And those Gurkhas with the British army, the Algerian, Senegalese and Kanak fighters who got themselves killed for their conquerors? "Why, Flavie? Because in mingling his blood with his master's the servant raises himself to his level? To set himself free, perhaps? To surpass him, even? To dominate him in turn? What do you think, Flavie, you the Vendéan?" "Listen, that's very interesting what you're saying, but all that, you know, is politics. I have to tell you that it doesn't interest me very much. Me, I take care of the wounded, you understand? I help them to survive, that's already a lot. But won't you have a coffee before going back?" I would have liked her to be more cultured so she would understand that it was the Vendée of history I desired in her body, but her innocent charm was ample compensation.

I delayed my departure on purpose, and thanked God when the curfew came into effect. She fed me a little and I accepted the webbed cot in the infirmary. I realized that my ideas meant nothing to her, and so I decided to make a last-ditch effort. Having no wound to enlist her sympathies, I told her I had been syphilitic. "Show me," she said matter-of-factly. We went behind a curtain, and she pronounced my cure complete. Putting on my pants, I told her that I desired her. "Yes, I noticed," she answered, with a smile that spoke volumes. "We can see each other again if you get leave. At Droucy. I know a little hotel." To obtain this leave, I immediately wrote a letter declaring my mother dead.

I would have loved to see her undressed. But the sky was so grey, the earth so brown, the air so chilled by all those cadavers that lay across our path, that she could not even bring herself to remove her wool stockings, and so as for the rest... Mediocre lover that I had always been, I was conscious only of my own pleasure, and I had never seen it written on the face of a woman. Flavie was a sphinx-like mask undone by pleasure. As soon as I slipped between her thighs, she was seized by spasms and emitted sighs of contentment that made me twice as manly. I was very flattered of course, but she was the one who was gifted, not me. "I'm like that with all men," she said, to excuse herself. I, the ninny, thought I had the right to be offended.

There was also the dawn, bluish for once, when I watched her sleep, still astounded at my luck, and when I caressed her cheek, saying, with my mother's false French accent, "Flavie, my love, my only love..." she awoke, laughing heartily: "Don't be silly, my sweet Canadian. Go get me the chamber pot, I really have to pee..." There too I pretended to be affronted by her sauciness, but I could never keep up the act in her presence for very long.

I did, however, push my new-found sincerity to its limits by proposing marriage the day I became a lieutenant again. But now, she who loved to laugh turned sombre. "No, really, you can't say such things! My fiancé is a druggist, he's with the army in the East, he's a good man, and I want to keep him! His father is a well-known shopkeeper in Nantes, I swore to his mother on her deathbed that I would marry this boy. Our two families have been close for a long time, the Kochs and the Rosenthals, and we've been promised to each other since childhood. So no, please, don't joke about that, you're breaking my heart..." Her unit left the sector the following month, and I never saw her again. But I have blessed her transit through my life many times since. At school with her I learned a little about what it is to speak the truth.

Flavie had moved me on once more. If I had not met her I would not have known how to behave towards Essiambre d'Argenteuil the day we saw each other again. He'd been much talked about since we had separated. In particular,

I remember the act of sympathy that so endeared him to the men. A sergeant in his company, an orphan from birth, had had his skull shot away right beside him by a German shell, and for a month he wore his perforated cap as a sign of mourning. After being awarded the Military Cross and two or three other distinctions for bravery, he obtained a leave from the Princess Pats to join a propaganda unit whose responsibility was to encourage enlistment in Canada. Promoted to major, he travelled around in a Daimler with a chauffeur and shot films about the front; he had set himself up in a castle that was requisitioned when his team moved into my sector. He had heard about my resurrection and invited me to drop by and see him.

I was trembling like a leaf by the time I arrived. No one answered when I knocked, and so I walked into a grand salon. Still no one. I opened the door to a room, and a beautiful naked woman of a certain age let out a piercing cry. I learned afterwards that she was the owner of the castle. Essiambre appeared immediately and came towards me smiling, his arms open wide, a glass of champagne in one hand, his cigarette holder in the other. As if nothing had transpired, he introduced me to the lady at some length as she got dressed. Without thinking I shook her hand while she pulled on her silk stockings. My compliments, Baroness…

We went into his office. He spoke very quickly, lighting cigarette after cigarette, writing non-stop while reading a dispatch out of the corner of his eye. It was clear from the way he busied himself that he wanted to stop me from talking. In fact I said almost nothing. I listened to him the way one listens to someone once loved but now become anonymous. You understand the language he is speaking, but you no longer speak it yourself; you nod your head when the meaning of certain words comes back to you, and you smile when you don't get the drift. That was our conversation: he spoke, I listened.

"I heard about your little troubles," he said, more or less, "but you've survived them, so let no more be said. And you've made lieutenant again without a senator pulling any strings, congratulations! Now listen, I need you. I have trouble writing in French, I'm more at ease in English, and I need a secretary. You'd write letters, speeches for the troops, appeals to our fellow citizens so they'll enlist en masse. You get the idea? I'm counting on you!"

I refused. He didn't react, but he stopped playing his nervous game. Heating water for tea, he began to speak to me of the baroness in terms so crude that I suddenly began to like him less. He went on to describe an orgy in which he had participated during a leave in 1915. It took place in a Scottish manor, where the guests were disguised as small children. Dressed as a little sailor riding around on a tricycle, he had found himself penetrating, in a standing position, a war widow in a crinoline with a ribbon in her hair and a shepherdess's crook in her hand. I counterattacked by talking about Flavie. "She's the one who showed me the way back," I told him. He did not let up. Displaying a Prussian iron cross, he sang the praises of a German officer, prisoner of war, Count Captain von Wille, who had wept for his dead mother in his arms. I replied that his tea was very good.

In the half light of the Capuchin church, I think again of Flavie, who, with the lack of modesty combatants acquire in the presence of death, went to the bathroom in front of me, crouched under her shirt. My whole body remembers her. Still drenched with desire as I recall the scent of perspiration that clung to her uniform, far too grey, I study Christ's Stations of the Cross to control my erection, otherwise I'll never be able to get up and leave. A lady in a flowered hat pauses in front of me and places a coin in my hand. I would thank her, but I rather resent being mistaken for a pious bum. And I would gladly drop the coin in the alms box on my way out, but I'm too thirsty.

ESSIAMBRE WON THE DAY ANYWAY, WHEN MY COMPANY
of Pioneers was grafted onto his regiment. Having sworn off
the comforts of the Propaganda Service, he had earlier asked
to be reunited with the Princess Pats, saying, "It's better to
make history than to write it." A motto that suited him well.

He had arranged for me to be attached to him as his
chief clerk, so I had no choice. I say that, but I was delighted.
Forced to spend time with him, I was again attracted to him.
I didn't desire him any more, I only wanted to be reminded,
by my closeness to him, of how he had so deeply shaken me

one late summer's day. I allowed myself to be intoxicated by this memory in order to keep the prevailing horror at bay. At the same time I had the impression that the affection the troops held for him, due entirely to his courage and integrity, spilled over a bit on me and haloed me; just by being by his side, I had the illusion of being liked a little by the others.

I wrote his dispatches, his orders of the day, his letters to the French authorities. And above all I fulfilled that responsibility which Essiambre abhorred: I had to read all the letters from the men to their families, and I censored them when required. I adored doing that for him, and I even kept those I found especially appealing, longer than I should have.

Dear Mama,

We have a new liutennant hes called Luzignan. A guy who dosnt seem one of us. I think he must have kissd major Esiambers ass to get here. What I dont understand is they say he has a French girlfreind. An asshole like him I don't get it. But what do you know, love, like uncle Alphonse says, is stronger than wanting to shit.

You tell Octave he can take my skates, he can have them. Yestrday we killed three germans and the major congrattilated us. Hes for real. The French cofee tastes awfil I miss yor tea. Pray for your boy who wants pece.

I let it all go through, obviously, and I sometimes wondered, troubled, if the Germans facing us made as many spelling mistakes as this poor boy from the Gaspé.

I also wrote to families who had lost one of their own from among our ranks: a stylistic exercise that tested all my skills, because I had to show compassion for men I had never seen in my life, or whose passing caused no regrets among the troops. To save time I copied some letters and sent them to several families, while making sure they lived far enough away from one another that no one would doubt the sincerity of my sentiments. Among others I saved this one, concerning Private Blondeau, because I must have recopied it at least fifty times.

Madame, Monsieur,

My responsibilities as Major of the Princess Patricia Light Infantry Regiment impose upon me a painful duty. It is to announce to you the death of your son, Private Jean-Baptiste Blondeau. A volunteer, he was with us from January 6, 1916, for he understood before many of his compatriots that the Canadian army is defending in Europe those sacred values which are justice and democracy. His zeal during basic training caught the eye of his superiors early on. A jolly companion, he had only friends, and he knew how to make new ones when death took them from him. In combat his courage knew no equal, and his future promised many honours and certain advancement.

His end, like his life, was exemplary, and I had the sad honour of being witness to his last moments. We had received the order to launch an attack on the trench, and he had insisted on being the first in line. He fought like a trapped bear, and when we returned from our mission, he, as usual, brought up the rear.

Always the first to set out, the last to return. We had all regained our shelter when a last German bullet, traitorous and deadly as the rest, entered his ear and lodged in his brain. It took us some time to realize that he had surrendered his soul to God. He was simply seated on the ground, we could not see the thread of blood that flowed from his ear, and he had a distant look, like a man who is searching within himself for a precious memory. His last thought must have been for you, his dear parents, about whom he had only good to say.

I ask you to accept, Madame, Monsieur, the deepest sympathies of a regiment that feels itself, henceforth, orphaned. My sincere respects, etc.

Private Blondeau was even more of a thief than my friend Tard, and he cheated at cards to boot. The third time he was recaptured after deserting, the non-commissioned officers quarrelled over who would command the firing squad. They played a little poker, and the winner had the honour of shouting "fire."

Essiambre never read my compositions, I had his confidence. In going through his papers one day I discovered the other letters from Amalia Driscoll. Just as before, none had been opened. And so I began to write to this lady, and it is really thanks to her that I earned my stripes as a ghost writer in uniform. I had to feign for her a tenderness that Essiambre had never felt for anyone. To write sincerely I only had to think of Flavie, and the ink flowed freely. Her replies enchanted me.

·
·
·
·
·

NOVEMBER, 1915

Essiambre, help!

I am becoming ridiculous.

My pretensions to nobility forbid me the simplest of deeds. If I enter an elevator and I am not alone, I would die rather than press the button for the floor where I am going. If there is no elevator attendant I wait until someone asks me my destination, I reply, and I let the other person act for me. I will take every opportunity life offers to assert my power. When I am alone in the elevator I press the button myself, but only because I have no wish, after all, to remain there for the entire day...

The same thing for the streetcar. I never run after it, there is nothing so vulgar as those people who climb on panting, all dishevelled from their sprint. I prefer to melt in summer from the heat or to freeze in winter while waiting for the next car. I never pull the bell cord to get off; I find that coarse. And those people who expose you to their body odour in accomplishing this act... it's disgusting! No, if no one pulls the cord for me, it's simple, I do not get off, I prefer to walk. That causes me certain inconveniences. For instance, last Saturday, as I was on my way to the A.L. Greene store, where I don't like to be seen but where one finds many pretty things at a good price, no one pulled the cord at Cumberland Street, and I had to continue four more stops to the Château Laurier. Happily the day was fine, and the little unplanned walk did me good. At least I did not violate my principles.

All these stratagems are beginning to seem like an enormous idiocy. For the moment I believe I am the only one to see it, but sooner or later I will have to resign myself to living like everyone else, or I will end up in the asylum. More and more, I am isolated. In the time of my splendour it cost me little to break with an Adelaide over a question of religion, or to bar someone from my circle for adultery, but the fact is that these exclusions have resulted in my being viewed as a kind of conceited Pharisee. After having fled the sinners whom I thought to dominate with my moral superiority, which I am the first to acknowledge was bogus, it is now I, the right-minded one, from whom others flee.

It is as though all my secrets were out in the open. I see the smiles gliding over my clothes, dulled by time. I look less good than in the past. I grow pale, and my youthful blemishes have reappeared, forcing me to plaster my cheeks on certain days of the month.

Poverty muzzles me as well. The other day, at the home of Mrs. Gibbon, the senator's widow with whom I play music and who invites me regularly to her teas, I dared not reduce her to silence when she complimented me on the whiteness of my skin. "You still have the complexion of a young girl. Why, you remind me of those nuns who have smooth skin all their lives. As they have never known a man, their faces are innocent of all the grimaces of pleasure or the pain of unrequited love. That is why these happy creatures never have wrinkles like married women. You are so fortunate, my dear friend!" For a moment I thought I was being mocked for the protracted virginity all ascribe to me, but I bit my tongue. And just in time, I thought to myself. If I launch one of the cruel retorts of which I am capable, or if I break with her, it will be known and I will be the laughingstock of all my friends. I chose to attribute her words to her customary thoughtlessness, and to pardon her like the good Christian I am. I have been reduced to that: I remain silent, as to break with Mrs. Gibbon would deprive me forever of my Wednesday outing and my only good meal, which I take with her on the first Sunday of the month. (My mother's cooking is as bland as ever.) These calculating silences cost me dearly.

Even my talents as an actress have begun to desert me. Before, if I was thirsty, I would only have to look thirsty, and someone would instantly appear to offer me something to drink. That is over. My sighs no longer function. My friends no longer offer to fetch me when we go out, whereas once I always had a carriage at my disposal; even, at times, an automobile. Now I must ask, otherwise I have nothing. Fortunately there is the telephone, it is less embarrassing.

No one is disturbed any longer by your extended absence, either, my dear Essiambre. For a long time people felt sorry for me on that account, and it earned me many marks of friendship. I accepted them with gratitude, having no others.

It is not you whom I lamented, but rather other men, but I could not talk of those secret sorrows. To you, my initiator, I can tell everything. When Hilton was killed at Cambrai, I wept in silence. I did not want it known that I was partial to him, especially since he had married in England three weeks before joining his regiment of Grenadiers. The same thing when Richmond lost his life at the Dardanelles. I said nothing, I only reread with emotion the two postcards he had sent me from there. Fortunately you are alive, Essiambre, otherwise I would only be left with the dead to love.

If I may speak more freely of you in what remains of my circle of friends, d'Argenteuil, it is because you have again begun to write me on a regular basis this past time, and I have seen to it that that be known. It is also because we agreed to play at being betrothed. When I knew you I was interested in Major Camden, one of the aides-de-camp of Prince Arthur. To attract his attention I wanted to be invited to a reception given by the Militia Minister, Sam Hughes. I had just come back from Bark Lake, and I had to renew my network of contacts in society. Having seen you again at my sister's, and having learned that you would be there that evening, I agreed to accompany you. I knew instinctively that you would consent to being my ally in these society games.

It was a very successful evening for you, who walked out of the minister's salon with your lieutenant's commission in your pocket. Much less so for me: Camden didn't even look at me, all my sighs fell on deaf ears.

Seeing my discomfiture you understood immediately, and that is when I took the measure of your feminine sensibility. Escorting me home that evening, you excused Camden's behaviour, saying that he too was despondent at not finding a regiment, and that that explained his indifference to me. "If you want I can talk to him on your behalf. We have friends in common, he and I. Just say the word, and I'll take care of everything..." In return for your collaboration you wanted me to introduce you to Sarah Cummings, daughter of the judge, an intrepid horsewoman and accomplished poetess. We have a deal, you said, smiling, as if to ensure that I took it as a bit of a joke.

Bolstered by our little conspiracy, if you remember, we made ourselves inseparable for three weeks, and it is that, doubtless, that heightened the speculation surrounding our liaison. Which was all perfectly fine. In a few weeks you would be off to the front with the Princess Patricia Regiment, I would perhaps have my rendezvous with Camden, and you, for your part, might have a chance to court Sarah Cummings. We amused ourselves greatly with the rumours that circulated on our account, and I confess I enjoyed being seen on your arm. With your ease in society and your informed conversation, you added a great deal to my charm, and it pleased me to make the rival ladies jealous.

The hunter and the huntress made a good team, but the results were hardly brilliant. Camden clearly preferred your company to mine, and despite all the trouble you went to, I was barely able to claim two waltzes with him during those festive weeks. He was far from treating me with the coolness of our first meeting, but he responded to none of my languorous gazes. I know that you had no luck with Sarah, who, thinking you were with me, did not dare approach you. Her indifference did not seem to upset you.

Keeping company did, however, allow us to get to know each other better. One could not conceive of two people so unlike one another, and you left me with more questions about you than certainties. There are things you will have to explain to me one day. For example, the more I try to enhance my own nobility, the more you prefer to associate with the common man. You have nothing but indifference for the blue blood that so attracts me. I went into raptures over the nobility of your fellow officers, Colonel James, the great surgeon, the Doctor-Major Stephenson who had given up his seat in the Commons to enlist, but you, Essiambre, you preferred talking to cowboys, insurance agents and tinsmiths who served in the ranks. You might have spoken to me from time to time of your Seigneury of Argenteuil, one of the most important in Quebec, but not a word.

You had the same disdain for your illustrious ancestors. I, an Irishwoman in love with the suffering of my forebears, would have liked to hear you talk about your grandfather, the celebrated orator and patriot who paid for his militancy with a long exile in Australia. No, the only one of your predecessors about whom you spoke with enthusiasm was that Anne Dupuy of whom I had never heard. If I remember right, she was the daughter of a tanner who accompanied de Champlain, and a servant woman, and she was carried off at the age of nine by the Iroquois, with whom she lived for ten years. Adopted by the Onondagas, she took several husbands while living with them and almost forgot her mother tongue. She was found during the expedition to the Iroquois of Monsieur de Tracy, but she had become an Indian to such a point that she did not want to return with the French, and hid in the woods. She only emerged from her hiding place because she had glimpsed in a dream Mother Marie de Saint Joseph, one of Catholic Quebec's vestal icons, and she wanted to meet her. Otherwise she would never have followed her rescuers to Quebec. With the Indians she had learned to believe in the truth of dreams.

Shortly afterwards, Monsieur de Tracy provided her with a dowry, and she accepted the hand of one of his soldiers, Sergeant Essiambre, the first of his name in New France. She had twelve children by him, and, a widow, remarried at the age of fifty. She died when more than eighty years old in the arms of her fourth husband. Is it this woman with her insatiable appetites whom you admired? I would never have revealed the existence of this ancestor turned Iroquois, but you, you boasted of her everywhere. In the end, Essiambre, I still don't understand you: you who speak French with your clipped accent and English with that of Oxford, but who are consumed by the most terrible egalitarian passions! It is that, above all, that distances me from you.

You were even capable of unseemly baiting on that point. Such as the time when you brought to the Addisons that magnificent officer of the Scottish Grenadiers in Montreal, who had the manners of a young leading man in the movies. He was beautiful as an angel, that boy, and even in his kilt he was manly enough for three. The women swooned before him, the men wanted to shake his hand. It was only when the evening was well underway that you raised a toast to the health of your friend, Lieutenant Jude Cohen. An icy silence descended on us all, and you, Essiambre, were all smiles.

The next day I reproached you in no uncertain terms, for which I ask your forgiveness today, and I told you that if you insisted on bringing that gentleman everywhere, I would see you no more. Deft as you are you said nothing, but in your silence I could gauge the depths of my sordid racial prejudice, and I felt extremely foolish.

When the Princess Patricia Light Infantry Regiment left Ottawa, I agreed to accompany you, to make a little fun of our fine society that judged me incapable of finding a husband. That day I wore my mauve taffeta dress, my mother's mink stole and a pearl grey felt toque that had cost me months of scrimping. You looked like a general in your lieutenant's uniform. We made a lovely couple, I must say, and when the train pulled out, I blew you a kiss with my hand. I even waved my handkerchief like a real wartime fiancée. But the truth is that I wept for other men, even Camden, who wanted nothing of me. For you, never.

· · · · ·

I AM NOT SORRY TO HAVE LEFT THE LITTLE ONE BEHIND
at the Hotel Couillard. The way things were going she would eventually have unmasked me.

She told me she had gifts. I believed her a little, she actually reminded me of Flavie on that score, and it was that in her that frightened me. "I can stop the hail. It's a gift that the fathers pass on to the daughters in my family. They say it comes from the Indians. It's the only thing my father gave me. I also have the gift of curing burns. That I got from my mother. I can even cure burns over the telephone, talking to the person who's been burned. I also know how to get rid of children mothers don't want. My friend Virginie showed me how. When a woman in the Flats doesn't want a child, they call me. But I don't ask money for that, otherwise I would lose my gift, you understand?" She also has the gift of making herself loved by men who are not drawn to her. That I can corroborate.

Before the war she and her friend Virginie met men while waiting in line to take Communion, or at the monthly euchre game organised by the Zouaves. But never married men, because the women who live in the Flats would never have pardoned such immorality. Then one day Virginie met a man who got her pregnant. She married him, and the little one lost the partner she'd had in her escapades. Fortunately the war began, and Ottawa filled up with new men passing through.

She exploited the situation to the fullest for a long time. Too much, even. Once she came down with a sickness that could have got her thrown in jail had her doctor not been more understanding. It's because of this sickness that she can no longer have children. She doesn't think God wanted to punish her for being so foolish. "No, the Lord is too good to punish a woman like that who has the gift of making herself loved by men who wouldn't want her otherwise. It's just nature's fault." She restrained herself for a while after that, but her desire returned along with her health.

I once asked her how she had managed to meet me.

She burst out laughing.

"I did with you like with the others. To collect men, I went to the station. I looked lost, I walked up and down in the waiting room like a girl who has just arrived in town and doesn't know where to go. It never failed. A man always came up to me and asked if he could help. I asked him for the address of a hotel I knew, the Couillard, here in the Flats. If he offered to accompany me I accepted, and to thank him I invited him up to visit my room. Three times out of four the man asked me if I had money to pay. I replied I was not sure I had enough. If he offered to pay for the room, I was sure we would spend the night together. What is funny is that no one asked me where I had left my suitcase, as if a girl could travel like that. I don't know how many times I played the trick of the girl lost in the station. There were so many soldiers in Ottawa wanting to go with the first girl who came along that I could even choose. And I loved the uniforms so much that I found almost all the men handsome.

"Sometimes it didn't work, when I happened on honourable men or faithful husbands who really believed the story of the poor country girl lost in the big city. They were very gallant with me, they even paid for my room, and then they left, proud of having done a good deed. That annoyed me a little, especially if they were good-looking, but I couldn't really blame them.

"When I met you I had just stumbled on a good Samaritan like that. He had paid for the hotel room, and he had left immediately because he was embarrassed to find himself there and to be having bad thoughts. The hotel receptionist, a tub of lard with the face of a rat who I didn't like, had laughed at me. 'So, no luck tonight...' That made me mad! 'Go to hell, you!' I replied. 'I'm going to find me another one right away, it won't be long! Just watch!' I took the first streetcar going to the station.

"When I saw you walking around in the middle of the station like someone who can't decide what train to take, I went right up to you, and this time I asked you if you were lost and if I could help. The room was already paid for, I could do the favour that someone usually did for me. You said you were hungry. So I took you to the station restaurant. It was while watching you eat that I went all soft and started to want you. I felt sorry for you, and suddenly I wanted to be your mother. It's not by reading my palm that you seduced me. I'd already had that done to me, I knew the trick. I'd wanted a man for weeks, I would have taken anyone, but you were my first choice for sure."

She interrupted her story. Her face went dark. It was as though she wanted to change the subject. "You were in the war. Maybe you knew Anselme?" I told her no. She looked disappointed. Anselme had been killed in 1917 but she didn't know where. She only knew that even if he was good for nothing, he had still died a hero. It was her friend Virginie who had received the customary letter of condolence, but it was the little one who had had to read it out loud. A beautiful letter, she assured me. So beautiful that Virginie had given it to her and she had kept it for at least a month before throwing it away. Now she knew it by heart: "We had all regained our shelter when a last German bullet, traitorous and deadly as the rest, entered his ear and lodged in his brain. It took us some time to realize that he had surrendered his soul to God. He was simply seated on the ground, we could not see the thread of blood that flowed from his ear, and he had a distant look, like a man who is searching within him for a precious memory." I didn't tell her that I had written the same letter to a hundred tearful mothers, but I confess that the coincidence left me somewhat ill at ease.

To change the subject myself, I asked her how she had learned to read. "At Bark Lake," she replied. "I beg your pardon?" "At Bark Lake, the summer before the war," she elaborated. In the darkness she didn't notice that I was blushing. "I was maid for the Atkinses, who had lent their vacation house to a couple, and among the friends of this couple was a very nice lady, Miss Driscoll, who made me into a real woman." I didn't have to ask her for details, she told me everything with all the enthusiasm that stemmed from her gratitude.

"That summer I wasn't happy to have been sent to Bark Lake because it reminded me too much of the woods that surrounded Nazareth on Allumette Island. I was afraid of missing the city, Virginie, my other friends in the Flats, and my outings. But it wasn't long before I was put with Miss Driscoll, and nothing was the same after that. There I was really with a grand lady.

"I had a nice little room in the attic, with a mirror. The first thing I had to do in the morning was visit all the rooms to collect the pails of piss and shit and to empty them into a big tank outside. That was normal, I was the newest on the staff. Then I tidied the rooms, I made the beds. The last room I did was Miss Driscoll's. She's the only one who didn't leave when I went in, and she always invited me to rest a little. Then she talked to me while making herself up and combing her hair in front of the mirror. I liked her fair skin, her long hair, and to stay longer I offered to help her.

"She took away my shyness right away by talking to me in French. In those days I'd not yet practised my English with the soldiers, and often I didn't understand the orders people gave me. I made the best of it with stupid smiles to give the impression I understood. Sometimes that made my bosses angry; they would rather I told them I didn't understand. One day I was sent for flowers and I came back with cauliflower. Miss Driscoll felt sorry for me, and that's how she became my interpreter.

"I never knew where she'd learned her French. In books maybe. Anyway, when she talked to me, it came out all by itself. Of course she was a very very educated woman, you could tell. Even today I would like to talk well like her, but there's no chance of that, I started improving too late. I don't know why, she liked to listen to me too. I made her laugh, I think.

"Sometimes she asked me to tell her stories from home. She laughed till she cried, even if she didn't understand everything I said, because we didn't speak French the same way. Once I told her that the neighbour's maid didn't like me because she already hated Mrs. Atkins before knowing me. 'What can you do, Miss? When it rains on the priest, it drips on the beadle. That's the way it is...' That made her laugh for three days. I didn't think it was funny, but I laughed with her so she wouldn't think I thought she was laughing at me. But I was careful with her. I never used bad words: fart, ass, shit, fuck, nothing like that. I wouldn't have wanted her to think I was vulgar.

"Everything she taught me I still know today. Before meeting her I didn't know how to do my toilet, as she said. With her I learned the trick of washing my menstruation cloths and drying them at times of the day when men wouldn't see. It's thanks to her that I know how to eat cherries like you should: you put your hand in front of your mouth and take the pit and put it carefully on the plate with the spoon, instead of spitting it as far as you can like we always did. Useful things like that show you have class even if you're poor as dirt.

"But more than anything, she taught me to read. Almost every night, when I'd finished my day, she had me go up to her room to help her get undressed, and she brought out her big picture book and asked me if I wanted to learn something new. I always said yes. It was as though it gave her pleasure to play the schoolteacher with me. But to me it meant even more, because with her I could become the little girl I never was.

"She liked me too, I know, and it made me feel funny because I wasn't used to it. She even seemed happy when I told her I couldn't read. You would have thought she wanted to do something to pay me back for admiring her so much. That night she showed me the letter *A*, as was only proper. The first time I read a word I hadn't written myself it was like Jesus Christ in person had come back on earth to perform a miracle right in front of me: A-P-P-L-E. I started to sob, and she did too. I didn't sleep all night. The next day when I reread the word, I was amazed it had stayed in my head, because I thought I wasn't intelligent. I would have loved my family to see me reading my first sentence: 'Jane likes po-ta-toes.' Especially Viatime and Ermille. After reading them my sentence, I would have shoved the potatoes up their asses. Anyway…

"By the end of the summer I was signing my name, I was reading whole pages in the big book that belonged to the children in the house, I read the labels on the tins. Since then I've never stopped reading, and thanks to that I've just found myself a job in a bakery. I'll never again be a housemaid, never again.

"I so much didn't want that summer to end. The week before everyone left, a night when Miss Driscoll was all alone in the house, there was a terrible storm on the lake with thunder and lightning, you would have thought it was pissing nails on the roof. Miss Driscoll was afraid but not me, I was used to storms in the country. She asked me to sleep with her as if I were doing her a big favour. I was very honoured, I who had slept with my two sisters my whole childhood, including Thérèse, who farted in bed like a man.

"I think it was the most beautiful night of my life. She fell asleep right away, and she snuggled up to me like a little child who's cold. It was the only time I felt stronger than her. Now I was protecting her, I was her mother, her best friend on earth, she would die without me."

I hadn't been listening to her for a good while. It was more than I could take. She seemed not to have noticed my inattention. I had only one thought in my head: to go away, because I was afraid I would confess to her that I also, in my own way, knew this Miss Driscoll she so admired. I decided to wait until she was asleep before sneaking off. It was as though she knew what I was up to. "Would you come to me again, please? I'd like some more." I wasn't sure I wanted her again, but she was very persuasive, and I didn't even have to think of Flavie to give her what she wished.

She also said, "You know why I love that so much with you? It's because you have class. Before, I only knew one other like you, who talked well, who had enough education for two. I've always dreamed of meeting another one like him. He was such a good man," she went on, "that my friend Virginie never wanted to believe me when I said I'd slept with him."

"It was the year before the war. I was walking around Sandy Hill when I stopped in front of a house where there were people playing music. It was so beautiful that I started to dream of the day when I would settle down in the Flats for good, when I wouldn't be a maid in people's houses any more, when I would have work in a factory and an apartment all to myself. Then I would buy myself a beautiful player piano to make music with, and I would invite people to my home and serve them a lovely cake with tea. Like people with class.

"A good-looking gentleman stopped beside me and asked if I was invited to the house where they were playing music. I said no but I didn't blush, because I was dressed that day for going to mass, so I did not look so much like a maid. He asked me if I wanted to walk with him. I didn't say no and we ended up in his bed, where one of his friends lived who wasn't there. He is the gentleman who was the first to read my palm. It was the first time also that I'd slept with a man who called me 'Miss.' The next morning I went off before he awoke because I was afraid my beautiful dream would come to an end. I didn't want our night to lose its magic, and for that he couldn't know I was only a servant. He told me he was a lawyer.

"Believe me or don't believe me, I saw that man again once. It was at Bark Lake. He arrived one fine evening for supper, even more beautiful and prouder than when I'd known him. He spent four days in the neighbourhood, and not once did he seem to remember me. Sometimes he looked at me straight on and he didn't bat an eyelid. As if I were a total stranger. I, of course, did the same.

"That's when I understood what class really is. He must have remembered me, but he didn't want to show it so I wouldn't lose my job. If they'd known at Bark Lake that we knew each other, I would have been called a slut and been sent off right away.

"I realized how right I was not to say anything when I saw that my mistress, Miss Driscoll, found the young lawyer to her taste. So I was best not to boast that I knew him. And since I'm not the least bit jealous, I encouraged my mistress to go out with him. I did everything to praise the gentleman. I don't know if they went together after Bark Lake, but I wanted it to happen. They would have gone so well together, those two.

"I never told Virginie that I saw that man again at Bark Lake, because I was afraid she'd say to me: 'He didn't recognize you so as not to look bad himself, stupid! No man who sleeps with you recognizes you afterwards anyway, so don't put on any airs!' Maybe it's true that he didn't recognize me, but I prefer to believe he did."

I wanted to ask her if that man had skin as smooth as a woman's, velvety even, and covered with freckles; he even had them on his member. No need, she told me herself. "I remember him because he had freckles on his weenie…" No doubt about it, it was Essiambre. I told her that I thought I'd known that man during the war. She jumped, all happy. "Is he still alive at least? I don't want him to be dead, he was so kind!" She wanted to know his name. I told her he was called Latrémouille, as though he could have been anyone. I added that he had been horribly mutilated, and that he'd been living in a monastery ever since.

She lowered her head for a moment, then she recovered just as quickly. "It doesn't matter," she said. "Anyway it's you I want now." It was not hard to believe her. Everything she did showed how attached she was to me, but I was suddenly afraid because she had been too close to this Amalia Driscoll I coveted and to my Essiambre whom I had truly loved.

She often said she was a bit of a witch. She didn't know how truly she spoke. A witch who would have made off with parts of my life, and not only that, who would have lived them better than I did. Suddenly even her goodness ceased to charm me. I had only one wish: to get out of her life.

"Adieu Concorde," I said to myself.

I'VE JUST BEEN RELEASED FROM PRISON.

The judge sentenced me to eight days for public drunkenness and vagrancy. I was in the midst of an argument
with my drunken ghost when I suddenly detected in his
gaze that glimmer of unsettling lassitude one might find
in an exhausted knife thrower. I asked him to lean his
head towards me so that I could whisper in his ear, but it
was really to give him a punch in the face, which he royally
deserved. I'd had enough of his moralizing. He bent down, I
swung at the air, and ended up in a pool of vomit. A passing

policeman led me to the station, and it would seem I was not very polite. I was thrown into a cell where two fugitives from conscription were already confined, unfortunates still being hunted down even though the war has long been over.

It could have been worse. It turned out that the court bailiff was a former Princess Pat. He came to see me the afternoon of my arrest, and advised me to play dead. "Listen, if you plead not guilty, you'll have a formal trial. I spoke to the officer who arrested you and he'll testify that you were having a lively conversation with a lamp post when he picked you up. If the judge thinks you're crazy he'll make you a ward of the Ontario Lieutenant Governor. You understand what that means? You'll be shut up in an asylum, and you may never get out. So don't make a fuss, plead guilty and get the hell out. Take off, because if they grab you again, your goose is cooked. I know you're not crazy, only halfway, but they don't. So..." Even a chap who's half drunk can follow good advice. I pleaded guilty, I cited my service record, and I got off with a short sentence.

It's too bad all the same, this minor setback. I had been doing so well for the last while. Concorde had given me back my strength, and with the cash she lent me I had sent a telegram to the postmistress in my village so that my father would send me a bit of money. He replied three days later: twenty dollars and two words, "Come home." I wrote him to explain my situation. Instead of insisting on a pension or a job, I'd decided to take advantage of the new federal government program aimed at veterans. Any former soldier who could demonstrate some knowledge of farming had the right to a plot of land in the West, and a grant to purchase agricultural equipment. The West, a farmer, I liked the idea! To learn the ropes I just had to find work as a hired hand on a farm out there. They were looking for people, why not me? A small loan, I explained to my father, would help me to live, pending my departure for the Prairies. The postmistress, the worst of gossips, must have told my father I was lying. Never mind, I believed so firmly in my new scheme during those penniless days that I didn't even think of courting Miss Driscoll.

I rented a room on Preston Street, in a neighbourhood where I was sure no one would know me. My life was exemplary: when I drank beer it was just one glass even though I had to cross the river to drink in Hull, and I came right back like a fat faithful husband. I ate well. The landlady had forbidden me to cook in my room, and to save money I'd decided not to avail myself of the meals she offered, for a fee, at her table. But I managed. I kept food cool in a little box I'd attached to my window with a brick on top to discourage birds, I borrowed an electric iron from the lady, a marvellous invention, I balanced it between two marble bookends and plugged it in. That way I could heat up the canned goods I snuck into the house. Of course, the landlady wasn't too happy at times. "That smells like cooking, no?" I just had to look offended for her to leave me in peace.

As proof of my new moral standing, I even went to the Odéon to see a play likely to keep me on the straight and narrow: *The Finger of God*, starring Léonard Beaulne, and directed by Wilfred Sanche. I remember, because I sent the program to the postmistress so she would read it to my father; just to get her goat, the old cow.

What followed was all the fault of the circus. The Robinson Circus was set up on a vacant lot at the corner of Somerset and Preston. But before the big premiere there was a parade along my street. It was wonderful, much better than the theatre. At last I saw real lions in cages, leopards, giant monkeys, clowns, strongmen, bearded ladies and dwarfs. There was even a wagon with a steam organ on board, whose music made me feel like the war was really over.

I was in such a good mood that I accepted a neighbour's invitation to go to the local blind pig, one of those illegal bars that existed even before prohibition and that are called speakeasies in more polite circles. There they sold liquor we were encouraged to consume at home, but when the owner was in good humour she let us drink on the premises. I was just curious, and when I was offered a small glass of rye whisky I said yes, but just to taste, thank you, no more.

I tasted the whole bottle. The proprietress got irritated when a gentleman in a boater began to talk about the war. "Ah, no! None of that! It always ends up in a fight, those discussions, and it's not good for business!" Just a minute later two fellows started hammering each other in the corner. I had done nothing. I don't know how it happened, but I found myself outside all alone.

I must have walked for the better part of an hour, because I couldn't remember where I lived. All of a sudden someone took my arm. It was Concorde. I was a bit embarrassed to see her again, I didn't quite know what to say, especially since I wasn't all that lucid. She took me back to the Couillard, where I stayed with her awhile.

I only remember that I found myself suddenly back on the street with my drunken ghost, and I was so confused that I almost didn't recognize myself. He rebuked me, and I ended up in prison. I've had no more news from my twin sot. Never there when I need him, obviously.

·
·
·
·
·

:

I PICKED A BAD TIME TO GET OUT OF JAIL. LIFE IS
hard in Ottawa.

Again yesterday, I got thrown out of the railway station. The policeman on duty warned me that it was the last
time he wanted to see me there. I went, however, with the
best of intentions. In July I'd read in the newspaper that
they were looking for fifteen hundred men to bring in the
harvest in the West, and I wanted to sign up. "It's November, the harvest has been over for weeks! Get out!" It's got

to the point where I am not even welcome in churches: the beadles toss me out because I seem to be begging, which is not true. I'm praying, that's all. The only place I'm tolerated is at Adrienne's blind pig, because I'm a valued customer. I buy my bottle of whisky and I leave immediately.

The other morning we were alone, Adrienne and I. She must have been bored because she offered me a drink, something she does only for a very distinguished clientele.

The vivid recollection of Essiambre came to me there, in her living room, when I expected it least. I think it was while stroking Adrienne's cat that I was caught off guard by the memory.

On the eve of the Battle of Passchendaele, I imitated Essiambre's handwriting for the last time, to send news to Amalia Driscoll.

My dear friend,

I am so sorry to hear that Mrs. Fitzjames' little dog is dead. It's true that to mourn the death of a pet is a silent grief that only a compassionate soul like your own can understand.

I too have at my side a faithful companion whom I would not hesitate to recommend to you should he have the good fortune to return to Ottawa. He is Lieutenant Lusignan of our company of Pioneers. A cultivated gravedigger, which is rare, also an aristocrat in the Nietzschean sense of the word, who disdains received ideas and who is a master at the art of expressing himself, with an appalling respect for the truth. You will like him. I like you too, but more.

It was the first time I'd spoken to her about myself. I added three or four pages on the cold, the mud, the blood in the trenches, things of which I still cannot speak but that I managed to write about with ease. I had been sent to the rear, and he had gone on to the front, certain that this time he would not survive. I guessed at his premonition by the ferocity of his last embrace. If he had stayed a second longer in my arms I would have been struck with spasms, like Flavie.

It took days for them to find him, and I was not there when it happened. The men had been more zealous than usual in their search, because they loved him. Half of his body was gone but they recognized him by his leggings, which he did not wear like everyone else. True to himself, Essiambre told me one day that he wanted a funeral no different from that of his men, and if he were killed, that his body be thrown into a common grave with the others. I disobeyed him. I had him buried with all the honours appropriate to his rank, which made him one of the rare combatants to have a grave and a cross all to himself. I could not have done otherwise.

I didn't shed a tear at that time, I didn't drink a drop either. I watched my men gather up his belongings with respect, as though they were the relics of a saint. They put together a package that I sent to his mother; I only kept Amalia Driscoll's letters. I wrote all the letters of condolence to his relatives and friends. Not one tear, nothing.

I cracked eight months later. Essiambre had a cat, Jezebel, which one of my men picked up. One day she had a litter, and we left her alone in the bunker for the day. When we came back she had disappeared, and her kittens had been eaten by rats.

I don't remember what happened afterwards. The last time my men saw me I had just drunk more than my ration of rum and had wandered off unarmed in the direction of enemy lines. When I was found I had been taken prisoner by the Germans. Incredible luck, because otherwise I would have been good for a court martial and the firing squad. My men covered for me in memory of Essiambre.

I was wailing so loudly that Adrienne asked me to leave. "Tell me another story next time. I've heard that one six times already." As we left, my drunken ghost and I decided it was the last time we would set foot in that den of iniquity.

I KNOW NOW WHAT'S LEFT FOR ME TO DO.

Since my return to Ottawa I've made no effort to find
Amalia Driscoll, I've been content just to think about her.
But now I have to take action, especially since winter is on
its way. Not that I'm afraid of the season, I even like this cold
that makes us all equal, as does desire. That said, I prefer to
sleep where it's warm. On that score I've been lucky, as it
continues to be pleasant, even if November is well advanced.

At night, in my dreams, to feed myself, I take the sling-
shot I'm going to make one day, shoot down pigeons and

gulls in the parks, and cook them up in empty tin cans over a little fire. They're delicious, especially when the can once held tomatoes, you don't even taste the rust. This morning, just as I was about to sit down at the table, I was abruptly wakened by two authentic alcoholics who had slept beside me under the Pretoria Bridge. They must have been after my breakfast. I didn't give them time to wish me bon appétit.

Fortunately they were even drunker than I was, and I was able to shake them off easily. After my flight I sat down on a park bench. A few steps away a buzzard tearing apart a dead rat reminded me I was hungry. Someone had left his newspaper on the bench. For the sake of appearances I began to leaf through it. It was the paper *Le Droit,* and in the society section I saw a public invitation that confirmed me in my conviction that God the Father in person was watching over me.

> Tomorrow, November 11, there will be a celebration in the gardens of Saint John the Baptist Church, to mark the first anniversary of the Armistice. The good Dominican Fathers are planning a notable event. The Papal Zouaves will be taking part. Their band will play a number of selections to entertain the guests, and the battalion's most dexterous members will give fencing and bayonet demonstrations for those who enjoy the display of arms. Corporal Beaulieu will recite "The Cross of the Dying Soldier," and Sergeant Daoust will sing "The Song of Prohibition," a composition by Chaplain Pelletier.

Also on the program are fortune tellers, some games of skill and chance, and a lottery. There will also be a counter where one may purchase, at a reasonable price, tobacco, candy and lemonade, and even ice cream if warm weather prevails. The star of the program will be, as usual, the singer Amalia Driscoll, who will interpret extracts from Gounods's Mass in C, accompanied by the Children of Mary Choir. All are welcome.

"That's it, she's mine," I said to myself. "I must find this woman to bind myself to Essiambre forever."

I will go to see Liebermann, the pawnbroker on the Flats. I'll leave him my watch, my officer's ring, everything I have of any value, including my clothes and the suitcase that contains Miss Driscoll's letters. I will only keep my uniform and the necessary underclothing. With the money I will treat myself to a good room and a meal at the Hotel Couillard, I'll take a nice warm bath, brush my uniform, and when I arrive at the celebration I will be in top form, all my faculties sharpened for the assault on the trench. I will listen to Miss Driscoll sing, and as soon as she has distanced herself from her admirers, I will approach her. I know what I'm going to say to move her, she won't resist me. I will assume the proper attitude to offer my condolences, and immediately afterwards I will draw her to me for life. So as to be sure not to do anything foolish, I am going to repeat what I must avoid saying to her: "Mademoiselle, pardon me for existing, but I have something to tell you. I am the former Lieutenant

Lusignan, once the lover of the man you loved. Yes, the same who drank down my pure essence on a certain afternoon before a Quebec City ablaze with light. I still think of him when I pleasure myself alone at night. He loved you very much, and I would love you even more if you would procure for me the pension that would enable me to live a life of leisure until my death. Or, if this course of action repels you, I would accept a post doing nothing in Parliament. If I do not please you, you are in no way obliged to love me, even less to sleep with me. On closer examination, you do not tempt me very much either. I would be happy then with a small loan, enough to get through the winter in the hotel. Let us say, a hundred dollars. Or twenty or ten. Or whatever you have in your purse. I'll also accept the clothes you've put aside for the poor, those of your deceased false fiancé or of your dear father, I'm not fussy. Give something, anything, and I will immediately go and devour half of what is left at the buffet, and for a beverage the water in the flower vase I see over there will suit me fine. I will wait for you afterwards in some disreputable venue on the Flats, until my last breath, my dearest love. Finally, restore to me my letters, those I wrote in Essiambre's handwriting, and which are mine, not yours."

There, I've exorcised the wicked in order to be good. And to be certain of that, I only have to refrain from drinking alcohol. Not a drop.

It should have been a very good plan.

I entered the Dominican Gardens with my left hand closed over my right cuff to hide the forbidden daisy. I do believe that lent me a rather seductive martial air. But I was so thirsty that my tongue was stuck to my palate.

Miss Driscoll sang, and as soon as she left the platform I placed myself in her path. I would not be moved. She had a cigarette case in her hand, I remember. A plump young woman in an apron was following her like a little dog, carrying a tray larger than herself. Beside me there was a kind of churchman who was trying to talk to me while making extravagant gestures with his arms, but I understood nothing of his mute sermon.

When Miss Driscoll reached me I thought of Lieutenant Jude Cohen, that Grenadiers officer from Montreal who was so courageous in battle that his companions in arms renamed him Mac Cohen. He had taught me how to say "kiss my ass" in Yiddish. Those are the only words I was able to pronounce when Miss Driscoll asked me what I wanted: "Kisch mir'en tokhes!" I can't help it, my memory does what it wants and I obey.

With that, the servant fainted and the glasses on her tray shattered, to deafening effect. Miss Driscoll retreated, emitting a scream worthy of a true songstress, just like in the theatre, and the priest immediately knelt to bless the girl. When I came to after the commotion, the three individuals had disappeared and the celebration had resumed its festive hum. There was in the air a scent of eucalyptus, but I could not detect its source. I was alone.

I'M NOT SURE WHAT HAPPENED NEXT.

All I remember is that my drunken ghost reappeared all of a sudden right in the middle of the Flats, to which I had returned, I don't know how. I had a hard time recognizing him: his head was shaved to resemble Christ's crown of thorns, he had a beard and he was wearing a brown robe and sandals on his feet. I asked him what he was doing disguised as a Capuchin. I didn't even recognize my own voice when he started talking to me: "But I'm not your drunken ghost. I am Father Mathurin. Come." It took me a while to place him. He was the little priest I had glimpsed at the celebration. The deceptive November warmth had disappeared, the wind was cold and it was dark.

Father Mathurin told me the rest. He had led me to his monastery not far from Saint Francis of Assisi Church. He said I was very compliant. He served me tea and biscuits in the parlour, then he moved me into the little basement bedroom where I am still. I slept four days running. That was a year ago. Things are better now, much better.

Father Mathurin is the monastery's oldest resident. He's been here since he was ordained at the end of the last century. He has done everything: been vicar of the Saint Francis of Assisi church, taught Bible studies at the Seraphic School in Ottawa, taken care of the monastery's finances. He occupies the humblest room because he remains convinced that the day will come when his Order will send him abroad as a missionary. Then, perhaps, if God wills, he will know the glory of martyrdom. He has been waiting for twenty-two years.

He was my first history teacher at the Nicolet seminary. It's because of him that for a long time I thought myself the descendant of the fairy Melusine and the King of Jerusalem. He only stayed one trimester at the College of Nicolet, and he left us in order to don the Capuchin vestments. I had totally forgotten what he looked like. He remembered me as if we had parted the night before.

After I regained my strength he took me on as beadle at good Saint Francis's church, from which I had once been evicted for begging. It was now my turn to send beggars away from the church, but I was not a very diligent beadle. I sometimes skipped the Angelus, and I confess that I preferred my theological discussions with Father Mathurin to my domestic tasks. With the coming of spring I was kept on as the monastery's gardener, and caretaker for the Seraphic School. My salary is symbolic in the extreme, but I have my own little corner, a bed and three meals a day.

My voluntary captivity with the Capuchin Fathers is good for me. I never step outside without being accompanied by one of them, sometimes Father Céleste, sometimes Father Candide, often Father Fidèle, all upstanding apostles who speak with a Toulousian accent. Mathurin himself brings me my meals in my basement cubbyhole. The fare is frugal, but I can't complain: bread and coffee in the morning, stew and cheese at noon, soup and fruit in the evening. Sometimes I cook spaghetti on the hot plate at the foot of my bed; Mathurin then brings me a small carafe of wine and we talk through the night. My only window, which gives on the garden, is opaque. I never see the weather, and during my first months at the monastery it was only on the day Mathurin brought me an orange for dessert that I guessed winter was approaching.

Mathurin is my ambassador in the world, and the tales he brings me distract me more than the pious readings he urges on me.

The other day he said to me, "You, a man of letters, will understand what has happened to me.

"Before meeting you, my life was so dreary that all my memories belonged to books.

"Even today, however, that is where I prefer to seek them. My own are not interesting enough, I am so insignificant. I am the very embodiment of that humility proper to my Order, and humanity, in the future, will remember more clearly the scent of a dead flower than my passage on earth.

"For all that, it is not as easy as I would like for me to remain in the background. My habit sometimes elicits laughter from Protestants, and even Catholics. At such times I tell myself that I ought to become a Trappist in order to live sheltered from the eyes of the world. I would be happy to remain inconspicuous, as the Capuchin rule dictates, but there are times in one's life when it is impossible not to attract attention. For example, the other evening, my superior, Father Céleste, sent me to the home of Madame Vaillancourt, one of the parish's benefactors, who had organized a recital of religious poetry. 'Go ahead, a little outing will do you good, Father Mathurin. Those events bore me to tears. You'll tell me about it afterwards.' I obeyed.

"The reader was Y..., the Marian poet of Trois-Rivières, who must have written more than two hundred thousand verses dedicated to the Virgin; he has done nothing else his entire life. He was accompanied by a violinist whose playing, according to the two ladies seated behind me, was perfect. As for myself, I never have any opinion.

"Mary's bard's poetry was in all respects faithful to the dogma of Our Mother Church, to that I can attest, but it was somewhat repetitive, and I began to find the evening rather long. As we had been served cabbage at the refectory, our customary Friday night dish, I experienced a sudden need to take a short digestive stroll outside. And so I rose, and still bent over, I made my way to the first door I saw, opened it and immediately shut it behind me. But this door did not give onto the street at all, as I thought: I found myself in a pitch-black storage room. Only the sliver of light from under the door enabled me to make out, dimly, the shapes of the objects customarily found in such places: brooms, pails, rags.

"Once I had recovered from my initial shock, I reproached myself for having planned my escape so poorly. Then I thought of the spectators, especially Madame Vaillancourt, who must have been asking themselves what bizarre impulse drove me to shut myself up in there.

"They say troubles never come one at a time, and it's true. The more I thought about the absurdity of my botched exit, the more I felt like laughing, and I crouched down to bring part of my cassock to my mouth in order to stifle my giggles. It was an unwise manoeuvre that only exacerbated my digestive discomfort; I had to press my other hand to my posterior in order to muffle the noise that I felt was coming. I finally had to back into the wall in order to deflate myself discreetly; the odour of fermented cabbage only intensified my childish hilarity. Impossible to recover my dignity after that. No sooner did I regain control than I was seized with renewed spasms of laughter at the thought of the spectacle I was about to make of myself. (My flatulence has always made me laugh—an aberration that, no matter how many times I have confessed it, I still cannot explain.)

"Within four minutes I devised a hundred plans for making my way out of there without arousing too much curiosity from the parishioners. None were any good. But I had to act! The reading over, they would surely come knocking at the door to ask what I was doing, would discover the sickening odour, and would spread all over the parish that I am the Capuchin father who hides in the dark to giggle and fart while art and the Virgin are being honoured next door. Ah no, not that! So I shook myself all over to chase away the bad smell, I pulled myself up to my whole small height, and I opened the door briskly to return to my seat in the most natural way possible. I had to put on a serious face, and so I thought very deliberately about my little sister Sophranie, who died of consumption thirty years ago.

"All eyes were on me but I didn't waver. I had adopted the air I would normally assume while administering the last rites to a pious woman. I could have been taken for a great actor making his first appearance onstage, except that no one applauded. But when my eyes met those, furious, of the Mariologist, who was just then extolling the odour of our Virgin's sanctity, my laughter, too long suppressed, was torn from me like the moaning of a maniac. The reader went silent, the violinist stopped playing, the spectators glared at me and I had to flee with my head down and my hand on my mouth to smother the laughter that shame could not contain. (I laugh loudly, another of my great failings. My superior says I bray like a donkey, and I cannot contradict him, never having seen a donkey in my life.)

"I told the whole story to Father Céleste the next day. It took him a good five minutes to gain control of himself before pardoning me. All the same, I felt ashamed as I left his office, for the excellent reason that this story was not entirely my own. And that, my good Lusignan, you are now the only one to know: the real truth is that I needed to relieve myself and that I chose the wrong door twice before making my escape, but the rest I borrowed from O..., a great poet whom I admire but whom I am forbidden to read, not having received permission from my superior. I don't know why I plagiarized myself before Father Céleste. Is it because I read too much? What do you think, Lusignan?"

I said nothing, I had too great a craving for a glass of beer on that occasion to think of anything else. Before leaving my cell, Mathurin embraced me and said, "You never laugh at me. That's what a friend is. Without you I would die of boredom here." It's true that I never laugh at him, and I am very careful not to tell him that I am holding myself back all the time. Sometimes it's difficult.

THREE YEARS I'VE BEEN LIVING IN THE MONASTERY.

I'm treated very well. The Fathers now let me go out alone. I never leave the Flats, I don't recognize anyone and no one knows me. With my church caretaker's clothes on my back and my rake in my hand, I nod mutely to the people I pass. They smile at me with the benevolence one reserves for an inoffensive immigrant who doesn't speak the local language, and it stops there. It's better that way. If they spoke to me I wouldn't know what to say.

Mathurin is as good to me as ever. I remain his indulgent confidant. Sometimes I suspect him of telling me the story of his life because he wants me to be his biographer. It doesn't matter, I listen all the same. I have nothing else to do at night.

I feel that at last I've been delivered from the future. The life I have is enough for me. The government has perhaps changed since I've been here. In any case, I could not say who the Prime Minister of Canada is. It's very pleasant not to know such things.

During these years of exemplary living, I've almost stopped thinking about Miss Driscoll. I've concluded that I will never love her, I only loved a woman on paper, she who bared her soul in the letters she wrote to Argenteuil.

Father Mathurin has retrieved them for me from the pawnbroker. Reading and rereading, constantly, Amalia Driscoll, I can better resist the temptation to move on again.

March, 1916

My friend d'Argenteuil,

Prepare yourself. Today is a day of admonishments. I'm speaking of your letters, of course.

Oh, you write me, yes! But your correspondence more resembles a military bulletin than the affectionate bantering a friend deserves. I can already foresee the next I am to receive: "A brutal awakening this morning, The Boche is not far off. A shell killed twenty of our men yesterday. I smile, all the same, when I think of you." There. It's not very inspiring. Take care: I will end up reading with indifference the missive announcing your death. Love me a little, my good friend, because I miss you all the same in this land where there are no more men to love.

I confess that I now regret having prolonged for so long the little joke of our make-believe betrothal. In the salons where I was still quite celebrated, the lecherous ladies urged me to take them into my confidence, and I managed to titillate them while leaving them unsatisfied. The virtuous ones insisted on being reassured as to the morality of our relations, and I reassured them. You, Essiambre, who are a better actor than I, would certainly have appreciated my responses.

All things considered, the past year has unfolded well for me, despite the constant bad news we receive from the front. The dead, numbering in the tens of thousands on each side, have unfortunately paled next to the names of those few we had the good fortune to know. Lieutenant Curtis, who was the Military Attaché to Governor General Connaught, and who served as Usher at Rideau Hall, an office he performed very well with his stentorian voice: killed at the controls of his airplane in a duel with a German pilot. I knew the others better. Captain Newton of the Princess Pats, whose lisp we used to mimic: killed by his own sentry before the Battle of Ypres. Your regiment, you told me, lost eighty men in this engagement, and for days my heart was sore because it seemed I knew at least half of them. Prendergast, killed by that gas you call yperite; Johnston, pulverized by a shell along with four of his men: they never found his remains; Simmonds, who drowned in a shell crater. The first was the best tennis player in his club, the second a whiz at bridge, and the third a talented flutist.

I myself suffered a great loss when Prince Arthur was repatriated. It was perfectly proper, the son of Queen Victoria ought to be with his army, but I lost the best of my protectors. When I learned that Lord Devonshire was going to replace him, I asked myself, anxiously, if he too liked skating. Well, no, he does not, and I have just lost my principal attraction to the court.

It's my friend Dorothée de Villers, Princess Patricia's lady-in-waiting, who warned me in secret about Connaught's recall. Naïvely, I thought this confidence hid some good omen for me. Perhaps the Duke might want to take me to Buckingham as part of his suite. And why should my fantasies stop there? A series of unfortunate developments, not infrequent during a war, could upset the order of succession to the Crown, Connaught would find himself King, and I would be governess to his grandchildren. Then a rich suitor would ask for my hand, I would be a Duchess, my fortune would be made and I would reign a little over the Empire in my fashion. I would myself have knighted you one day. History, as we know, has seen many such fabled destinies, and so why not mine?

I attended all the events that preceded his Royal Highness's departure, I exhausted my sister's wardrobe and all my savings. I made him my last curtsey in the course of a private interview, he kissed my hand lightly with his lips and addressed to me a few very kind words; it was the last time I saw him. No one telephoned me at the last minute to tell me I was to be part of the voyage. I had dreamed for nothing. I experienced Connaught's departure as a disgrace.

I receive no more invitations to Rideau Hall. Only the servants remember me. My salvation resides in the relations I have maintained with the military attachés. All are handsome young men whose only failing is the ambition they all share to go off and *be killed for the King. If it is not permissible for them to invite me to Rideau Hall, they are pleased to take me to dinner in town or to a picnic in the countryside. I owe their invitations to their predecessors such as Hilton and Richmond, who told them I was someone to be reckoned with in Ottawa's best salons, and they count on me to initiate them into the ways and customs of our little colonial society. I do them this service willingly. For a time I thought my return to the court's favour was imminent, and that I would again be called the "royal favourite," as in Connaught's day. A vain hope, like so many others.*

Among the aides-de-camp, there was Porter. I must tell you about him. He was a young colonel who had been to Oxford and Sandhurst; his family owned mines as well as a vast estate in the north of England. He was here to rest. Towards the beginning of the war, twice decorated for courage under fire, he was taken captive; after four months in a Cologne fortress he was freed in an exchange of high-ranking prisoners. He was not anxious to return to action, as he told me bluntly. He was the first I had heard speak badly of the war. A horror, a civil war, a beastly carnage where modern man used technology to commit organized murder: his revulsion was total. In those days when one only spoke of military glory and suicidal sacrifice, such words were rare, and so were voiced only in the strictest intimacy.

As he was still recuperating from his war wounds he could not participate in all the winter sports I practised, but I did introduce him to sleighing. I can still recall his childlike laughter when our sled capsized at the end of its run; I remember his joy awakening my maternal instincts. There was also that ball at the Roxborough Hotel where he almost slipped, and to stop him from falling I had to hold him by the waist, an intimate gesture that troubled me greatly.

He was the first man I desired as a real woman. As the little maid said at Bark Lake—she was not, like me, afraid of words—to have that man, I would have played the whore. I knew he was married, but I loved him so much that I was in no way jealous of his wife. I even inquired after her, often. It was simple, I wanted to appropriate everything he touched, and when he spoke of her I committed to memory all his words, the better to analyze them later. I sought hints of distancing, signs of indifference, and when my search proved fruitless I even enjoyed the tears his faithfulness wrung from me.

All told, it was love at first sight, but dawning slowly, with no blinding flash. I have no photo of him, only a note for me that he wrote in the program for the opera we attended at the Russell Theatre, La Bohème. He wrote: "Art is a friend who never disappoints." Not very original, I know, but for a long time I would have liked to be buried with this piece of paper in my hands.

After his introduction to diplomacy in Ottawa, Porter returned to England, and King George made him his equerry. He is now the head of a family. I never dared write him. I loved Porter. To you goes the credit for making a woman out of the old young girl I was, but it was with him that I became the woman you never had time to get to know, she who has learned that true love also consists of suffering.

I have acquired in my unhappiness a taste for vulgar frankness. You are the only person in the world to whom I can confess these mad thoughts that plague my private life. Do you know what I do on those nights when I shut myself up at home? You know that attraction at fairs where one places one's face atop cardboard figures to be transformed into Louis XIV or the Queen of Sheba? Well, I sometimes push perversion to the point of borrowing your body, the only one I have known, and joining to it Porter's face, to bind myself to him in my imagination. The worst of it is that I say nothing of this to my confessor; I even experience no shame at the thought of these games, which comfort me a little. A little.

Next to Porter, my other memories of these two years of war are extremely pale. It amuses me now to remember the time when I frequented all the teas given in honour of our glorious soldiers. To show my solidarity I muted my appearance, and wore grey or black dresses, like a widow. I went everywhere carrying my canvas bag with its wooden handle and floral motif, and as soon as I had a minute I did like the other ladies, I knitted socks and balaclavas for the brave boys of the Princess Pats. I also loved the evenings organized to collect money for the Belgian refugees, where it was de rigueur to speak only in French. I smile now at the thought of those stout dowagers who would have had themselves crucified rather than speak two kind words to the French-Canadian baker, and who suddenly were addressing each other as "ma chère," and "vous prendrez bien une autre part de gâteau, ma bonne amie, n'est-ce pas?" with an English accent you could cut with a knife. But the war was only beginning, and we meant to do good.

We also organized masquerades and spectacles, including an adaptation of the Rubaiyat of Omar Khayyám in which I played the role of a card reader with a gypsy air. According to

Porter I performed very well, and as for me, I took pleasure in at last being someone other than myself. You would have liked me in that disguise, Essiambre. You might even have been tempted to conquer me all over again, and I must say, I would have consented.

What remains to me of Porter is an amber cigarette holder with which I smoke my eucalyptus cigarettes for my asthma. I take it with me when I go out into the world: I feel as though the smoke that drifts from it haloes me with the charm I dream of clothing myself with for life.

Essiambre, the last months have been hard. You will perhaps find it difficult to recognize me one day. And beware: you will doubtless court disapproval if you take up with me again in public.

You see, I have lost the war. Since last January 25, I am in the camp of the vanquished.

It was another charity gala designed to raise our soldiers' spirits. It was at the Château Laurier no less, and the entire Ottawa political and financial elite were present. I attended on the invitation of my last official suitor, ex-Captain Duff, who had lost an eye in France and who had just been named Senate Clerk. He's a friend of my younger brother, I was sure that I interested him, he had even provided proof: on a day when my mother gave a tea in our home, a memorable event in itself, Duff offered me the aid of his hands to reshape my ball of wool. A daring proposition, as you may imagine, but I accepted! I wanted the ladies present to see me for what I have become: a free and modern woman. Uneasy, my mother whispered in my ear: "But what would Major d'Argenteuil say if he saw you? You have just taken the first step towards infidelity." I smiled, and said nothing.

Since I'm talking about you, let me say that the news from the front has not escaped me, and where you are concerned it has been excellent. You were twice promoted for your courage, which is considerable, and I am proud to say so. But it is also rumoured that you have capitalized on your glory to indulge in excesses that would have led me to break with you were I really yours. Thus, during an evening at the Savoy in London you are said to have danced with the wife of a Canadian minister and then to have escorted her to her table, only to plant the poor lady there in order to pursue a woman more your age and more to your taste. Furious, the minister refused to receive you afterwards. You were, it appears, very drunk that evening. Later, you apparently spent a night with Sarah Shaughnessy, widow of the heir to the Canadian Pacific Railways. Is that all true? No, say nothing, I believe everything that is said about you.

I received this information from Duff himself, who seemed to admire you deeply, and even to approve of your misdemeanours.

Men seem to like you enormously, my Seigneur d'Argenteuil. You must tell me your secret one day.

I was very happy to be invited by Duff. It had been so long since I had seen the great ballrooms at the Château Laurier, and this outing would do me a world of good. For the occasion I bought myself silk stockings at Murphy & Gamble, and I brought out my blue tulle dress that suited me so well. A bird of paradise in my hairdo completed the effect. I was ravishing if I may say so, even Duff agreed.

But had I known who had organized the evening I would have stayed home by my fire. It was a band of little hussies who take advantage of their place in the world to cause scandals wherever they go. They are called the Naughty Nine. Young women of the best society, but in my opinion, utterly common.

They had already begun to make their mark in Ottawa. They were always seen hanging about together, and their rude stunts were beyond counting. The one called Sarah Colborne distinguished herself, among other things, during a cocktail at the Roxborough, by stuffing her mouth with olives like a squirrel. Everyone laughed at this clownishness, but not I. Another, Amanda Kelly, made a name for herself by doing a cartwheel in front of everyone during a tea at Rideau Hall! Some of them even smoke cigars in public to show they are equal to men. But what most irritates me in their conduct is good society's indulgence on their behalf: all their idiocies are tolerated, they are found charming, they are said to be "refreshing." They have free rein, whatever they do. Had I behaved like that in times past, Prince Connaught would never have wanted me at his table.

Nevertheless, the evening began well. The ladies were almost all as elegant as I was, and I know I was much observed. The gentlemen were also well attired, in their silk top hats and their beaver coats. The meal was delicious, an excellent rib of beef cooked in its juice. I was literally swimming in the scent of wealth and distinction, it was exhilarating.

Then the spectacle began. The Naughty Nine had mounted a parody of a New York evening called The Vogue Cabaret. The orchestra played popular tunes, that modern American music that is now insinuating its way into everything. The Nine first erupted from different parts of the room disguised as Ziegfeld Follies dancers, with their hair in short urchin cuts under black velvet toques, wearing short sequinned dresses, so short that one could see their naked legs and the detail on their delicate shoes. Each held in her hand an amber cigarette holder identical to mine, a present from Lord Porter: I was so ashamed that I immediately put the object away, and smoked all my after-dinner cigarettes without using it. Each one sang a little song of her own, and they all converged on the main stage, performing lascivious dance steps.

Thunderous applause for the entrance of these ladies! Even Duff, at my table, clapped his hands and whistled in admiration. I could not believe my eyes. The rest of the evening followed suit.

A masterpiece of vulgarity. Cheeky little political sketches, American songs, obscene dances, nothing was missing. After the intermission they returned in white satin dresses that revealed everything of their bodies, wearing plumed toques and glass jewellery that looked very nouveau riche, if you ask my opinion.

That is exactly what I said to Duff, who replied, "Hush! I want to hear what they're saying. They're hilarious, the girls, don't you think?" I was so furious with him that I did not even taste the dessert, which, however, looked delicious. I didn't want anyone to think I was enjoying myself, and this little sacrifice was a sign of my disapproval.

The worst were those dances they executed with shameless pleasure. The foxtrot, the one-step, the two-step, not to mention the tango two of the girls performed, and that was to constitute the high point of the evening. I almost got up to leave at that point, but I had not a penny for a cab, and I was to return in an automobile with Duff. Otherwise...

More thunderous applause at the end, and even two encores. I must have been the only one in the room not to have applauded at all, and of that I am proud. But to see such a distinguished audience show such enthusiasm for those indecencies cut me to the quick. I did not hesitate, you may well imagine, to say exactly what I thought of this disgusting spectacle at a time when our thoughts ought to have been with those of our number who were being massacred in Europe's trenches, and, and... I ended up at a loss for words. At one point, perhaps irritated by my sermon, Duff tried to reason with me. "Really, it was only a little entertainment! Why are you being so high and mighty about it? These are fine girls who are trying to cheer us up in these sad times, that's all. A little charity, Amalia..." I cut his reprimand short. "Miss Driscoll, Captain Duff. I would be most obliged if you would resume your distance. From now on it will be Miss Driscoll..." Now it was he who exploded, he made a scene, he said I had ruined his evening with my moral preaching, etc. He brought me home, but we did not exchange a single word in the automobile.

I did not call him back, not even to thank him. In the interests of making peace, however, I was prepared to forgive him were he to telephone me and present his excuses. He never called. My descent had begun.

However I might campaign against these girls, boycott the salons where they were invited, nothing made any difference. Their popularity was impervious to my cruellest barbs, and when I mocked them, people sang their praises. It was as if the earth had ceased to turn. Overnight, what one might wish on one's worst enemy had one no Christian soul, was inflicted on me: I was suddenly outmoded, I had aged and the world around me had grown younger without me. The Nine appeared everywhere, and above all, they never missed a soldiers' departure so they would have the perfect excuse to embrace as many as possible. And one found that charming, innocent. When Lord Devonshire settled into Rideau Hall, the Naughty Nine were invited, I was not. Although I had once reigned over this world, I no longer existed. I was even the object of ridicule in town: it was said that I was constipated, old hat, a hypocrite, anything at all. Given your prolonged absence, our betrothal was no longer taken seriously, and in the salons I was even called the virgin widow (but if they only knew). I was poorly positioned to complain of this treatment, I who had in my turn spoken ill of my neighbour in those circles where charity is unknown, and had more than once laughed heartily at the misfortunes of those highly placed in that world. The world does not punish you differently for having done its bidding; the dagger you wielded yesterday becomes the foil that runs you through today.

Since that time I have experienced the worst of solitudes, which is isolation. To invite me into one's home is no longer a sign of friendship, but of courage. My own sister, Rose, I am ashamed to say, prefers not to see me when it is her day, and she no longer lends me clothes for my outings. Since May I have received no invitation to the soirées that count in Ottawa. None.

The only pleasure remaining to me is to go to say farewell to the soldiers leaving the station by entire regiments. I wave to them and pray for them, handkerchief in hand, but I know none of them. Their grateful smiles console me a little. It is to that that I have been reduced.

Essiambre, my good friend, it is official: I am feeling better. And so be kind and write me at last a true letter, as you know how. That way I will be less alone with my small happiness.

The unthinkable has happened: I have accepted a real job. It had to be, otherwise I would have died of boredom. My last hope has presented itself in the person of the Ottawa Citizen's new editor-in-chief, Edmund Garry, who interviewed me for an article he was writing, in fact, about you, d'Argenteuil. He said he knew you well, you were both lieutenants with the Princess

Pats. His wound obliged him to return to Canada; he had been a journalist before the war, and thanks to family connections and his legendary capacity for work, he quickly moved up the ladder in his newspaper. Garry told me he wanted details about you that I was the only one capable of providing. I think he hoped to make a hero of you; I don't know if he has written that article.

And so we made friends, he and I, and it wasn't long before he told me that he didn't much like the society columns I signed "Deirdre Hawthorne," and that he preferred my sketches to my style. He then offered me more serious work on the paper, that of advertising artist. I would earn a real weekly salary, like a man. I said yes immediately.

One more reason for my detractors to welcome me into their world no longer: I am working. Too bad. At least I am now comfortably paying my way.

Thus, you have come to my aid without my asking. And so thank you, Essiambre, you have been my salvation in these so difficult times.

One more thing, and it is important. Three days ago I awoke in the middle of the night with your name in my head, only, strangely, I could not remember your face. I no longer saw your body either. Now I understand why.

It's that I've begun to see other men. There is the Chilean poet and diplomat Rainer Obadia, a wealthy man who wants to take me to live in Paris; there is also the painter Alfred Thompson, who is of Welsh origin but who lived for ten years in California, where he acquired a free mode of behaviour that would have shocked me before I knew you. These conquests compensate for my worldly disgrace. Doubtless you would say, my dear Essiambre, that all that is salutary, and you would be right. Voluptuousness induces oblivion. The carnal act is the universal solvent of regrets.

Come back alive, Essiambre. You will discover a woman whom pleasure has rendered tolerant. Since I do not believe I have come to the end of my discoveries, we perhaps still have things to say to each other.

Goodbye, Essiambre.

I'VE LEFT THE MONASTERY BUT I'VE NOT BUDGED from the Flats.

It's Mathurin himself who urged me to leave. I had adopted certain practices of the Capuchin Fathers, such as shaving without a mirror, and he thought that inappropriate for a man with no vocation. And so he found me a room with a woman of a venerable age, as well as a job as bookkeeper for Baker and Brothers scrap metal.

I do not abuse my newly regained freedom. I have readopted certain habits at Adrienne's blind pig and a few drinking spots in Hull, but I retain my dignity. The proof? My drunken ghost walked out of my life, and I have never seen him again.

Mathurin would very much like me to see Miss Driscoll once more, but I dare not. It's been five years since our botched rendezvous at the Dominican Fathers' celebration, but I remember it as though it were yesterday, and I fear that she recalls it only too well herself. Although I am perhaps mistaken in attributing to her memories identical to my own.

She lives at the Hotel Couillard, room number 27, the same I occupied with little Concorde. She has been there for about the same amount of time that I took refuge with the Capuchins. The day after the celebration she did a charcoal drawing for her newspaper depicting the scene that brought us face to face. It was titled *Commotion*. I was there in profile with my military uniform, the young servant was lying on the ground, Miss Driscoll held the pose of a frightened singer and Father Mathurin had one knee on the ground and his crucifix in his hand, with something in his gaze that reminded me of Goya or Velasquez. Mathurin brought me the reproduction in the newspaper. I would not have been up to taking notice of it at the time.

She is a prominent advertising artist, again according to Mathurin, who knows everything. She draws what is sold in Ottawa. The Milk Fairy for Producer's Dairy, their milk rich in lime; Stanley's tweeds for the elegant man; lined, galvanized and white enamelled iceboxes for twenty-four dollars at Caplan's, 135 Rideau Street; Victrolas and player pianos. Ladies' clothing: brassieres, blouses in crepe de chine, kid gloves, silk stockings at H.J. Daly's, Connaught Square; not to mention satin petticoats and washable taffetas, poplin dresses and camisoles, always reasonably priced at Robinson's, at the corner of Sparks and Metcalfe. Olive oil is hers as well, as are Gin Pills for the kidneys, Alabastine water, biocrate of Magnesium, so good for the digestion, and Tarol oil made from cod's liver, which cures all respiratory ailments: the flu, whooping cough, bronchitis. Peg Top cigars, four for twenty-five cents, Gauvin cough syrup made from wild cherry, I think she does them all. I forgot the desserts: Madame's Caramels, the after-dinner mints and jellybeans; along with those, Primus tea or Dalley coffee, depending on your tastes. She also does courtroom sketches in the paper for trials where the accused are in danger of being hanged. All I have to do is open the newspaper, I am sure of finding her.

That's not all, there's better still. She is also playing the piano in the cinema, an old dream of hers if my memory of her letters serves me well. She is practising her art in Ottawa's new theatre, the Capitol, a palace with gold gilding on the walls, attractive imitation marble, thick carpeting throughout, a real stage with an orchestra pit and a magnificent velvet curtain. It only takes fifteen cents admission for you to feel like a king or a millionaire proprietor of all these luxuries; the entire common crowd has been ennobled in one fell swoop. You would think you were in a once-splendid Austro-Hungarian castle; that's what the newspaper says, anyway. I go sometimes, not for the films, but to hear her play. Most of all, to see her.

One might suspect that these outings are not advisable for me, given the fragility of my condition. But the opposite is true. Before the showing I position myself near the stage door to be certain that she will be playing on that night. She always arrives veiled, with a large velvet hat and a long coat. As soon as she goes in, I buy my ticket and sit as near to her as I can. Sometimes I just listen without looking at the film. I follow her home after the show and then I head back myself, without stopping at Adrienne's blind pig. Miss Driscoll heals me with her art; I feel better when I see her.

Sometimes, when films from Russia or France are being shown and another artist plays the music, she explains the film to the audience. On these occasions she lifts her veil and makes large, delicate gestures with her white gloves. She is an excellent performer, although I suspect she cheats a little. I say that because those films are not always as interesting as she says. It doesn't matter, she is the one I want to see.

Something tells me that Essiambre d'Argenteuil would be very proud of her. For want of the worldly and romantic success to which she aspired, she has become an artist. But first she had to break with her class. To agree to work first, then to practise her art.

Mathurin, who talks to her sometimes because he calls on her occasionally to play the organ at Saint Francis of Assisi Church, told me what I hoped to hear. In the months following the celebration, Miss Driscoll's mother returned to Ireland to claim a legacy; there she died. To care for his heart, her father went to live with his doctor son in Niagara Falls, where the climate is more temperate. He did not last long either. As the Blackburn Street apartment was too large and too expensive for her, Miss Driscoll sold the little that she had and moved into the Hotel Couillard in the Flats. The Couillard is not the Roxborough or the Château Laurier, it is even a bit shabby now. But Mathurin tells me that she has rented a suite where she has set up her drawing board and her materials. She orders all her meals from the kitchen, and she has a faithful admirer who provides her with excellent contraband sherry and boxes of cigarettes. She doesn't do any cleaning, she has all her sewing done for her, in short she lives the life of the failed princess she always knew herself to be.

Miss Driscoll has become a great lady in moving down to the Flats. Everyone knows she is an artist. People step aside when she strides down the sidewalk, men lift their hats, the scrap workers at Baker and Brothers stop swearing when she goes by, it's as though she imposes a silence on the pedestrians and the passengers in the horse-drawn vehicles. She is greeted by the Calabrian knife grinders whose speech is incomprehensible, by the vendors who peddle their apple or raisin pies from house to house, the vegetable and fruit sellers, the milkmen, the icemen. Her haughty gait skirts, as though by magic, the dung from the Dominion Transport stables on Cummings Street, and every time I pass her she leaves in her wake the Canada Bread bakery's bouquet, which smells of good wholesome bread. Nothing unpleasant ever happens to her. Even the little neighbourhood boys fight for the honour of doing her errands.

She parades through the streets in her outmoded outfits that suit her so well. As though fashions had frozen in 1916, the year she found herself excluded from good society. And, according to Mathurin, who is truly a valuable informant, when her clothes can no longer be used because of wear she goes to a nearby dressmaker, who makes her the very same, in identical colours and cloth. It is as if she has of her own free will enclosed herself in the past. I don't know if her obsolete attire adds to the admiring aura that follows her everywhere, but she certainly seems to hold on to it as to a talisman. In any case she is charming as a woman of yesteryear, and I suspect she will always be the age she was when she changed her life to become an artist.

On a number of occasions I have found myself seated in front of her on the streetcar or face to face with her in the grocery store. With the scent of eucalyptus that follows her everywhere, I could recognize her with my eyes closed. Only one thing about her disturbs me: that gaze of a woman who doesn't know her husband is cheating on her. Some days I want to introduce myself, take her by the arm and walk a little way with her. I always restrain myself in time. Whenever I am tempted to approach her, the thought of Essiambre making love to her stops me. I experience a pang of jealousy, quickly followed by a sense of relief, as though our shared memory of Essiambre's embraces had united us in a bond of blood.

Be that as it may, I will soon depart. I am doing too well to stay here much longer. Father Mathurin, who is very attached to me, does not want me to leave, but he feels it would be for the best. I hear his unspoken prayer. I will go away after the new bell for Saint Francis of Assisi has been blessed. In his capacity as the eldest of the monastery, it is he who will have the honour of officiating. He has accepted the name that I proposed: the bell will be called Flavie.

·
·
·
·
·

MATHURIN OFFERED ME HIS SUITCASE, WHICH HAD never travelled. The one I deposited with the pawnbroker was sold a long time ago with everything it contained, except the letters that Mathurin was alert enough to salvage. I left with the only suit I possess and the thirty dollars I had saved by almost ceasing to drink. Mathurin's new suitcase, all in tawny leather, with its still-shiny clasps, made me look like a gentleman who knows where he is going.

The story of this suitcase adds some richness to my life, which from here on in will be devoid of interest, as I wished.

Mathurin received it as a gift from his mother on the day of his ordination, in anticipation of the day he would take up his life as a missionary. It was during the period when he dreamed of falling into the hands of bloodthirsty pagans in China or Africa, and dying as a holy martyr to the faith. It didn't matter whether his torturers were yellow or black. Only one thing counted: to be canonized, and to have a day to himself on the calendar: Saint Mathurin, priest and martyr.

I asked him one day where his vocation as a martyr came from. "You see, when I was small, I dreamed of being a prophet. But as I soon realized I did not have that gift, I thought it would be easy to become a saint by having myself massacred in defence of the faith. I know what you're thinking. That it's pride, all that? You're absolutely right. My only dream, when you come down to it, was to be included in a book that would talk about me. Life has cured me of such vanities. Here, take my suitcase, it will be of much more use to you than to me."

He said he had joined the Capuchins because it was the only order that would take him, given that he was not highly rated at the seminary. He was very disappointed to end up in Ottawa as a teacher at the new Seraphic School, he who had dreams of more exotic perils. All his colleagues were from the south of France, and he was, as is still the case, the only Canadian of the group. He was very bored, and that is why he almost swooned the day he was summoned by the Father Superior: "Father Mathurin, you have asked to be sent abroad. Between now and the end of summer, you should have some news." And so he would have spent only twelve months in Ottawa; a horrible year, but one that was over.

Without knowing quite why, he was sure he would be sent to Uganda. Doubtless because he had loved the sound of the name ever since the day when as a young seminarian he had visited the Quebec chapter of the White Fathers of Africa, where he had seen a stuffed monkey, elephant tusks and spears. As a child he had dreamed of being decapitated at the feet of the Emperor of China. For ten days in a row he thanked God for His goodness by fasting every night. There was only one thing that tempered his enthusiasm: he had not yet received the duly signed order for his posting. But, no longer able to restrain his joy, he had in the end confided to a colleague that a wonderful change in his life was imminent, and that from now on he would have to pray a bit harder for black Africa. Three days later, the round of confidences having done its work, all his colleagues embraced him in turn, telling him how much they envied him. At night, in his room, he caressed his leather suitcase before falling asleep.

After an interminable waiting period of three weeks, he at last received his posting. He was being sent to Japan. No matter, he was still happy. To this day he cannot say where exactly the city is where he was being sent, and no matter how much he pored over a map of the country for several days, he could never pick it out. "It doesn't matter," he thought, "when I arrive in the first Japanese port I will ask my way from a passer-by, who will surely have the charity to come to the aid of a little Brother of Saint Francis. I would do the same for a Buddhist missionary who had been sent here."

The order stated that he had first to go to the mother house in Toulouse to be trained for preaching in a foreign country, a matter of four to six months. He would then go to Rome to study Japanese, which made him somewhat uneasy, as he had always been weak in languages, even dead ones. (He has never been very strong in French either, and he still has to mask his spelling errors with handwriting only a pharmacist can decipher.)

Including his instruction and his apostolic mission, he would be gone for seven years. His departure was set for the month of November, and so he had six weeks to pack. It took him a few minutes.

He capitalized on the waiting period, however, to ask forgiveness from his colleagues for all the sins he may have committed concerning each of them. As is the custom, he had to kneel before everyone individually for public absolution.

This exercise, painful enough in itself, caused him considerable difficulty. He had to say, "My brother, tell me in what way I have offended you so that I might ask your forgiveness in the name of our Lord Jesus Christ." He then learned to his stupefaction that his fellows had endured for months shameful failings that only their charity had concealed from him. Father Céleste forgave him his noisy eating at the table; Father Fidèle said he had closed his eyes to certain bodily odours that had been following him around since adolescence; three others confirmed his observation; Father Candide, whom he thought was the most charitable of all, was the most severe: his gluttony, his inattention at evening prayers, the fact that he picked his nose when someone else was saying mass, his resonant naps in the library, his thick laugh and his predilection for puns, which he repeated over and over again because he forgot he had already come out with them, there was no end.

The exercise at least had the advantage of teaching Mathurin to know himself a little better. He resolved to improve himself to the point where his colleagues would one day not even recognize their missionary brother. Looking back later on those faults attributed to him, he had the less charitable thought that his colleagues had perhaps accelerated their approval of his request for posting at a foreign mission.

He wrote a long letter to his parents, pious and edifying the way his mother liked them, taking care to make certain that it would be read aloud to all family members who did not themselves know how to read. His father had an answer sent to him: "Send us stamps from over there, your brother is making a collection." Then he decided to write his friends to say goodbye, but he realized to his great sorrow that he didn't have any. All his former colleagues had scattered, and he couldn't even count on former students who might remember him fondly. The emptiness of his life appeared to him in all its desolation, and he prayed more ardently than ever so that the impending martyrdom to be inflicted upon him by the Japanese emperor might one day rescue him from oblivion.

The first stop on the journey that awaited him was Montreal, where he was to board the ocean liner that would take him to Liverpool, and from there to Cherbourg. He was well received at the Montreal mother house; a little party had even been organized to mark his departure, a courtesy he had not been vouchsafed in Ottawa. The boat was to leave the next day at nine o'clock. A lay brother had been delegated to take him to the port.

He never knew exactly what happened. One thing is certain, he slept very badly, and woke at dawn only to go to back to sleep, convinced that the night was still young. But the lay brother who was to fetch him had been called away elsewhere during the night, so that no one took the trouble to make sure he was awake. He awoke alone, very well rested, and it was while crossing the empty refectory, suitcase in hand, that he realized with horror how late it was. At the exit he passed the bursar, who asked him, in a voice too gentle for his tastes: "Ah! Father Mathurin, you are still with us? Are you only leaving this afternoon?" Somewhat embarrassed, he confessed that he feared he was a little late. The bursar had a car come immediately, and ordered the driver to take him to the port without delay.

The boat had left. Sheepish, Mathurin returned to the monastery. Making inquiries left and right, the best the bursar was able to do was to have his ticket reimbursed.

Impossible, however, to reserve space on another steamship. The bursar then asked him, in a voice that was not gentle at all, to return to Ottawa and there to await orders from his superior.

His Ottawa colleagues were very decent towards him. No one was so indelicate as to mention in front of him the schoolboy blunder that had deprived him of his glorious destiny. It should be said that they felt a bit shamefaced to have revealed to him his faults with such frankness. They would have been less zealous in their admonishments had they known he would be back so soon.

He paid for his error with a renewed waiting period of fifteen years, without budging from Ottawa, without even changing his cell. He who had inherited the most humble room of all on his arrival, certain that he would receive another posting any day now, refused all those that came free and that were more comfortable. He had almost lost hope when he received his new posting as a missionary. This time they were sending him to Africa. He had changed continents during his wait, but that didn't matter to him, because he did not know this time either what the country of his martyrdom was. He thinks it was Senegal. Or Tanzania? No matter.

He had to submit himself again to the ritual of being pardoned by his brothers, and it was even more painful than the last time because he knew what they were going to say. And so he heard the same list a second time round, and his colleagues appended all the faults they had omitted the first time, plus new ones he had acquired. Before this ordeal he would never have thought he would be so eager to see Africa one day.

The day of his departure, unlike the previous occasion, there were four to accompany him to the station; I think they wanted to be sure to see him go. In Montreal he refused the hospitality of the monastery; he would wait all night on the dock, he would not miss the boat a second time, and he would catch up on his sleep aboard the steamship.

When he presented himself at the ticket office the next morning, circles under his eyes, he found it in turmoil. The lay Brother charged with seeing him off went to see what was going on. Catastrophe: Canada had declared war on Germany and her allies a few weeks earlier, and the boat had been requisitioned to transport troops and supplies. He protested of course, he demanded another reservation, but nothing could be done. Some other time.

He went back to Ottawa at once, certain now that the martyr's crown had been tressed with another in mind. "Take my suitcase, Lusignan, I've lost hope. Take it now and go to see your father." I did as he said.

·
·
·
·
·

AFTER A PROLONGED SEARCH FOR A BEAUTIFUL COUNtry through which I might wander to expiate my cowardly acts, I have become an exile in the village of my birth.

I couldn't help it. I had to come back to this land that had always dwelt within me.

But first, I took a little detour. It took me three years to make the trip. I didn't speak a word of French during my roamings, I was no longer the Lusignan I had known so well, I had everyone call me Lou. I almost managed to forget who I had been.

To earn my living I became a peddler. I liked being welcomed into people's homes. Often they didn't need anything, or they didn't have enough money to buy anything, but they invited me in anyway, saying: "Come and sit down just for a few minutes. At least we'll have some news." I told them news I made up along the way, I gave them my views on politics with an assurance that even astonished me a little; to move them or to give them an illusion of prosperity, I talked to them of the famine and wars that were devastating Russia and China; I also passed on gossip from neighbouring villages, which they very much enjoyed. In short, I told them all they wanted to hear, and I was liked. I willingly stayed to eat and sleep, and I rewarded my hosts with quantities of free samples, especially for the children and widows. As a result, my jobs didn't always last long.

I still have fond memories of the Toronto sugar company whose molasses I sold. My clients were for the most part orphanages, convents and colleges, and I sold tons of molasses by convincing the buyers that the price of sugar was going to increase tenfold because of the imminent war. As this war was late in arriving, my clientele began to complain of such tactics, more worthy of a campaigning politician, and I soon ceased to be the company's star salesman.

Then things began to go downhill, in part due to drink. Twice I found myself in prison for vagrancy, one short time for theft, which was a miscarriage of justice, I swear.

Back in Quebec, I ran into difficulties. I, a lover of railway stations and of taking trains without bothering to pay, lingered a bit too long in Montreal. I had not eaten for three days and so at the station restaurant I ordered a meal, which I devoured, and then refused to pay for on the grounds that the food was inedible. The chef did not find that funny, and we had a bit of an altercation. The police were called, and the next day the judge threatened to commit me to the asylum. That's when I decided to visit my father.

He was waiting for me. He didn't even seem surprised to see me. He thanked me for writing him, because it was my rare letters that helped him to become more intimate with the postmistress, she who always thought the worst of me. She's a widow, and she and my father see each other in secret. His eyes light up when he talks about this shrew, who is not all bad. I will at least have provided him with this small happiness, one that eluded him for so long.

I got to work right away. Tools were no longer foreign to me. My first project was the making of a coffin for a man in the village who was to be hanged in the Trois-Rivières prison; if I understood rightly, it was for the murder of a moonshiner, the owner of the best still in the region, a very respected man.

I did most of the work on my own. My father helped me out with his advice. I would have been happier had I not known the identity of the hanged man. He was my child-hood playmate, Hector, who mimicked so well the cry of the Iroquois that we had never heard. After watching his exe-cution in the public square at Trois-Rivières, I almost went back on the road. The state of my father's health held me back. Instead of running away, I fashioned his own future coffin, without any help. He was very happy with me, he even said I had surpassed him in his craft.

I never left him again. I was at last a real son to him. I organized his order book, I collected all his debts, some of which went back to my birth, I chased off the village youths who came to hunt at his blind and to laugh at him before and after their hunt. I even took back from the Poitras family the old carriage that my father had disguised as a coach with a coat of arms, but that had never been paid for. I drove my father around in it every chance I got, and gave him a tour of the parish while playing the cranky coachman. When I went with him to the general store, no one called him Good Saint Joseph any more, they said "Mr. Lusignan," so fearful were they of my excesses. We began to cook as my mother had, to remember her better.

He died peacefully, with no memorable last words, in my arms like a man loved. Father Mathurin hastened to our side, a faithful friend. I didn't want to bury my father in the asylum graveyard with my mother, I didn't want him to spend eternity with visionaries of my ilk. No question either of putting him in the cemetery belonging to the village that had mocked him all his life. Mathurin obtained a dispensation from the parish, and we buried him beside the house at the duck blind. Only Mathurin and I were at the burial; after saying the Mass for the Dead, my friend helped me put him in the earth. By the time we had filled the grave we were bathed in sweat under the July sun, despite the wind off the river that made us cold. I took my revenge on this beautiful day's indifference to my grief by forgetting the date.

That night we made a campfire to pay him a final homage. Under the ashes I cooked potatoes and eels I had caught in the river the day before, and Mathurin managed to wheedle a jug of communion wine out of the priest. We feasted like true comrades, while laughing merrily at my past lapses and his bygone yearnings.

Mathurin spent several days with me, and while I was working with wood or cooking, he talked. When he left for the monastery where for thirty years he has known no one, he seemed much better. He'll come again when he can.

Mathurin is happier since he has renounced his martyr's halo. He no longer dreams of that book wherein would be chronicled his edifying life. Before leaving Ottawa in 1924, I told him a bit idly that the best thing he could do would be to write a book himself: "I don't know, you could write the life of a saint who has been unjustly ignored." I should have thought before I spoke.

He began the next day. He thinks only of that. As he has performed all the duties imaginable at the monastery, his Order is giving him all the free time he needs to pursue his research at the National Archives. He is convinced that his efforts will lead to his being named postulator for some saint, and to a long residence in Rome. He will escape Ottawa's industrial gloom and will turn his back forever on the small world that never acknowledged his worth.

First, he took his merry old time choosing his subject. He began with a long inquiry into Marguerite Bourgeoys, who preferred the itinerant life of Mary to one of contemplation, and threw herself into the world to do good by educating young girls and treating the sick. The story of her first miracle fascinated him: suffering from migraines, the painter of the dead assigned to do her portrait slipped a lock of Marguerite's hair under his wig, and the pain vanished immediately. A postulator colleague at the National Archives advised him that Marguerite belonged to the Sulpicians in Montreal, and they would not much appreciate seeing a Capuchin usurp their candidate for sanctity. Fourteen months of work for nothing.

By the next day he was delving into the file of Jeanne Le Ber, that contemporary of Maisonneuve who with her own money had a cell built into a church in Montreal, where she walled herself up alive. As a willing prisoner of Jesus Christ, she accepted one meal a day and devoted her life to prayer. Mathurin was certain that no one else would be interested in this poor contemplative. Wrong. Another Sulpician shooed him off as though he were a little boy stealing apples. One more year lost, but he had no regrets.

He only has time now for Marie de l'Incarnation and Catherine de Saint-Augustin. It's as though, once he immersed himself in seventeenth-century New France, he ceased to live among us. It makes him happy. I did warn him, however, to beware: those two belong to the Jesuits, and another disappointment looms. He pays no attention, his happiness is too great. His eyes mist over when he talks of Marie's letter in which she tells of summoning to her convent a traveller about to return to France, so as to reassure her son that she is still alive. Behind the grille in the visitors' room, so the man will see her well and memorize her face, she removes her veil. It's a very tender scene, it's true. From time to time, to give him pleasure, I ask Mathurin to repeat the story of Marie's veil. He needs very little urging.

He has just spent months recopying passages from *The Life of Mother Catherine de Saint-Augustin*, by Father Paul Ragueneau. I confess that I only half listen when he tells me that Catherine swallowed the rotten and smelly phlegm of the sick in order to mortify herself, or that she threw herself into the snow up to her waist to drive away the impure thoughts that tormented her. I prefer to hear him talk about how in a dream, to ease her suffering, she suckled at the Holy Virgin's nipples, an experience, it must be admitted, that not many of us have shared.

He has now reached the passage where Catherine has been carnally united with God, and also with the Holy Ghost and Saint John of Patmos, episodes whose interpretation has caused him certain difficulties. But Mathurin has no doubt that Catherine will one day be canonized. The most difficult task remaining to him is to unearth miracles in case the heroic account of her virtues should prove inadequate. He does not much care for the reports of healing attributed to her intercession, because they are for the most part instances of hemorrhoids and scabies, which are not very interesting, but for the time being he is making do with what he finds. I encourage him as best I can.

When he comes to see me, we spend long days discussing his project. Or rather he spends long days talking to me about it. During that time I work with wood, as my father did while listening to the outpourings of the notary Poitras, happy in a past that only he was bringing back to life. He gives me his texts, and I correct his spelling mistakes. He leaves, contented, with his thick dossiers under his arm.

Even now it's hard for me to stay in one place. I still take to the road for months at a time, but I have become prudent. I go away less; the last time I got no farther than the Delaware River and I had no problems with the authorities.

When all is said and done, I'm happy in the village. I've been here now for two years. Every day I avenge the memory of my parents by terrorizing my fellow citizens. They still see me as a dangerous madman, and so of course I take full advantage. I only need to set foot in a tavern for all the clients to fall silent; some now try to be polite to me, but I don't encourage them very much. I prefer them to see me as that crazy Lusignan who scares everybody, the man you point to when warning your children: "If you don't work hard at school you'll end up like that drunk Lusignan down by the river..." It's my new role in the village theatre, and I want to hold on to it.

What I've also come to understand is that they fear me because I actually fought the war. They were all draft dodgers here. Of thirty-nine who were conscripted, thirty-six obtained exemptions from a judge, and three others hid in the woods, where they ran the region's stills. All three were amnestied three years after the war. In their guilty memories, I am the survivor who reminds them of their cowardice and their nastiness towards my parents. The horrors of war they've learned about from others invest me with a cruel courage I do not really possess. And for once I am smart enough not to correct their misconceptions. It gives me great pleasure to see them pissing themselves with fear when I prowl through the autumn rushes and alders, dressed in my army coat, with my Lee Enfield that no longer shoots.

I have also, in a small way, taken the place of Poitras the notary by turning myself into a jurist. My career began last year when I filled up my long winter evenings reading ancient notarial works whose contents I now turn to good use. On Sunday, after mass, the only time when the villagers feel free to bid me good day, all I have to do is linger a while on the church steps for someone to ask my advice on local issues. I cite articles in the Code, I draw on the jurisprudence of New France, I juggle Latin and English words and I confuse my questioners by inventing laws that will only exist in happier times. I even settle disputes from time to time, and I don't charge a penny, so as to confuse them even more.

I also earn a good living, I have plenty of work, and I get along well with the river. Fishing and hunting are still good, the vegetable garden is productive and provides me with as much tobacco as I can smoke. With the summer's profusion of berries I concoct a heady wine that costs me only the odd nocturnal headache.

One day I will remain here for good.

·
·
·
·
·

LEFT TO MYSELF I WOULD HAVE STAYED LONGER IN MY cabin on the river, but Mathurin almost forced me back to Ottawa. He said I needed a rest and that the timing was good because there was something he absolutely had to show me.

I had just come back from one of my wanderings when the spring flooding inundated the blind and carried off my father's coffin. Rushing to my aid, Mathurin helped me search for it. When we found the box floating amid the ice, it was empty. I don't know where my father is now. He has perhaps followed the underwater current and made his way to the sea. He will turn up one day on a beach in Brittany or Jersey. Well, he always dreamed of escaping the village, now he's got his wish.

Mathurin was my saviour once more. In any case, he stopped me from setting fire to the house and throwing my tools into the well. When I had drunk up all my reserves of berry wine he said, "Come back with me to Ottawa, I need you." We left the next day at dawn after storing the coffin under the gallery. When my turn comes I'll be laid out in it; Mathurin has promised me that he himself will sink it in the river afterwards.

I only stayed in Ottawa for a few months, and I left again as suddenly as I had arrived. Mathurin found me a job working on the roads, a lucky break as work has become hard to find here, and I entertained myself by going often to movie theatres and to concerts. And it was a good thing, as I again saw the lovely Miss Driscoll.

She hasn't aged, perhaps because she has once again changed professions. As she can no longer, since the advent of the talkies, accompany films on the piano and as advertising illustration seems doomed in the short term, she bought the equipment that belonged to the Flats' photographer, Marcil, after his death. The family had to sell it to pay for his burial. The gentleman who plays the role of Miss Driscoll's faithful admirer has had her apartment at the Hotel Couillard enlarged to accommodate her darkroom. She is now a photographer at the paper, and even does portraits.

She has also begun to paint. She has joined the Association of Christian Artists, called Le Caveau, founded by the

Dominicans at Saint John the Baptist Church. For the most part she paints canvases of religious inspiration. This is what Father Mathurin wanted to show me: a painting representing the martyrdom inflicted on the Sulpician Lemaître by the Iroquois, for which a Dominican colleague had served as model. "I too would like to pose for her in a religious tableau," he told me. "She always takes Dominicans, as if we, the Capuchins, were not good enough. Perhaps you could persuade her to choose me."

And that is how we met at last. Mathurin made an appointment with her, he took me along as interpreter and we had tea in her room, number 27, which brought back so much. I of course made no reference to these memories; at times I can still be tactful. Nor did I mention the lover we'd once shared, Essiambre. To Mathurin's great joy, she asked us to serve as models for a copy she wanted to make of Goya's depiction of the martyrdom of Brébeuf.

We both posed in the painting studio the Dominicans called the High Room, under the church's roof, beside the steeple. I'm not qualified to say whether the painting is well done; I can only say that I don't find myself very convincing as an Indian with a tomahawk. Mathurin is much better as Brébeuf. Be that as it may, my old friend was delighted with himself; even if he will not be immortalized in a book, he will at least live on in a painting.

I almost identified myself to Miss Driscoll, but I stopped in time. It was a day when she was painting a nude model in order to derive from it later a Canadian saint, Marie de l'Incarnation or Catherine de Saint-Augustin, I don't remember which; I only know that it was Mathurin who proposed the subject. Mathurin came with me on that occasion, but the naked woman in the room made him ill at ease, and he left. She finished her work, and the model departed as well. Miss Driscoll and I chatted a little over a glass of port in the twilight of the High Room. I had a sudden urge to proposition her, if only to lay my cards on the table afterwards. But the poor light from the oil lamp was hurting my eyes, and more importantly my heart wasn't in it, because it was Essiambre's memory I desired in her, nothing else. I wanted to take his place, just once.

There were long silences between us, and each time she lowered her head I searched her face, wondering if she had the slightest inkling of the sordid game I'd played with her, passing myself off as Essiambre the letter writer. I couldn't read her eyes, and I am almost sure that, myopic as she is, she guessed nothing about me. I was the Invisible Man circling his prey, about whom he knows all. Then the silence became so intense that I took my leave a bit abruptly. I left the studio as troubled as if I were the one who had been misled. The cold night made me hurry my steps as though I were fleeing them, Essiambre and her.

I was making my way towards the little room I was renting on Booth in the Flats, when a man surged up before me. I didn't recognize him at first. He held out his hand. It was Garry, older but very elegant. I had been most embarrassed to see him again ten years earlier, when he had saved me from prison and a certain beating. Now I was happy because

I had thought him dead, like so many other former Princess Pats. He invited me to follow him. His chauffeur and car were waiting a few steps away.

We went for a drink at the bar of the Grand Hotel. We didn't talk much because there was no point, we just listened to the little jazz ensemble playing music I don't know well, but that I like. At the piano was a young black man with magnificent features, whose coal-black eyes burned with suppressed anger.

When the show was over, Garry said, "I am the one whom Amalia Driscoll calls her faithful admirer, or her salvation, depending on the day. I now own the newspaper that employs her. I watch over her in Essiambre's memory. She is all that remains to me of him. She gave me the letters she received from him, I often reread them. Even now that he is dead, I cannot bring myself to leave him. You understand? The others, Obadia and Thompson, for example, didn't bother me, in fact they served my purposes. She even refused to follow Obadia to Paris; she said her art was here, and so I was reassured. With you it's different. I can't help myself, I'm afraid you're making progress with her and that worries me. I'm terrified you'll take her from me, and I want to hold onto her. Doubtless because of Essiambre's memory. Would you be prepared to do something for me? To go away, I mean. If you need anything, I can help you…" The bar had emptied, the musicians were putting away their instruments, talking softly to each other. The last round was over, but Garry, as the rich and respected man he had become, ordered more whisky without worrying about the rules.

I grabbed the line he tossed me. The time had come to free myself from Essiambre's memory. I didn't want to have that widow's look in my eyes all my life, as Garry did at the very mention of his name. I also coveted the money he was offering me. To temper the venality of his proposition, Garry spoke of a loan. I proposed, in exchange, to give him the letters I'd received from Miss Driscoll. He emitted a little cry of joy, pressing his hands together. I noted his address to send him the letters, and I pocketed the bills with a coolness that astonished me. It felt good, as though Garry's money had devalued once and for all Essiambre's memories for me, while increasing their worth for him.

A gallant man, he offered me his chauffeur and car to drive me home. I replied that I preferred to walk, no doubt to regain a bit of dignity. "I'm going to stay in the bar a little longer," he said. I pretended to stride away briskly from the hotel, and I hid behind a bush to observe what I suspected was going to follow. Twenty minutes later, Garry and the black pianist left the hotel arm in arm. I had guessed right: Garry filled the void in his heart with music, the happy man. I blessed their union.

I decided to leave without waiting for morning.

I DIDN'T GET VERY FAR.

A woman's voice called to me from the darkness: "Sir, sir... if you please..." I who thought myself so clever in spying on Garry from my bush was in turn being shadowed. The voice was agreeable, she called me by name asking me to follow her, and I had no reason to be suspicious. When we came to a street light she planted herself in front of me and, smiling, fixed me with her gaze for a moment, like someone harbouring a nice surprise. She had neither the physical attributes nor the clothes of those girls who ply their trade in the streets, and I really couldn't understand... Her smile vanished. "You don't recognize me? I guess you don't remember my name either. It's all right, I'm used to it..."

Even when she told me she was the lady who had posed nude for Miss Driscoll, I didn't recognize her; I was even a bit embarrassed. "It doesn't matter, don't worry about it. You didn't recognize me naked, so why should you recognize me clothed. I told you, I'm used to it. It's the story of my life. Come on," she said, "we'll go to my place. I'll make you a nice cup of tea, and we'll talk a little. There are things I've wanted to tell you for a long time."

Even though I wanted to leave Ottawa right away, she persuaded me to follow her when she said, "My name is Concorde. Before, when I was young, I was called Philomène. During the week we spent together at the Hotel Couillard, you explained to me that my first name came from the Greek *phil*, which means to love, and from the English, *men*. Philomène, who loves men. I've had lots of time to verify it: it's not true at all, you made it up to impress me, or to make fun of me, I don't know. Or maybe it's because you were drunk, as usual. It doesn't matter. In any case, you'll see that I'm less of an idiot than when I was looking after you. Don't just stand there, come!" Yes, it was she all right: the same cheerful voice, the same sense that she was a woman who has forgotten all the suffering life has dealt her. My departure could wait.

It took us a good hour to get there on foot. She lives in the Flats also, not far from my rooming house on Booth

Street. To compensate for having forgotten her face, I proved to her that I remembered all the rest. Allumette Island, Anselme, her friend Virginie with whom she had chased after men, her dream of getting into the laundry at Rideau Hall...

It was all for nothing. "I'm used to it," she repeated. "I'm the only one who remembers everybody, no one remembers seeing me. I don't think the good Lord wanted it that way, that's just the way it is. It must be because I look ordinary. I don't know how many times in my life I've seen people who I used to know well but who forgot my name, didn't remember how we met, what they'd said, what we'd done together; I remembered everything, all the little details, but they, nothing at all.

"That's not all: when people remember my face, they forget all the rest. They call me by other names, or they say I look like somebody else they know: a cousin, a friend, anyway, people I've never heard of. You'd think I looked like thousands of women.

"At first it broke my heart to be the only one who remembered, then I understood there was no point suffering because of that. People forget, it's not their fault. Me, I remember, I don't deserve any credit, my mind is like a trash can where other people toss their memories. But I forgive you. You're not the only man in the world who's slept with me and then not remembered. Especially since you were half drunk all the time. If I'd been drunk when we knew each other, maybe I'd be looking blankly at you too. I say that but I don't really think it, because you, I came close to loving you for real back then. I couldn't forget you.

"You're not the only one to have forgotten me. Miss Driscoll, who is the woman to whom I owe everything, she didn't remember me either when she hired me to pose naked for her, and I don't blame her either. Of course I weigh forty pounds more than in those days; I had false teeth put in too and I dye my hair blonde; in other words, I've changed. It may also be because we're speaking English now. When I knew her at Bark Lake, I didn't know three words of English, she's the one who started teaching me, and I was so proud to show her the progress I had made.

"I would like her to remember me, but perhaps it's just as well that she doesn't. Maybe she would not be happy to know that the little maid of Bark Lake has become a woman who poses naked. So I prefer to hide behind my English.

"The little Capuchin who came with you to the studio, Father Mathurin, he can't place me either, but that suits me too, only you don't know why. It's because when I was young my friend Virginie and I went to confess to him at the Saint Francis of Assisi Church.

"Poor Father Mathurin. What we did is we got on our knees behind the little grille in the confessional, we changed our voices, and we told him about our dirty sins, including some that didn't exist. 'Father, there's a boy who came to look after the house the other night. While I was playing the piano for him, he put his hand on my thigh, and then... I don't know how to tell you... anyway, we ended up in bed.

He took me once in the front and once from behind.' The poor little Capuchin, we could almost hear him blushing behind his grille. All he said was, 'ah yes?' or 'and then?' We knew he was hard as a stallion. He could barely babble his absolution when he gave us penances, which we just ignored. I always went first, I laid it on as thick as I could, then Virginie went into the confessional to finish him off. After, we ran away laughing our heads off. Now that I think, it wasn't very nice to do that, but we weren't being nasty either. We stopped after a year. Virginie stopped first because she started having children. Being a mother, that makes you virtuous. I know. I have principles too since I've had kids.

"Still, I always liked him, that little Father I mean, and so the good Lord would forgive me for all the tricks I played on him, he's the one I went to see when my little ones had to be baptized. From one child to the other he never remembers my name, but that must be because there are so many children to baptize in the Flats, so I forgive him because I don't feel right about being dirty with him back then."

She talks, she talks, I love listening. I'm not aware of my fatigue from walking, or of the cold that's starting to close in on us. Winter will start tonight in Ottawa, I can smell snow in the air. I don't know what to expect when we arrive, and I really don't care. I feel good in the company of this woman who is the extended incarnation of my own memory, she who remembers for two.

She lives in a neat little house in the Flats. Even before going in I guess that it must have two floors, a bathroom downstairs beside the kitchen, a concrete basement, a little yard with a shed. A workers' house like the others. I roomed in a little place like that when I came out of the monastery. Before putting her key in the lock she asks me not to make any noise; her husband and children are sleeping. I hesitate. She insists. There's no danger. We're going to chat, just chat, but not too loud, so as not to wake anybody.

The house is tidy, welcoming. We go right into the kitchen. She makes us black tea and offers me oatmeal biscuits. And if her husband were to wake? She reassures me: her neighbour must have put him to bed at the same time as the children, and he sleeps soundly since he got hurt and is unemployed. He broke both his arms, that takes time to heal. He's called Martial and he's a barber "at Monsieur Fournier's, the best barbershop in the Flats," she adds proudly. It's because her husband has lost his livelihood that she's been modelling at Miss Driscoll's. She always pronounces "Miss Driscoll," drawing the words out as long as your arm, as for the name of a venerated saint.

"I don't know what we would have done if she hadn't taken me as a model," she says. "My husband won't work again for quite a while. Besides, there's a lot of unemployment these days, all the men are losing their jobs, the morning paper says we're in a depression. In my street alone, out of fifteen families, there are eleven men who have been let go. In the street behind, it's worse. Even the Italians in the neighbourhood, who are so hard-working, don't have work. So when I saw the advertisement in the paper for a painter's model, I answered right away. It's funny, but I was sure there wouldn't be a whole lot of women in Ottawa who would agree to show themselves naked to a man, except a doctor of course. Well, I nearly fell on my behind when I saw that the painter was a woman and that it was Miss Driscoll. That's not all. She told me she'd received a hundred and ten applications. That shows how badly things are going in this country, or maybe women around here are less prudish than I thought. I'm proud to think she took me out of a hundred and ten. She says my body makes interesting shadows, and I know she's not just saying that to be kind. It's nice to hear.

"And it pays well! Five dollars a day, three days a week for three months, maybe four. It's almost as much as my husband earned in a good week. With that money we can have a turkey at Christmas, the little ones will have presents in their stockings at New Year's, and they won't take our house. And by then maybe my husband will be better, he'll be able to take back his chair at the barbershop; it's a good profession, because even if the country is going badly you always need barbers to cut hair properly. Of course, he doesn't know how I'm earning our keep these days. I told him I'd gone back to cleaning. It's lucky I said that because he had a fit: 'My wife working! You're going to stop that right away! Because what are they going to say, my clients at the barbershop, when they find out my wife's supporting me? Did you think of my pride?' He wouldn't calm down. I told him to shut his mouth. He's like that, my Martial: he gets mad about nothing, but he gets over it just as fast. It's best not to pay too much attention. A barber likes to talk..."

I stifle a little yawn. She suggests I lie down on the couch; she'll get me up early, before her husband anyway, but she won't send me off without making me a nourishing breakfast, she says. She herself will not sleep this night. The fact of having followed me through the streets of Ottawa and having found the courage to make herself known to me has worked on her nerves. She's going to make her bread and prepare tomorrow's meals; she's used to skipping nights of sleep, it doesn't tire her. I offer to keep her company during her night of insomnia. I want to listen to her, and her tea will keep my eyes open. There will still be time to leave at dawn.

While she is gaily busying herself in the kitchen, a sliver of memory comes back to me, and I think of adding to her good humour by telling her that she reminds me of the little servant who was at the celebration and who lost consciousness. My observation falls flat. She replies curtly that it was her, yes, but she doesn't ever want to talk about it. It's in the past.

There is a sudden silence. It's two in the morning. The night will be longer than I thought. She takes me by the arm and leads me to the living room. On the sideboard are pictures of her children and of her husband with his soldier's cap. She has one boy and three girls.

"Don't leave right away, my beautiful captain. I've been waiting too long to talk to you."

I want to know why she refuses to talk about the commemoration, she who remembers so easily. She lowers her eyes. "We have all night," I tell her.

"I DON'T MUCH LIKE TALKING ABOUT THE CELEBRA-
tion because...

"I didn't want to be there. In those days I went to mass
on Sundays with the Capuchins because for a long time I
believed my friend Virginie, who said that a common girl
like me had no business in Saint John the Baptist Church.
And that having no education, I wouldn't understand the
Dominican sermons anyway.

"But I have to tell you that when I met you, I'd also started
going out with another boy. He came from Lower Town,

he'd been drafted at the end of the war, but he'd landed in Europe the day peace was declared. So he'd returned to Canada on the first boat. But to hear him now he was at war for over twenty years and he just about won it all by himself. That boy was Martial, the same who's snoring in the next room. At the barbershop, when he wants to win a political discussion with a client, he says, 'I fought the war, Monsieur.' It's his secret weapon, you understand? Poor Martial...

"When the war was over, I didn't mind. I'd got so much out of it by meeting so many handsome men that I couldn't complain. I can say that I enjoyed the war a lot even if I didn't fight it. The only thing I didn't like was that I caught a sickness that meant I couldn't have children, according to the doctor. That made me less amorous, if you get what I'm saying..."

I tell her that I remember that detail. She smiles.

"With peace, I calmed down even more. Then there was the Spanish flu that was spreading everywhere and killing a lot of people, so that you had to be careful not to catch the germs of the men coming back from Europe. That's what they said, anyway.

"After a while I'd been calm for so long that I began to feel deprived. That's when I met Martial. I'd never have got interested in him if I wasn't missing a man so badly. Because he's not that good-looking, and especially, not that bright. At the time he was delivering ice in the Flats. He cut up the ice on the Ottawa River, and he delivered it door to door with a horse-drawn wagon. That's how I met him.

"Once when he was delivering to Madame Gariépy, who I was rooming with, I took pity on him for working so hard, and I enjoyed watching him shovel sawdust onto the blocks of ice he put into our icebox. I felt pity for him also when I saw he was having trouble reading the names in his delivery book because he hadn't been to school for very long. So I offered to help him read his book, and then one thing led to another and I made a pass at him. I've always liked delivery men, I don't know why. Martial was my first delivery man; I tell him that sometimes so he'll forgive me for the other delivery men who came after. I was his first woman; I took his virginity. I think he's always resented me a little for that. Anyway...

"What I also liked about him was that he was alone in the world. His only brother had drowned in the river, not far from the Flats, his sisters had died young, his parents had been gone for a long time. I who was an orphan by choice because I didn't want to have anything to do with my family, I loved the orphan who hadn't asked to be one, and who missed his family so much that he reminded me of a little boy. Seeing him so deprived of affection, I became maternal. It was like that with you too. When you climaxed with me you moaned like a child alone in the world for life; that's why I so much wanted to love you for real. You'd have to think that when I met you both, I wanted to be the mother of someone.

"You, the beautiful captain, what I loved in you right away was that you seemed like a gentleman even if you didn't have a penny in your pocket. You understand, it was important to me that a man had style. In those days I wanted to believe that there were spotless women in the world who didn't have to wipe themselves after sleeping with a man. I also wanted there to be men so refined that they didn't smell when they shat. I always knew that I was not just who I was, it's that thought that gave me some happiness in life, otherwise I would have stayed the poor little ugly girl from Allumette Island. You understand?

"I just wanted to tell you tonight that I came close to loving you madly. I didn't understand all your big speeches, I also thought you drank a lot, even that you seemed to like drink more than women, but you had something other men didn't. I also think I was attracted to you because you reminded me of a lawyer I had known, a real one, who was classy enough for two.

"For the first time in my life, also, I felt guilty cheating on a man. I wasn't like I was before, when I thought nothing of going out with three men at the same time. I wasn't a girl any more, I'd become a woman. I'd had enough of boys, I wanted a man.

"After having been with you, my beautiful captain, it seemed that I looked on my Martial with more tenderness, as though my cheating had made me want to be even more loving towards him. Then one day the circus came to town, and I went to watch it go by on Preston Street. When I saw those beautiful African animals that seemed to have come out of Miss Driscoll's beautiful books, it made me think of the cows and mares that used to mate on Allumette Island. After that I had only one thought in mind: to find you so you would do the same thing to me. I was dying for you to take me from behind. The men around here think you have to be a whore to want to make love like that; I knew you wouldn't judge me.

"I searched for you everywhere in town, I found you, and I almost forced you back to the Hotel Couillard. That was our last night together. I had my work cut out to excite you, because you'd drunk too much again. But I loved that so much that I was afraid to start over, and I swore I would never see you again. You disappeared, as I wished.

"After that I tried to be kinder to Martial. It was as though something had changed in me. I wasn't the same, I was all tender with him. He had just joined the Zouaves at the cathedral; they took him, not because he had been a soldier, but because he knew how to play the bugle. He was very proud of that. They had invited his band to play at the Saint John the Baptist Church's celebration. He asked me to go with him, but as a volunteer servant. I was not too happy putting on my maid's uniform again, because I'd been work-ing for some time at the Flats' bakery, but for once I wanted to make him happy.

"Once there I was happy too because at last, after so many years, I saw Miss Driscoll again. She hadn't changed, not a whit. The great lady, with class to spare. She had become a singer, and not of just anything, she was singing opera! I would have liked her to recognize me, the girl who knew how to read because of her, and who had not stayed a maid all her life. I thought that with my servant's clothes she would place me right away, but no! I could have been someone else and it would have made no difference. Never mind that I planted myself right in front of her and followed her everywhere with my tray, she didn't see me. And yet I had changed as she had wanted, but I don't think she would have recognized me in any case. My heart was bursting as I followed her around. I would have liked her to say she was as proud of me as if I were her own daughter.

"It almost turned into a disaster. Suddenly Miss Driscoll's way was barred by the little Capuchin Virginie and I had played tricks on by making up dirty confessions. So I kept very quiet beside my great lady. The last thing I wanted was that someone speak to me; I didn't want to open my mouth for fear that the Capuchin might recognize my voice. I was in a hurry for Miss Driscoll to leave him standing there, but no! You had to turn up also, the beautiful captain! With your uniform that wasn't as fresh as before, and the look of someone who'd been drinking all night, you were a pitiful sight. Before the Dominican's commemoration, I'd always thought it was a curse always to be forgotten by everybody, but this time I thought it was more of a blessing. Not only did you not recognize me, it was as though you didn't see me. That was lucky, because had you talked to me you might have mentioned our adventures at the Hotel Couillard, the Capuchin would have remembered me and Miss Driscoll would have abandoned me forever. It was as though I had changed into a statue. I was modest like a real maid, I looked down at the ground, I didn't say a word, I just waited for Miss Driscoll to leave you both behind. It was hot, I could feel that my face was all red.

"Then, I don't know what happened, all three of you started to talk at the same time, I didn't understand anything you said. I only remember that Miss Driscoll's eucalyptus perfume was making me feel sick.

"When I woke up you'd all disappeared, I was lying on the ground, and Martial's face was just an inch from mine. He looked worried. He helped me up, and there was so much kindness in the way he did it that I started to sob on his shoulder. I wasn't used to a man being good with me. I immediately passed out again.

"Martial went to get two Zouaves to help him, and they took me back to Madame Gariépy's; the doctor came and I slept for twenty hours. The doctor came back, and I had the surprise of my life: I was expecting a baby. And yet it was the same doctor who'd told me I couldn't have children. He didn't seem surprised. 'The body changes, my little girl. You were cured of your sickness, and your body resumed its normal functions. If I knew how that happened, I would long ago have been practising medicine somewhere other than Ottawa. But you must be happy, no? You'll soon find yourself married.' I wasn't so sure I was as happy as all that.

"I slept again a little, and when I awoke Martial was standing beside my bed, dressed as a Zouave like the day before. He looked upset, and seeing his innocent face I was so ashamed of having cheated on him that I told him we ought to get married, he and I. So my little one would have a father, I told him. He started to cry, and he said yes.

"I may seem hard on Martial, but what people don't know is that I'm very careful with him. For example, I never told him that I wanted so much to make mommy and daddy when I met him that I took the first in line who wanted me. I couldn't help myself; I wanted a protector for life. Martial or another, it didn't matter. I never told him that, I didn't want to hurt him.

"It was a good thing that I asked him to marry me, my big Martial, because I'm sure he wouldn't have thought of it himself. He was certain that the child I was expecting was his, even though I wasn't so sure. It's when he was born that I knew exactly where I stood, not because of his looking like you, but because it was exactly nine months since the circus had passed through Ottawa, which was the last time we saw each other, you and I. I've always known the moment when I made each of my children; I've got a real woman's memory for that.

"Martial insisted it be Father Mathurin of Saint Francis of Assisi who married us. I didn't say much, I didn't want him to know about my youthful excesses, but no fear, Father Mathurin remembered neither me nor my voice, which shouldn't have surprised me. The ceremony went well. Monsieur and Madame Gariépy took the place of my parents, Virginie was my maid of honour and she prepared a good meal. It was a nice little wedding. It's true, I was pregnant by the captain and I married the Zouave, but I soon resigned myself to that. You keep on loving those who are absent through the companions life puts in your way. Our memory works all that out, like a deaf confessor.

"We called our son Édouard, like the old king. It's only later that Martial learned he wasn't his. (Virginie told him one day when she was angry with me because I'd sent her husband packing, Lucien the asshole, who tried to sleep with me all the time because he thought I did it with anyone at all.) Martial was furious, but he calmed down after a while. He was afraid I would leave him. He even says about Édouard, 'He's the one who will keep the family name alive.' I don't react when he says that, I prefer to stay silent."

She continues to talk, but I haven't been listening for a while. I get up and go over to the sideboard to look at the children's photos. In the semi-darkness the little boy's face says nothing to me, he's a child like the others. I begin to wonder if I heard her right. Suddenly, I don't know any more. She goes on with her story as though she hasn't noticed my discomfort, and she returns to the kitchen. I follow her.

"The first, my only boy, is yours, my beautiful captain of once upon a time. My oldest girl, Anita, is the daughter of Giuseppe, who is just called Joe. He lives not far from here and is married now to someone else. A little man, strong as a bull, who paves the roads with his Italian cousins. I met him when they were working in front of our house. He smelled of tar, a hot smell that I like. His wife resents that I had a child by him, but she has no reason to squawk, he wasn't even married when I knew him. Really...

"The third I had with Amédée Dubé, a cute little Syrian whose real name is Achmed Dubaï, but who changed his name to be like everyone else in the Flats. That time there was a big to-do with my husband. He hadn't said anything about Joe because he was afraid of his big muscles, but with Amédée, he went to see him at his grocery store to tell him to leave his wife alone. In front of all the customers! I was so ashamed of him that I'm the one who got angry! Especially since Amédée was so frightened that he never wanted to start anything with me again, but it was too late, the little one was already on her way. At least Amédée has class, as I always say to my husband: every year at Christmas he and his sister bring presents for the little one, and they do it for the other children too, as though there were no difference between them. My husband still gripes anyway.

"I had her baptized Virginie, in memory of my friend who had the same name and who died because she went to see someone other than me to get rid of the baby she couldn't support; she didn't come to see me because we'd had a stupid argument, she and I. I still blame myself for that. It's to keep her alive that I gave her name to my daughter.

"My fourth, Ginette, is from Mailhot, the MP. He was one of my husband's customers, but I found it curious that he went to have his hair cut at Fournier's salon, he who could have had it cut for free by the Parliament barber. At first I thought he went to Fournier to meet people and to get their vote in the next election. But it's my vote he wanted. He got it. I found him so distinguished, so educated, and he took me to hotels because he was married. Even to the Château Laurier once. I loved that! Him too. But when he learned I was expecting because of him, he disappeared. He was never again seen in the Flats. What a bastard! I'll never vote for him again.

"Of course, all these affairs don't go down too well at home. My husband isn't happy about it. I promised him many times to stop, but I can't help it. It's hard for me to say no to a man who says he wants me. My husband even said to me once, 'You love yourself too much!' For once I think he was right. When a man desires me I become a woman again who desires too: I'm no longer the mother of my children, the wife of my husband, the daughter of my father, only a woman making love to a man. I'll never change. At least Martial has stopped making scenes in front of the children. You have to watch what you say when you're a parent, because you never know, they could repeat things at school.

"I got pregnant three times with Martial, but I had a miscarriage every time. I think it's because he's only my protector that it doesn't work with him, as though my body can't quite open itself up. The devil has to get into me before I can make a child with a man; the good Lord does the rest.

"It's not much fun for Martial and I know how he must feel, because there are men who laugh at him because of my behaviour. Even at the barbershop. It's all very well for me to say to him, 'Listen, their wives aren't angels either. They're jealous of you because you have a good trade and you speak well.' Once it all went too far.

"I'd gone once with big Champagne, the plumber, just once because he wasn't as good as he said in bed, but afterwards he spent all his time boasting that he'd had me. He even made really crude jokes about it. One time after Martial had cut his hair, he said to him, 'Martial, when you kiss your wife, imagine you're kissing my ass!' The whole shop burst out laughing. What can you say to someone so low he can come out with disgusting things like that? And my poor Martial is not strong enough to take big Champagne into the alleyway and fight him. Because of that affair people were laughing at him all over the Flats, and it ate away at him, for good reason. It got so he wasn't eating, he wasn't sleeping. I couldn't just go and knock big Champagne senseless with my cast-iron frying pan, like I did with Lucien, Virginie's asshole husband (I can't say it too often).

"So I had to take things in hand. I went to see Joe the Italian at work, and I said to him, 'Listen, I've never asked anything for your daughter, but it's time you did something for the honour of the man who's fed her ever since she was born.' That same night my Joe beat big Champagne to a pulp in the Hotel Couillard's tavern. People stopped laughing at my husband, and the son of a bitch Champagne was never seen again in the Flats.

"It still hurts poor Martial that I run around. So I try to console him as best I can. I tell him, for example, that he's a good father, that he's the one the children love, not the others. Also, that there are things I do only with him. Even though I tell him all that, sometimes he's sad for a long time.

Then it passes, and he doesn't talk about it any more. Until the next time.

"Just recently he did something unforgivable. He wanted to smash the face of Ti-Pit Langevin, the milkman, who has the strength of three even if he doesn't look it. My husband came back from his evening with the Zouaves, had one drink too many at Adrienne's blind pig, and threw himself on Ti-Pit because we'd started seeing each other from time to time, him and me. Ti-Pit broke both his arms. Not only that, in the fight, he tore his corporal uniform from the Zouaves; I had to sew it up again. So he not only can't work as a barber, it looks like my Martial won't be promoted to sergeant in the Zouaves, his life's dream. Anyway I was so mad that I went to find Ti-Pit and I told him it was over between us. Let him go back to his wife who doesn't much like screwing. That'll teach him to beat up my husband.

"That's the way it is. With my husband not working, and unemployment everywhere, I've no choice but to pose naked for Miss Driscoll. It doesn't bother me, but I'm a bit worried about our family. I don't let my husband see that, so as not to hurt him. After all, he's my husband before God, I care for him and I'd never throw him out. And he, he'd never leave home, he's not resourceful enough for that.

"In our house, in any case, thanks to my working as a naked woman with Miss Driscoll, we have plenty to eat, but everywhere around us you feel that people are hungry. Even the animals in the city and in the forest are hungrier than they were. In Ottawa, especially in the Flats, near the river, we're used to seeing wild animals eating out of the trash cans, mainly skunks, foxes, raccoons. But now it's worse. You hear them fighting at night for trash cans with nothing in them. Now that it's autumn, when you get up in the morning, we see that our cats and dogs have disappeared, probably eaten by the animals from the forest. There are not even any more rats in our houses and streets. It's got so the bears come out of the woods to eat in the city. They walk through our streets as though the town had always belonged to them. We feel like tramps being chased off by a ravenous landlord we'd forgotten existed. One morning last week we had to kill a bear that was eating apples in widow Perras's yard. All the men took out their hunting rifles and went after it. Even Martial went out to help them with his helmet and his gun from the war. All the children in the Flats were laughing like crazy, they were so afraid.

"The real proof that everything's going badly is that not only has the bakery closed, where I worked after I stopped being a maid, but the foundry too. Even the Hotel Couillard almost shut down because the men have no more money for drink. But the real proof is that every morning our yards are full of tramps we don't even know. There are some so miserable you're afraid to look at them. You don't let them into your house. You'd think poverty had made us less charitable.

"One morning we got up, and guess who we found lying in our yard? My two brothers, Viatime and Ermille! I don't know how I recognized them, they were in such a pitiful state, both of them. They were dirtier than they'd ever been, their clothes were all torn, their mouths were all black because they had no more teeth, and as it was cold as the devil this autumn, they'd torn up their underpants to wrap them around their hands and their ears so they wouldn't freeze. I brought them in, I couldn't stand to see them like that. After they'd eaten, they told us about their troubles. They'd ended up drinking away all the land they had up north. Because they drank, they'd lost their jobs as lumberjacks. They had nothing left to their names, so they'd jumped on a train to come and see their sister in Ottawa, because they'd heard I was doing well.

"They stayed with us for a while. They got properly washed, I found them some second-hand clothing, I fed them, then I told them where they might find work other than here. Martial wasn't happy to see me giving them charity. 'After what they did to you? I thought they were assholes, those two?' He was right, but I couldn't help it, I'd forgiven them. I couldn't let them die outside in the cold. What I didn't tell Martial was that it did me good to forgive them their beastliness. Since that time I've a lot more trouble remembering how nasty they were.

"As you might expect, while they were here they slept in the basement, and I locked them in every night when they went to bed. Then I told them that if they touched a hair of my daughters' heads, I'd kill them with the gun my husband had from the war. They saw I was serious, and they behaved.

"They gave me news from where I grew up. I learned who was dead, who'd done what. Once they said, 'Don't go back to Nazareth. The place we come from doesn't exist any more.' All the land around there has been abandoned. The men who left for the war were killed, or they stopped somewhere else on their way back, or they died of the Spanish flu. The government took back the concessions because the taxes weren't paid. The municipal corporation went bankrupt. Nazareth no longer exists, it's been wiped off the map. The houses still standing were scavenged for firewood by layabouts from the other villages. After that the trees started to grow back all by themselves. The wild animals returned. Now there are wolves, foxes and bears that roam on the land we cultivated. Nothing's left of us. We were just born there, no one remembers us. I don't know why, that hurt a little. But it doesn't matter, I've made other memories here that are much nicer than those I had before."

Concorde has grown silent so as to concentrate on what she is doing. Dawn is breaking at the window. Outside, the beautiful snow that fell last night is starting to blacken from the coal fires in the houses. It's warm and cozy in the kitchen. It smells of baking bread and simmering stew. "What should I make you for breakfast? I can make pancakes or good porridge with thick cream and molasses. A nice slice of homemade bread toasted on the stove along with that, and a little coffee. Would you like that?" She is radiant with goodness, like during our nights at the Hotel Couillard, and the desire I felt for her then revives in me all of a sudden. I desire her face gleaming with sweat in the heat of the stove fire, I even find magic in her flowered apron. But her air of a woman occupied keeps me at a respectful distance, and I exorcise my longing for her by thinking about my friend Tard, who would so much have enjoyed my describing to him the scene I am part of now. I would like to eat something to make her happy, but I have no appetite. I ask her if I can come back later in the day to see what our son is like. Her answer sounds like no: "Martial is his papa. You're just his father."

I'm going to go, it's better that way. I feel in the inside pocket of my jacket for the roll of bills Garry gave me, a comforting gesture that brings me to my feet.

She doesn't hold me back. "Goodbye, Concorde." For once, she doesn't reply.

·
·
·
·
·

IT WAS SEVEN YEARS SINCE I'D LEFT OTTAWA. AND
I was doing quite well. Sometimes Mathurin gave me news.
The new village postmistress told me there was a war in
Spain.

One day when I was working peacefully in my workshop and I'd left the door open because of the bad smell, two
people appeared on the gallery. I couldn't really make them
out because of the September sun that was setting the river
ablaze, but I soon realized it was neither the bailiff nor the
sheriff.

They came in just like that, a plump, well-dressed lady with a big boy. The lady reminded me of Miss Driscoll, with her head held like a singer and her assured manner, but without the scent of eucalyptus; the young man was the spitting image of my grandfather the market gardener. I would gladly have greeted the lady by name, but words failed me. It must have been two months since I'd spoken to a living soul, and my mouth had gone numb. She easily beat me to the punch: "Concorde... You still don't recognize me? I knew it..." I was going to say something polite when she told me that the young man was my son, and I almost swallowed my pipe.

Then she went out to leave us alone, him and me; and also, I expect, because the smell was truly awful. It's not only because I had smoked out the house with my pipe. I had also taken a few eels out of the smokehouse a few days earlier, then had gone for a walk and had forgotten to come back, as sometimes happens with me. The door had stayed open and some animal, a fox or a raccoon, had come in and gobbled my meal, leaving in return the stench of a sated beast. The year before a bear had rendered me the same service, and I'd had to kill it because it became a regular guest. It's the sort of thing that happens when you live alone. It also reeks because when I forget for too long to bathe in the river, I smell stronger than the bear I killed.

Still, the young man and I got along right away; he didn't comment on the griminess of the surroundings, which showed he was well brought up. He's called Édouard, and he's studying at the Seraphic College in Trois-Rivières. I promised to go and see him, to take him on some outings. To my great surprise, I easily kept my word; he's a sharp boy whose character, happily, is not at all like my own. For example, he has a good heart. I do not have a good heart. The proof? If I visited this boy so often at his college, which smells almost as bad as my house on the river, it was to bring me closer to his mother, whose enhanced persona so delighted me. That's how it was in the beginning. Afterwards I became fond of him in his own right, and I still go to see him even if his mother doesn't really like me. Which is of no importance; I love her, which is all that counts.

We didn't have a chance that day to get reacquainted, she and I. The two of them left as quickly as they came. She returned in October, without him. She wanted to thank me for going to see him twice. "Thanks to your visits," she said, "he's not so bored, and so I'm sure he won't run away from school, and he'll get educated the way he should. He says he likes to hear you talk about your life. I'm not surprised. His papa talked to everyone except his children, and that may have been something he missed."

She seemed moved when she said that, so I offered her a chair and a glass of my redcurrant wine. She stopped me right away. "First, go and fetch me some water from the well, we're going to do some dishes. Your glasses are so dirty, they look full. We're also going to open the windows. That will be a good start. And you should know that if I do that with anyone at all, I don't just do it anywhere. If you want us to sleep together either you come to see me in Ottawa or you clean things up at home. Either way, take the trouble to have a good bath." She didn't have to tell me twice.

There are times when I say to myself that if I'd known how she would change my life by coming back into it, I would never have opened my door to her. A moment later I say no, she's done me too much good. It's simple. I am a different man.

She too is not the woman I knew back then. Now she's a Madame. There's not much to say about my last seven years as a hermit and vagabond living quietly in my house. I've been happy just to keep myself alive and be a thorn in the side of my neighbours in the village. But she's come a long way without ever leaving the Flats.

"I had to," she says to me. "My husband couldn't cut hair any more because his arms were still bothering him. So when Monsieur Fournier at the barbershop died, I persuaded Martial to manage the shop and to hire barbers who would work for almost nothing because of the depression. I named him manager, and that made him the happiest man in the Flats. When business picked up I had him take out a mortgage on our house, which was paid up, and I bought the whole building for a pittance; I even enlarged the salon. Four years ago I bought the Hotel Couillard, which had just gone bankrupt. I started running it properly, I made Martial head manager, and it began making money like before. Martial was responsible for purchases, he spent half his time talking up his clients, saying 'I'm the business here... I was in the war...' I let him say what he liked, at least we were living better than before, when we were so poor I had to bare my behind to Miss Driscoll.

"Martial died two years ago. He was doing some errands when a car hit him while he was crossing the street. Poor man, he'd just been promoted to sergeant in the Zouaves, and people had stopped laughing at him because I was so busy at the hotel, I didn't have time to run around. He was buried in his new sergeant's uniform, with his bugle by his side.

"I've changed the name of the hotel. It's called the Duke now. It sounds classier. I got rid of the whores who used to bring their clients to our rooms, and we serve the best beer in Ottawa in my tavern. I can't serve there because I'm a woman, but I'm the one who throws out the drunks who start fights. Martial tried to do it a couple of times when he was alive, but he always ended up with his face all bloodied. They don't dare touch me because I'm a woman. I think I remind them of their mothers, so I use that to keep the peace and not have any brawls.

"The best is that I've inherited Miss Driscoll as a resident. She had kept her apartment and studio at the Couillard. She's doing a bit of photography still, but less than before because of her arthritis; she stopped painting when the Saint John the Baptist Church burned down in 1931. She doesn't remember me any more than she did when I used to get undressed for her pictures, but she's happy to have me as her landlord. I promised never to raise her rent, and sometimes, when I have the time, I serve her her meals myself in her room. I even let her install a bird feeder in her window. To thank me she tried to give me her paintings, but I didn't want that; I insisted on buying them. I did it to help her because she doesn't work much any more and she has less money. It's my turn to be charitable with her. The only painting of hers I don't have is the one where Mathurin posed as Brébeuf and you as an Iroquois. She gave that to Mathurin.

"Everyone in the hotel takes care of her. When there's noise in the rooms, I go up and tell the clients, 'Don't disturb Madame the artist.' They calm down right away. One day she even invited me to have tea in her room; I didn't dare say yes, obviously. But I did accept one thing she offered: that she take my photograph.

"I can't say I was happy with the result, but it wasn't her fault. No one had ever taken my portrait, and I didn't really know what I looked like. I console myself with the thought that there were lots of men in my life who desired me. But to see the photo, you wouldn't think so.

"We're friends now, she and I. As I've thinned down a little bit lately and she's gained a little weight, she gives me her old clothes, which fit me like a glove. More and more people say I look like her. Nothing makes me happier than to hear that."

She's beautiful, Concorde, as a Madame. I tell her that every time I can. She replies that I find her to my taste now that I'm no longer much to look at myself. Yes, she's just as frank as she always was. One thing is certain, I've learned not to be too lyrical with her. It irritates her. One day I called her "my muse." Her reply: "Oh yes, you amuse me too." In other words, she mistrusts me and the words that come too easily to my lips, probably because they come out of the books I spent too much time reading in my youth. That's what my friend Mathurin would say anyway, he who was for so long a victim of his own reading.

She has other reasons to be wary of me, and she's not shy to voice them. For instance, she thinks I'm interested in her because Miss Driscoll would want nothing to do with me now. However much I swear that's false, there are times when I fear that it's only too true. In my moments of doubt I remember that it's with her, Concorde, that I stopped dreaming of being other than I am.

To allay her suspicions, which I can well understand because I know myself too, and to please her, there is, fortunately, our son. It wasn't easy for me to get used to Édouard's affection for me. I already had one friend in Mathurin, and suddenly I had two, a difficult adaptation for me to make. His open friendship never failed to surprise me. And yet I have done so little for him: I have brought him a few sweets at college, I have listened to him, and I have told him stories from my life. The more I talk to him, the more he listens. I am passing on to him my memories and those of my village, which I'm sure he will never know. These words are his sole legacy. He won't even have the rights to the house on the river, which, when I die, will almost certainly be seized by the authorities for unpaid taxes. It doesn't matter, he tells me. He's still attached to me, and I can't resist. I can't help it, I love this boy now as if he really were my son.

I didn't think, either, that I would become so interested in his mother, but that happened too, and more quickly than I would have thought. On my very first visit to Ottawa, she took me into her widow's bed. I was the first to be astonished at my passion for her. And yet she's not, any more than before, physically or mentally the sort of woman who always haunted my dreams. But I love listening to her talk, laugh, complain or sing. When I am near her I am good to others, I help people out whom I don't know, I want to please.

But she was clear from the start: "If I sleep with you, it's just because I've found no one else. I like what you give me, that's all. I've never loved a man in my life. I came close to loving you twenty years ago, but you were too drunk. You missed your chance. We can't relive the life we've lost. It's too late. Come to bed." At first the freedom we accorded one another suited my temperament well. I only stayed a few days in Ottawa, and I went back home with no expectations.

Then I began to make the trip frequently and to stay with her for long periods of time. Sometimes she lets me invite my friend, Father Mathurin, and we listen indulgently to his stories of holy women. After supper we make music together, because Concorde, since she's become a bit rich, has treated herself to the gift of her life: a superb player piano with candelabras on each side of the piano roll. None of us knows how to play, but we pretend, with pieces of music that play all by themselves. Father Mathurin does Bach, Concorde does Schubert and I play "Roses of Picardy" over and over.

The house cat, Catou, is our most faithful audience, he listens without turning a hair, solemn as a judge. When we've finished he goes and lies down behind the piano; that's his home.

Concorde is right to say that life is good at times, when we want it so.

MY INCREDULOUS RAPTURE CONTINUES. IT HAS NOW been three years.

But as always, I had to make a fool of myself, with the result that my beauty has banished me to my native ground. Next time I'll be more careful.

The truth is that for the first time in my life I was too sure of myself, too certain of my happiness, however unhoped for it had been. I ought to have stayed anxious, it would have been better.

I was sure that I could fulfil Concorde's every desire. During my stays in Ottawa I took the place of her husband a little, in managing the hotel. She was also grateful to me for taking care of her children, whom I entertained with tales of my escapades as a backward adolescent. Finally, I had become in her arms the attentive lover I had always dreamed of being, and she rewarded me with caresses to which even her late husband never had access. Convinced that she had everything she could wish for, I felt I had the right to the same.

That was my mistake: to think that to make someone else happy, it was enough to be happy oneself. And God knows, I was happy with her.

I should have seen the clouds on the horizon, however. For some time, I'd felt she was on edge. She was afraid a new war was going to break out. "I feel it in my bones," she said. "I'm sure something's going to happen over there in Europe. It's as though they can hardly wait to start killing each other again. And you know what that means, eh? It means the war is going to take my Édouard away from me and I'm going to lose him." She burst into tears every time the subject came up. I did my best to reassure her. There was a civil war on in Spain when we first began seeing each other again, and as soon as she heard that a neighbour in the Flats had joined the brigade of Canadian volunteers, she was certain Canada would eventually be involved. I'd calmed her down by telling her I don't know what, me the intellectual with his fossilized knowledge, who in fifteen years hadn't read a newspaper. I might have been right despite myself in 1937, but this time my soothing words had no effect. I ought to have been concerned.

She was right, and she had guessed it all from afar. The day we learned from the radio that Poland had been invaded, our Édouard came home dressed as an officer, with his fiancée on his arm: Marie, Virginie's daughter, who was a chambermaid at the Duke. Concorde's congratulations were not very warm. She was happy to see her son marrying the daughter of her best friend from her youth, but she disapproved of his abandoning his burgeoning career in teaching, he who had the education she had so envied in others. He, a university graduate, was going to get himself killed for the French and the Poles he didn't even know? Ah, no... She was so sad that night that I chose to sleep on the couch so as not to disturb her.

The wedding preparations distracted her, especially since we had to hurry them a little. Édouard would soon be joining his regiment. Concorde had consented, on one condition: that the wedding take place in the Saint John the Baptist Church, which had been rebuilt from the ground up since it had been destroyed by fire some years earlier; even the bells were new, thirty-two of them, just arrived from Belgium. "It's not because we're in the Flats that we don't have enough class to be married at the Dominicans'," she told her son. For my part, I arranged for Father Mathurin to officiate. The Dominicans acceded to our wishes most graciously.

I thought that Concorde would regain her good humour in preparing for the celebration. She made much of the fact that she had asked Miss Driscoll to photograph the bride and groom. Miss Driscoll had accepted, even if her arthritis was causing her a lot of pain, but she would have as her assistant her perpetually faithful admirer, the very charming Mister Garry, the newspaperman. And of course, these two august personages would attend the banquet after the ceremony. When she told me these details, she could hardly contain her joy.

Her apparent happiness made me wax lyrical as well. And that night she loved me with an ardour I had never before seen; happy as I was, certain also of her feelings towards me, convinced as well, in my profound idiocy, that she had reached an age when it was almost impossible for most women to find a new partner, I proposed that she be my widow one day. She didn't reply, a bad sign. I hadn't understood that in making love with such abandon, she had just bade me farewell. In the morning she asked me to leave and never to return, because it was better that way.

I obeyed, but on my way to the station I must have turned around at least thirty times in the hope that she had changed her mind. I bought my ticket as slowly as I could, and I let three trains for Montreal go by before understanding that no, she had not changed her mind. (She confessed to me later that she'd had an abortion the next day.)

My disgrace was so sudden that I have still not suffered from it in the least. There is also the fact that I am more lucid, because I have come to recognize many things in the course of reinstalling myself in my refuge on the river. It's been two weeks now since she's thrown me out.

Now I see everything clearly, as when one encounters again a movie one liked the first time round, but whose true meaning one grasps only on second viewing. Concorde wants no more of me because she's in love with another. And this man is none other than my old companion in arms and in unrequited love, Garry, the official faithful admirer of Miss Driscoll. I realized that this morning while doing the washing.

Garry and Miss Driscoll were now for me only the last shadows of Essiambre on earth. I saw them again a few times during my last visits to the Flats, but I felt nothing. She still had her photography and painting studio at the Duke, but hardly used it; he remained rich and influential. As he is very generous with her, Miss Driscoll has at last become the idle lady of her youthful dreams. He escorts her to concerts or to the theatre every time something interesting is going on in town, and if I can believe Concorde, he's the one who settles the hotel bill every month. They go walking every Sunday in the summer season, she the elegant anachronism of 1916, and he the distinguished modern: a handsome felt hat, a well-cut suit, flower in his buttonhole, two-toned shoes and a cane of Scottish wood with a silver knob. In truth, they make a lovely couple. I suspect that it is this image that started Concorde dreaming.

When I passed them on the street in the Flats, I came to a halt. She, with her beautiful large myopic eyes, never recognized me. He greeted me nonchalantly with his cane, and for my part I presented him with the smile of a gentleman who knows the value of discretion. I don't know why, but the picture of their almost bourgeois tranquility gave me a salutary feeling, the assurance, perhaps, that the worst pain love can inflict comes to an end after all, and that even our most vain hopes bring their rewards.

And so this is the man Concorde loves? I will soon know the truth. Édouard is getting married on Saturday, Concorde has asked me to fulfil the role of his father. I hope she has not changed her mind. I have never been a father, I would like to try it once.

This will be my last visit to Ottawa. I know, because Father Mathurin wrote me this morning to ask me to return his suitcase, which has travelled with me such a long distance. He invited me, at the same time, to stay at the monastery on the night of the wedding. Well, no matter. I'll be there.

·

·

·

·

·

IT WAS FINE.

The bride and groom were as pretty as a picture, she in her white gown and he in his uniform as a lieutenant in the air force. Concorde was quite the great lady, even more than Miss Driscoll in her prime, and Mathurin was perfect during the ceremony, even if he seemed as sad as Jesus's disciples in the garden at Gethsemane. For my part, I was most dignified. The suit Mathurin had unearthed at the Saint Vincent de Paul outlet for the poor looked almost new on me, and Concorde had offered me a shirt and tie for the occasion. I hadn't drunk a drop the day before, and I restrained myself at the banquet.

During his sermon, Mathurin said that we shouldn't worry too much about the war that threatened, because Mr. Hitler and Mr. Mussolini were Catholics, after all. "By Christmas there will be peace," he said. I turned towards Concorde, thinking it might have pleased her to hear those words, but when I saw her tense expression I knew she did not believe our friend. Her mind was made up, there was going to be a war. I understand her misgivings. The last time, those killing each other were Catholics too.

As planned, Miss Driscoll took the photo, with the help of her faithful admirer. At one point Concorde left the group and invited Miss Driscoll to join us; they talked together a little, and, seen from afar, Miss Driscoll seemed to be saying that she was out of place. But Concorde insisted, and the chivalrous Garry agreed to take the photo with Miss Driscoll included. I remember the flashes going off on that beautiful autumn day, with the soft breeze that tempered the last November sun. Afterwards, we all went down to the Flats on foot, except the newlyweds, to whom Garry had generously lent his car. A real gentleman, that man.

We were in her office at the Duke. I had lingered for a few days in Ottawa on the pretext that I wanted to help Mathurin finish his book on Catherine de Saint-Augustin, which was partly true. The rest of the truth was that I was waiting for Concorde to give me a sign.

It was not at all the sign I expected, but I gladly bowed to it. She invited me to go to see her so she could show me the wedding photos. There was a bottle of rum open on her desk, we drank a toast to the health of the newlyweds, and I did not wait for the alcohol to work before asking if she was in love with Garry.

"Yes, but I have no hope," she said. "I can't love him because I can't steal him from Miss Driscoll, my conscience wouldn't let me, and he, he can't love me because it's her he loves. It's funny because I've been seeing them together for twenty years, and I was never interested in him until a little while ago. One morning I saw him in the street when he was bringing Miss Driscoll her carton of Craven A's and her bottle of sherry, like every week, dressed to the nines as always. And there, I suddenly remembered how I'd dreamed all my life of being loved by a kind and elegant man like that, who would call me 'darling' or 'my love,' as he does with her. I swear, it came to me like a lightning bolt in the middle of a sunny day. I can say it to you: I've never been so unhappy. I can't stop crying. It's crazy, no?"

I was careful not to trample her heartache underfoot by revealing to her Garry's preferences, and the true reasons for his attachment to Miss Driscoll. Instead, I served myself another glass of rum. She followed suit. We said nothing more.

To divert myself, I rose to examine the paintings on her office walls, the works of Miss Driscoll. The largest and the least successful was the one for which Concorde had posed nude back then. But she was not nude. Miss Driscoll had dressed her as Catherine de Saint-Augustin, in a scene where the devil is preparing to pour hot ashes into her ear to cure her of an abscess. Unfortunately, Concorde is unrecognizable as a holy woman. I didn't tell her. The most successful is the charcoal drawing called *Commotion*. You can't recognize Concorde there either, on the ground in a faint. My poor friend will have passed her entire life unnoticed.

She gets up and looks in the large wardrobe behind her for the two group photos from the wedding. I ask her why Mathurin looks like he's lost his last friend. "You don't know? He's leaving on a mission next week. His life's dream. I thought he would be happy too. But I think he got used to it here, and he came to like it." I learned the rest later: Mathurin was posted as a missionary, but not with the Papous, who might perhaps have crucified him as he had dreamed in his youth. He was sent to where land was being colonized, to Timmins, a little mining town in northern Ontario where the winter lasts eight months. He was made the priest, and he will be responsible for building the future Capuchin church. Concorde tells me that it's a town where there are no sidewalks and no toilets in the houses. Mathurin took with him only his suitcase and the painting in which he posed as Brébeuf. He said goodbye to no one, so hard was it for him to leave.

In the two photos I rather look like a decayed version of myself. In that with Miss Driscoll I am staring into space. Concorde asks me why. I mumble something. She doesn't believe me, but she's too discreet to say anything. The truth is that I didn't want Miss Driscoll to guess that I was thinking of Essiambre when she pressed the shutter release. In the photo Garry took, I am looking at the ground. There too Concorde wants to know why. "I don't know why, but the faithful admirer that day made me think of a journalist who lent me money and whom I'd never reimbursed." She gave me a beautiful faded smile, a sign that this last lie didn't bother her any more than the first.

Concorde deciphers the rest of the photo. It's a gift she has: she can predict the future from pictures.

"You see my Édouard? He'll die in the war, in his plane, after killing innocent people with his bombs. It's written. I can see also that his Marie is pregnant. She's expecting a girl but she doesn't know it yet. She'll be a widow for a long time. She'll remarry another soldier, she'll move to another country and we'll never see her again in the Flats.

"Miss Driscoll will die as well. She has two years left to live. Mister Garry will never get over it. You, I don't want to hurt you, but you won't last out the war either with your gassed lungs and your drunkard's liver. Me, I'll live to be a hundred, but I don't really want to. Life can be long when you have no one to love."

I ask her what she was thinking in the photo taken by the faithful admirer, with her gaze like that of a resident in a sanatorium. She smiles. "I was looking into his lens as strong as I could to tell him, 'You are my first heartbreak.' I don't think he heard me. But it doesn't matter…" She gets up and returns the photos to the wardrobe. Something tells me it's the last time she'll look at them.

Standing by the window she lights a cigarette, which she smokes with the amber cigarette holder Miss Driscoll gave her as a present. The bottle of rum is empty. My train leaves in an hour.

．
．
．
．
．

I FEEL THAT I WILL SOON BE UNDERTAKING MY LAST
migration.

It's thirteen months now since I returned from Ottawa,
thirteen months of winter, you could say. I'm now certain
that I will never see Concorde again, but never mind, at
least I saw her once, for the wedding, that's enough. I feel
like a man who has made his preparations for a long journey,
and I am very calm. Everywhere else the world is at war, but
here I am at peace with myself.

Now that Concorde has shut me out of her life, I know
I love her. In fact I have never felt so alive, and I tell myself

that the next time I fall in love I'll know what to do to stay that way.

In my workshop, where I am working better than before, I imagine I have her photo in front of me, and I talk to her every day. She didn't want to give me her picture, but I talk to her all the same. I give her the neighbourhood news, I tell her about the weather. To get to sleep at night I think back on her amorous caresses, and I go to sleep in her every time. I recently ordered from Montreal the same cookbook she uses, and I regularly prepare the dishes she used to make. That way I feel like I'm eating with her every evening. Her cod with tomato sauce, her compote with dried fruits, her garlic mashed potatoes, her pot roast: she comes back to life before my eyes with the aromas of her cuisine. Afterwards, we go into the living room and sometimes talk all night.

She's gone, and my desire with her. Before meeting again my love now fled, I occasionally called on the new postmistress, whose husband is a politician who travels a lot, and I didn't give a damn whether or not the village knew about it. She's the daughter of the former postmistress, the one who read my mail to my father and advised him to disown me. The daughter is better, but I've had enough of those love affairs between reasoning mammals who dress up their dead-end couplings with poetic declarations. I've broken with her. But I'm living an authentic love, one that triumphs over biology and reason. Yes, I have finally become a man worthy of the name, a man who loves a woman for nothing and expects nothing from her. It feels good.

That's not all. I take my bath every Saturday in case she should reappear unannounced like the first time. So as not to smell up the house, I now smoke my pipe outside. I sweep the floor after my day's work, I do the washing on Monday like her, I clean the windows once a month. Instead of letting the dog lick the plates, I wash the dishes every day. If I had her perfume, I would wear it.

The few parishioners who come to see me are no longer afraid of me; they even consent to drink some of my wine in glasses that are now clean, whereas before they always refused. As for those citizens who still fear me as much as before, I recently surprised a ten- or eleven-year-old boy fishing at the end of my dock. A pretty little man with red hair, who reminded me of my friend Rodrigue at college. He was trembling with fear, the poor boy, so I calmed him. We even got along. He told me the village had given me a new nickname. They call me Absalom now, doubtless because of my long hair and my prophet's beard. The name pleases me. I gave him some red barley sugar. That way he'll tell the whole village I'm not the ogre they think I am. They'll say he's a liar, but some will believe him, and all the confusion will only add to my mystique. It will serve them right.

I've just realized that for a moment I stopped thinking about her. That doesn't happen often. I never write her, because I know she won't reply. But I go by the post office at least once a week to ask if there's any mail for me, just in case she should send a letter. The postmistress always replies, curtly, that there's nothing for me, and I go back to the house smiling inside and saying to myself, "It doesn't matter. One day, maybe, she'll write."

My every gesture invokes Concorde's memory, and I firmly believe that these thoughts will bring her back to me. The more time passes, the more I am proven wrong, but I persist, I can't help myself. When I get up in the morning the first thing I do is see if she's at the door. I go to sleep each night telling myself that maybe she'll be there tomorrow. Yesterday, to please her, I wore my tie.

This morning, again, I woke up thinking that sooner or later she'll come back to me, or will call me to her side. That has put me in good spirits for the rest of day.

I am waiting. I have the time.

•

•

•

•

•

ACKNOWLEDGEMENTS

This novel is the literary expression of a collective memory that is slipping away more than it is spreading abroad. Phil Jenkins, a man to know, gave me the idea towards the end of the last century. He was then writing his excellent account of LeBreton Flats in Ottawa, *An Acre of Time*. Phil, the next pint of beer is on me, and thank you again for your case full of notes.

To my great regret, I never knew my other benefactor, the late Sandra Gwyn, author of *The Private Capital* and

Tapestry of War, those majestic reconstructions of the time when Canada was aping the British mother country. Mrs. Gwyn not only supplied me with anecdotes of a rare truthfulness, but she also opened to me the archival kingdom where Ethel Chadwick and Talbot Papineau awaited me, two figures as at ease in history as in the world of the imagination.

I would like also to thank Desmond Morton, Marcel Trudel, Modris Eksteins, Roger Le Moine and Gérard Bouchard, among others, who will certainly recognize their involuntary contributions; Gabriel Poliquin, my first reader, who had me read Toni Morrison and many others; Mario Gagné and Monique Perrin d'Arloz, whose constructive comments saved this book many times; the excellent Jean Bernier, my editor.

My last word goes to those who would be astonished to see themselves named here. I will mention only the lady who taught me that it is never too late to have a happy youth. Her name is Annette, and she is my mother.